Chasing Infinity

A Standalone Romantic Suspense Novel

WONDERSTRUCK

ARIA HARDING

Cover Design by: Graziana with Chris Covers

First Edition published 2023

ISBN Paperback: 9798988378433

ISBN Ebook: 9798988378426

1

———

WHITNEY

NEVER, in a million years, would I have thought that I'd ever intimately know the broom closet on the eleventh floor of the Nexus Realty Group building.

But that's where I find myself in the throes of a steamy dream.

With who?

I don't know, but that's beside the point.

All that matters to me right now, at this moment, is the way that this mystery man's lips are tracing over the curves and divots of my neck. Even though I *know* I'm in a dream, I can practically feel his hot breath trailing across my skin, eliciting goosebumps to rise all over my arms.

I moan as I tilt my face to him. Though he's standing right in front of me, I can't make out the features of his face. But I know deep down inside me that he's everything to me.

Whoever this man is, he likes as I verbalize my appreciation for him, and his ministrations become more intentional. His hands rest on the curve of my hips, and his thumbs trace underneath the seam of my shirt until he's touching my bare skin.

Though I'm still fully clothed, the idea of his touch sends my body into overdrive, and my pulse skyrockets, as does my pleasure. My breath is ragged and my chest rises and falls against his hand as anticipation builds within me.

I raise my arms to wrap around his shoulders, and I catch sight of the glittering ring on my fourth finger. This dream version of myself is *engaged*—likely to the man who is kissing my neck in this closet—and that realization makes this moment even more appealing to me.

A deep rumble emanates from his chest, causing goosebumps to rise on my arms once more. "I can't believe you're mine," he says in his raspy voice, confirming my suspicions that he is my fiancé in this scenario. "I can't wait to start our lives together, start a family."

The idea makes my chest ache, and I smile at the faceless man who is saying all the right words to make me yearn for this dream to be true.

As I rise up on my tiptoes to kiss him again, the distant sound of a phone ringing interrupts the moment. Before I can fully grasp what's happening, the man of my dreams starts to fade right in front of me. Panic strikes my chest, and I reach out to grab him again, hoping to hold onto him for just another few moments.

But it's no use. Against my wishes, I'm ripped from the moment as my phone continues to ring through the night's darkness, leaving me feeling alone and empty inside as I'm forced back into reality. The vibration of the ringtone echoing against my nightstand is a stark contrast to the quiet broom closet, full of hopeful kisses and whispered promises of everything I could ever want.

The minute I'm pulled back into consciousness, I reach across my pillows, my hand grasping at nothing for a moment until I feel the familiar outline of my phone. I pull it off of the charger and bring it to my face, squinting in the dark to see who would be calling at this hour.

STACEY PETERSON.

I REALIZE the only reason she'd be calling me at this time, and my heart drops.

Swiping the screen, I hesitantly hold it up to my ear. "Hello?"

The older woman sniffles on the other end of the phone, and I brace myself for the worst. "Oh, Whitney," she begins, her voice wobbly. "I'm so sorry to have to tell you, but Vance passed away this evening."

I nearly drop the phone. Though we knew this moment would be coming, hearing that my boss, my mentor, my friend, is *gone* is a bit of a shock.

My stomach churns and I close my eyes, breathing deeply through my nose. I can hear the rush of blood from my pulse in my ears, drowning out any other sound.

"Whitney? Whitney, are you there?"

Finally, the sound of Stacey Peterson's voice pulls me out of my stupor.

"I'm so sorry, I was just—" I pause, unable to come up with the proper words to explain how I'm feeling in this moment. "I'm so sorry for your loss."

"Thank you, dear," she says before sniffling again. "I wanted you to be the first to know so you can send out the appropriate emails."

I say a few more words of condolences to Mrs. Peterson, and then hang up the phone, trying not to let myself break down completely. My eyes burn as I sit in my bed, staring at the blank screen of my phone. Though he's been sick for a bit, knowing that I'll never see the man who was like a father to me for so long only amplifies the lingering loneliness I'm feeling from that weird dream of mine. Giving a forlorn glance at the time, I roll out of bed and get to work.

I try to bring myself out of the grieving friend position and back into my role as the personal assistant to the CEO. Despite how much Mr. Peterson and his family meant to me, at the end of the day, that's who I am. Even though it's still the dark hours of the night, my mind jumps into action, already drafting up the email I'll send out to the Board of Directors of Nexus Realty Group.

The next few days pass in a blur. I do my best to be supportive, jumping in and taking responsibility of as much as I possibly can, bearing the weight on my shoulders, all while trying to keep it together myself. But every night, after spending the day in the empty CEO's office, filling boxes of his personal items and memories he'd collected over the years, I go home and turn on the shower, curl into a ball, and let the hot water scald my skin as I cry for everything that we've lost.

That I've lost.

A few days before the funeral, I start sorting through some of my old, childhood boxes, searching for pictures or memories that Mr. Peterson was a part of. As I'm rummaging through a box filled with notebooks and pictures, my fingers brush a familiar leather cover and I pause, narrowing my eyes. I reach for it again, grasping the pink, leather bound notebook and pulling it out.

I absentmindedly flip through the pages, noting the names and the checklists on each page. Ever since I was fifteen and going through my first breakup—of many to come, unfortunately—I created a list of ten things that I wanted in my perfect man. I know it's restrictive and ridiculous, but I had dreams of finding a man who would meet all of these things, and then we'd live out our happily ever after together.

But I guess that never happened.

With a shake of my head, I close the notebook, putting it off to the side and shoving down the feelings of loneliness once more.

On the day of Mr. Peterson's funeral, I find myself standing in a rickety, old church, amongst all of the other people who loved him deeply. Our voices ring out as we sing a melancholy song and try not to give into the grief I know we all are experiencing.

When the melody ends, the preacher instructs us to be seated. Then, he begins his long sermon about how life is precious, yet even precious things must come to an end. I situate myself to be more comfortable as I listen to his deep, soothing timbre. The wooden pew is hard and unyielding against my spine, making the muscles in my lower back scream out in protest. We have already been here for around forty-five minutes. As much as I loved Mr. Peterson, I am itching to get out of here and into the fresh air.

The church smells of an interesting mix of death and hopelessness. It lingers over us, giving no signs of ever letting up.

Of course, I guess that's what you should expect at a funeral. I don't know why I thought it would be different. I hate funerals. Primarily because if I'm at one, it means someone I held very dear to my heart is gone—my mother, my father, and now, Mr. Peterson. The aura of my surroundings also takes its toll on me. I can feel the negative energy draping across the sanctuary like a heavy blanket. It's almost suffocating as it weighs us all down.

I fight back the tears as I glance around at all the guests. Everyone bows their heads or gazes at the preacher, listening intently. There isn't a trace of any color besides dark blues, grays, and blacks. I suppose it is the standard dress code for these types of occasions.

Mr. Peterson was a good man. He was kind to everyone who stumbled into his life, even if they didn't deserve it. He had been my boss for only a few years shy of a decade, but my friend for much longer. I was his assistant on paper, but our relationship was much more than that.

My father passed away when I was only ten. That was my first experience with grief. Then, only eight years later, my mother died, after fighting a vicious battle with cancer. After that, Mr. Peterson took me under his wing as if I were his daughter, welcoming me into his home and his family as if I was always meant to be there. With the Petersons, I had a safe haven. They were two people that I knew I could count on, no matter what. When he brought me on to be his full-time assistant at Nexus, I couldn't believe my luck. I actually enjoyed working for him. He had taught me everything he knew about the business world, giving me tips and tricks that I'm not sure I would've picked up elsewhere.

I sit there in numb silence, pretending to listen to the preacher drone on as I replay memories of Mr. Peterson over and over in my head. I keep thinking about how, come Monday, I will walk into our office and everything will be different. I will never see him again, and that's a hard fact that I'm unsure I'll ever be able to fully comprehend.

Though he's been gone from the office for the last few weeks, seeing the casket up there makes his absence feel more final. More permanent.

After what feels like an eternity, we sing one more song and the service concludes. Once we've all filed out, I find Mrs. Peterson and wrap my arms around her. She holds me tightly and then, when I pull away, kisses my cheek.

"You take care of yourself, dear. I know Vance would want

you to be happy. I do too." I smile at the kind, old woman and again give her my regards. She is going to be moving down south, where their *actual* children live, so I likely won't be seeing her anymore after this, though I hope we'll stay in touch a little bit. I was much closer to Mr. Peterson than I was to her, so I wasn't surprised when she told me she'd be leaving town. She has no interest in taking over Mr. Peterson's business, rather, desires to spend the rest of her time with her family. I can't blame her.

After one more hug, I let go of her and walk out of the church and into the new world, of which Mr. Peterson is no longer a part of. It stings, knowing that he won't be around to celebrate when I finally get engaged, or to walk me down the aisle at my wedding. He won't be there to cuddle my first baby. I won't get to see him look at them with so much love in his eyes that it makes his eyes water.

And all of these realizations hurt, like a thousand knives cutting me deep to the bone.

All this time, he's encouraged me to chase my dreams, and now, he won't even be around to see me finally achieve them.

As I walk to my car, one stray tear streaks down my face and I swipe it away, taking a deep breath and swallowing down the anger and sadness threatening to bubble up from inside of me. On a whim, I decide I need a little pick me up. My favorite coffee shop, Uncommon Grounds, isn't too far from here. My best friend, Leila, and I are frequent fliers there and know the entire staff by name. It opened up last year, and it quickly turned into the prime hangout spot when we are both off work, which is seldom, considering we both live busy lives.

When I'm a block away from the coffee shop, the sky opens up, unleashing a torrent of rain down onto my little car. My windshield wipers work furiously to clear my vision. I breathe a sigh of relief when I find a parking spot, which is quickly replaced by a grumble of frustration when I can't locate the umbrella I typically keep in the glove compartment.

Deciding to make a run for it, I hurry out of my car and sprint to the door, satisfied that I only end up *mostly* soaked to the bone. Right away, I feel the warmth from the small shop surround me.

Uncommon Grounds is such a quaint, little space. The shop itself isn't that large. In fact, it is relatively small compared to other places. It has an electric, stone fireplace on one side, surrounded by comfy leather sofas and little tables spread throughout the area.

Upon first walking in, guests are immediately greeted with the sweet aroma of fresh baked goods, like their infamous blueberry scones or the café's signature brew. The spectacular essence that the shop gives off never ceases to amaze me. The comfortable leather of the couches is always inviting. I rarely ever pass it up when I'm in the mood for something warm and cozy. Sometimes, I even come here after work hours to do some last-minute work for Mr. Peterson. I wonder if my new boss will require me to put in extra, off-the-clock hours like Mr. Peterson did.

Not that I minded; he always was grateful for any extra work I did on the side which made it worthwhile for me. And besides that, I do enjoy my job. There is something so satisfying about working with a powerful CEO and assisting in tasks to help further the company into new and exciting ventures. Though I don't hold an executive position, *exactly*, with Mr. Peterson, I was still a valued member of the executive team. He respected my opinions just as much as anyone else, and he was always open to anything I'd suggest.

Hopefully, I'll be able to prove that to the new CEO as well.

I walk up to the register and order my favorite seasonal

drink, a pumpkin-spiced latte. They make it quickly, and soon, I'm settling into my favorite two-seater booth next to the fireplace and the window.

The rain is still falling heavily outside, and I take a sip of my drink, watching it fall to the ground. This is exactly what I needed.

The last few days have been high stress, as we finalized all the details for Mr. Peterson's funeral. Mrs. Peterson helped where she could, but a lot of the responsibilities had fallen onto me. I was happy to help her through this, but now, I am feeling the effects weigh heavily on my shoulders. My muscles ache and I feel like I can barely keep my head up.

It is strange being forced to say goodbye to one phase of my life and immediately get thrust into the next one. Come Monday, I'll have a new boss, new expectations, and essentially, a new job. Nerves bloom in my belly, and I feel on edge about the whole change. I don't have any idea of what I will be walking into on Monday morning, and I hate to feel unprepared.

Curiosity gets the best of me, and once I'm settled in my booth, I pull out my phone and open up the search browser. I type the name, *Theodore Hurst*—exactly as it was spelled in the company-wide announcement email from our Board of Directors yesterday—into the search box and click the *go* button. After it takes a few seconds to load, pictures and articles come up about the man who I'll soon be working for.

My mouth goes dry as soon as I see his face for the first time, and I reach for my coffee to take a sip. It's a photo from what looks to be a gala. He's looking away from the camera at something else, but his face is lit up in a broad smile, which makes his dark eyes glitter, even through the stationary image.

You've got to be kidding me.

He can't be more than ten years older than I am, which is nearly unheard of for someone maintaining a CEO position.

Right next to the first few photos of him is a headline: *Theodore Hurst named next CEO of powerhouse commercial realtor, Nexus Realty Group.*

The realization that I'm going to be working for this man in a matter of days suddenly hits me, and a slight sense of unease settles in my chest. I wonder what he's like as a boss. Obviously, he must be a very driven person to have become so successful at such a young age.

I click on the webpage for his old company and pull up his details, itching to know more about him.

Another, more professional headshot appears on the screen, and I find myself staring at it for far too long. His face is almost too perfect, void of any type of blemish or flaw, and I wonder if they retouched the photo to make him appear more handsome than he actually is.

I drop my phone on the table and lean back in the booth, taking a second to fully process this. My best friend, Leila, is going to have a field day when she finds out that I'll be working for such an attractive man.

She's the epitome of a romanticist, always looking for the next epic love story. I have no doubt she'd jump on the prospect of this one. Not that I can really point fingers on the matter, either. I, too, desperately yearn for someone to love and call my own.

I read over Theodore Hurst's mini biography. I learn that he's thirty-six, and graduated from an Ivy League with degrees in business and leadership. He has worked for his previous company in Britain for the last four years.

The webpage goes on to describe his accolades and how he is well respected amongst his peers. The more I read, the more I wonder if this guy is even human or if he's an industry-made, professional business mogul.

I click around his website a little more, trying to get as much information on him as I possibly can. Unfortunately, aside from a few of his awards and general information, I don't find much else about him.

When I go to the contact page, I notice his assistant's email address. I copy it down in my phone's notepad and make a reminder to shoot them an email when I'm back home at my computer. Maybe they will be able to give me a little more information about what Mr. Hurst is like. I strive to be the best that I can be. Maybe if I make a great first impression, he won't treat me just like any other assistant, and he will recognize that I add value to the position too.

Once I'm done with my coffee, I decide that's enough sleuthing for today. I toss the empty cup in the trash and make sure I have all of my items before walking out.

As I leave the coffee shop to head towards home, I do a quick run-through of everything I'll need to do when I get there and over the next few days. Come Monday, we'll be welcoming our new boss. I'm a little on edge about that fact, simply because I feel like I'm walking into the unknown. Though it may be irrational, there's always the fear that with a change of leadership comes the change of staff. And I can't imagine what I'd do if I lost this job. I don't know who Whitney Palmer is outside of this position. I'm on my own now, and that's a scary thought.

I'll do everything I can to make sure that this new office is perfect for him. In this scenario, I fear that first impressions will mean everything, and I'll do whatever it takes to come out on top.

2

____

WHITNEY

I CASUALLY LOOK myself up and down for the umpteenth time in the body-length mirror hanging on my closet doors. Tilting my head to the side, I do a little spin, ensuring everything about my appearance is perfect.

Today is the day that my coworkers and I meet our new boss: Theodore Hurst. To be perfectly honest, I'm a little scared. I am afraid because I will be spending practically every minute with him. I'm going to be his assistant. And according to my job description, I will practically live and breathe anything he requires from me. If he doesn't like me, there's the potential that he can make my job miserable. Or, he could dislike me so much that he'd fire me, and where would that leave me?

Terrible thoughts of endless to-do lists and impossible tasks float through my mind as I imagine the worst-case scenario. I can't even imagine what it would be like to hate coming to work every day, and I have no intention of finding out.

It takes me longer than I'd like to admit to find the best outfit to wear to work. My clothing choice was never a problem when I worked with Mr. Peterson. He could have cared less if I showed up to work wearing sweats. But this guy? I have no idea what his expectations are. All I know is that I want to make a good first impression on him.

As I scrutinize my reflection in the mirror, I finally decide that this will have to do.

I decided on my favorite cream blouse to wear today. Then, I picked out a pair of maroon dress pants, and my tan, waist-length peacoat. I chose to wear a pair of my favorite heels. I'm not exactly short, per se, but even a little bit of a heel gives me more confidence than anything. Once I'm dressed and ready to go, I step out of my bedroom and into my kitchen to eat a protein bar before leaving. As I'm shoving my face full of the chocolate-peanut butter oat bar, I do a once-over around my space.

My house is about two miles from Chicago's Navy Pier, in a condominium complex with reserved parking. It isn't a huge condo—two bedrooms, two bathrooms, and a study—but it suits me. The empty room is for whenever Leila decides to spend the night, which isn't very often, but it is there, just in case. Glancing at the clock on my oven, I collect my phone, planner, purse, and keys and then hit the road for work.

I don't have time to stop for coffee, deciding that I can just get it at work. On a typical day with Mr. Peterson, I would stop at Uncommon Grounds or some other coffee shop for the both of us.

Once in the car, I pull up my favorite classical music playlist, letting the lilting notes calm my nerves. I got up early this morning, hoping to miss the heavy traffic, because nothing ruins my day more than having to sit in a traffic jam in the middle of downtown Chicago.

The shrill ringtone of my cell phone brings me out of my dazed state of mind. I would have jumped a mile into the air if it were not for my seatbelt, which does its job and holds me firmly in my place.

Considering that I am currently being held at a red light, I rummage around in my oversized purse, looking for my phone. I grumble to myself, wishing I had the kind of money to get a car with Bluetooth features. Finally, when my fingers graze over the vibrating device, I yank it out of the bag and place it to my ear.

"Hello?"

"Hey, there," the singsong voice that could pull me out of any dark space rings into my ear. My best friend is the epitome of sunshine and energy.

"Hello, Leila," I respond. "Nice to talk to you this early in the morning," I speculate while looking at my dashboard clock. It reads a quarter past six. Now that it's officially fall, the days are beginning earlier, so the sun is just barely rising through the sky.

"Yeah, well. The damn principal chose not to let us know that our school was out of power until just a few minutes ago. I guess something knocked it out over the weekend and they haven't been able to get it back up," she muttered, loud enough so I could hear. "Would've been nice to know earlier. I could've slept in!"

"Maybe he didn't know it wouldn't be back on yet?"

"Whatever, I'm still annoyed to be awake. It's fine though, I have things I can work on from home today. Anyway, are you free today for lunch? Cause I am in dire need of some Whitney time."

Furrowing my eyebrows, I try to picture my schedule for the day. I wish I could just grab my planner and see what my day looks like, but driving while talking on the phone *while* searching through your daily events doesn't exactly scream safe.

"This is kind of short notice, and today's kind of rough. The new boss is starting today, so I'm not sure, I'll have to double check my schedule. But I'm driving right now, so I can't look. I'll call you back when I get to the office," I tell her.

Leila groans on the other end. "*Please*, Whitney? I'll be going stir-crazy by the time lunch rolls around. I'm not used to being cooped up in the house for that long. Not to mention, I'm already frazzled knowing these parent-teacher conferences are right around the corner."

I can't help but laugh. Leila has been amping herself up for these conferences for the last few weeks. She still has a few weeks to go before she has to meet with parents, but she is just as organized as I am sometimes. She is already thinking ahead about what she will say about each of her students—the good ones *and* the bad. This is always her least favorite time of the school year.

"Where do you want to meet?" I ask.

She grumbles, "JTs? I'm dying for a chicken Caesar wrap."

Sighing, I nod, even though she can't see me. "Yeah, sure. I'll be there." She says goodbye and then disconnects the line.

I pull into the parking garage of our building and show the guard my badge. Then, I carefully park in my designated spot. It has my name painted on it and everything.

Reserved for Whitney Palmer.

I get out of my car, grab all my junk, and start my trek across the lobby to the elevators. I work on the eleventh floor, right next to the CEO's office. Our building used to be a hotel before they completely renovated it. The building had undeniable classic charm when the company bought it—way before I had joined the team—but it was dated and not at all safe for normal business usage. After doing a complete gut-job, the building was now sleek and modern on the inside, but still maintained the historic architecture that it used to have.

I walk into the elevator and click the button for the eleventh floor, where the CEO's office and my desk space reside. Nexus maintains the top three floors of this building, and rents out all the others to other companies.

"Good morning, Charlotte," I greet our secretary, who also is stationed on the eleventh floor. She greets me with a cheeky grin.

"Well, hi there, Whitney, you're here awfully early," Charlotte speculates. I give her a noncommittal shrug.

"Today's a big day. I have to have everything ready for Mr. Hurst when he arrives. Have you heard when he's expected to be here?"

Charlotte flips through her big book of notes that she has sitting front and center on her desk. She is diligent in writing down every little detail, so nothing gets forgotten. She scans her most recent notes and taps her long, painted finger on her chin.

"I got a message that he'll be in around eight-thirty," she informs me.

Letting out a sigh I'm not aware I am holding, I smile and thank her before heading to my desk. Mine is, of course, right outside the door of the boss's enclosed room.

I set down all my stuff and then arrange it the way I prefer. Carefully sitting down in my swivel chair, I boot up my desktop and sync my phone to the calendar so nothing gets lost from any work I finished on my own last night.

I have a bit of time still until Mr. Hurst shows up, so I click on my email and log in, hoping to get to work. As soon as my email is loaded up, I see the little red icon indicating I have a new unread message.

Narrowing my eyes, I click on it, only to see an email from Mr. Hurst's previous assistant at his old office over in London.

As I look closer and scrutinize the words written on the screen, it becomes clear that she created an entire profile on Mr. Hurst for me, including a list of all of his likes and dislikes.

Bless her heart! This will make my life as his new assistant so much easier. I scroll down and commit every little detail to memory as best as I can. Heaven knows how much time she saved me by forwarding this. Now I won't need to figure out his preferences the hard way—trial and error. I try my hardest not to wince when she notes that he can be disorganized sometimes and that he likes to close himself off when he gets too stressed out.

Being an assistant is not always an easy job. I've learned that business moguls can be high maintenance and can switch moods at the drop of a hat. It is always a good thing when you know exactly what they like and don't like or how they respond when the stakes are high. After working for Mr. Peterson for so long, I had his entire personality down pat. I could tell when we would have a good day versus just an 'okay' day, based on the way he would saunter down the hallway to his office.

And on those 'okay' days, I took it upon myself to find ways to turn it back into a great day.

But now, I'm starting all over again. Thankfully, this cheat sheet will give me a bit of a head start, but I know I still have a lot of work to do.

My gaze flies to the empty office before me. It's daunting not knowing who or what your boss is going to be like. But all I can do is show him the best version of myself—make sure he knows that I'm a capable assistant and I'm worth keeping around.

Slowly, the office begins filling up until soft chatter surrounds the whole area. We have a few departments who work up on this top floor with us, including HR. Taking a deep breath, I leave my desk and walk towards our break room to get some coffee. We have been off work for a few days in respect of Mr. Peterson, so now that everyone is back in the office, there is a bit of catching up to do.

In one of the cabinets, I reach for my personalized mug with the Nexus Realty Group logo on it and pour myself a nice cup of coffee. I haven't had any caffeine this morning and am already starting to shake from withdrawals and the nerves of meeting my new boss. I also grab a to-go cup for Mr. Hurst when he arrives. I add just the right amount of sugar and cream to it, as my email instructed. Two cups of coffee in hand, I wander back through the office to my desk.

I set down my steaming cup on my coaster and put the to-go cup in Mr. Hurst's office. Then I go back to my own work-space. I lean back in my chair, reach for my mug, and take a sip, letting the coffee warm me all the way down. I close my eyes and relax for a minute or two, focusing on the aromatic flavors of my hazelnut coffee. I don't even notice when the office grows eerily quiet.

"Ms. Palmer?" I'm mid-sip when a deep, husky, and *very* sexy voice says my name. I'm not expecting it, so I jump, spilling my coffee all over my favorite vintage blouse.

"Oh!" I shout as the hot liquid runs down my entire torso. I spring into action, placing the mug on my desk and reaching for the paper towels I keep in my drawer for accidents like this one.

After a good couple of minutes of dabbing at my shirt, I give up and swear under my breath. At that moment, I grow acutely aware of the sole cause of this event. He stands right in front of me, an unamused expression on his flawless features.

The most beautiful man I possibly have ever laid eyes on.

My hands fall limply to my side, still clutching the soiled napkins as I look the man over.

He wears a pinstriped, three-pieced, gray suit that looks

wonderful on him. The man's face is cleanly shaven, so his skin looks smooth enough to run my hands over.

His dark hair is styled, but I catch sight of a few stray curls, unwilling to cooperate this morning. He has a nice build: broad shoulders leading to a tapered waistline. His chestnut eyes spark as he observes me right back.

"I-uh..." I stutter. I shake my head slightly to clear it, and stretch out my palm. Then I try again, clearing my throat and saying, "Um, I'm Whitney Palmer."

He offers his own hand and grasps mine in a tight introductory shake. "Theo Hurst, nice to meet you, Ms. Palmer." His voice is deep and gravelly, which makes my insides turn to molten lava.

I give him a tight smile. "Please, call me Whitney, Mr. Hurst."

"As long as you call me Theo," he quips.

Nodding my head, I give a nervous laugh. "Of course."

Mr.—*Theo*—looks around the office area. "Do you usually drop coffee all over yourself when you meet new people?"

His eyes flick down to my bust area, and mine quickly follow his lead. I let out a sharp and loud gasp. My cream blouse, now wholly soaked with coffee, is also see-through. The lacy, nude bra I picked out this morning is now fully visible to the world. I quickly cover myself up with my arms, horrified.

With an amused chuckle, Theo hooks his hand underneath my upper arm and drags me away from my desk and into his private office. He closes the door behind us, then shrugs off his suit jacket and hands it to me.

Gratefully, I take it and wrap myself in it. He is much larger than I am, so it is like stepping into a cocoon, but either way, it offers me the coverage that I need. I'm immediately overrun with the scents of fresh laundry and a hint of eucalyptus. I try not to be obvious when I take another sniff. Theo, thankfully, isn't paying me any attention as he walks over and leans against the front of his desk, crossing his arms over his chest. He raises a dark eyebrow at me.

"I must say, this is some welcome, Ms. Palmer." His deep timbre is making my whole body tingle. He has a hint of a smirk playing on his lips that is doing weird things to my insides. *Who even is this man?*

"Whitney," I correct, and he nods. "I'm so sorry. I'm not usually that clumsy. You can be assured that it won't happen again," I ramble off quickly.

He gives me a smile that makes my heart flip-flop. What is the matter with me today? Do I need to go to Urgent Care and get an EKG done? "Don't fret about it, Whitney. It happens to the best of us." Theo winks at me and reaches behind him for the coffee cup he just noticed. He takes a quick sip and then scrunches his eyebrows together.

Again, my heart goes into what I can only believe to be cardiac arrest. And my brain falls into a mild panic attack as he savors the coffee. I can't read the expression on his face. Oh no! What if his previous assistant gave me bad advice?

"How did you know?" His tone is laced with surprise.

"Huh?"

"How did you know that this was how I preferred my coffee?" I exhale sharply and give him a little shrug, unwilling to reveal my secrets.

Quite honestly, Theo looks impressed. He walks behind his desk and places his black briefcase on the side. Carefully, he takes out his high-end laptop and puts it on the desk in front of him. Next, he pulls out a glasses case and sets it down on the top of the desk.

"Nice job, Ms. Palmer. I think we will get along just fine." He shoots me that crooked smile again, and I can't help but grin back.

"Thank you. Looking forward to it," I respond automatically.

He glances at his laptop as he sits down. Then he folds his hands and places them on his desk before his eyes find mine again. "Now, on to the next matter. How do you feel about lunch?"

I pause, caught off guard. "Lunch?"

"I thought we could get lunch to get to know each other better. Seeing as we're going to be working closely together."

I had gone to lunch with Mr. Peterson hundreds of times, so it isn't the suggestion that makes me nervous. It is a perfectly reasonable offer, but I am glad I said I would meet Leila for lunch today. Something about this guy has me feeling on edge, in the best way possible, and I don't want to embarrass myself even more than I already have today.

"Oh, sorry, I can't. I have plans with a girlfriend of mine. Maybe another day?" I ask him.

He nods his head, unbothered, as he looks back down at his laptop, reaching for the case and pulling out a pair of rectangular, black glasses. He slides them onto his face as he peers at his screen. I try to ignore the way those glasses have completely escalated his attractiveness. "Certainly. Not a problem. Well, go on then and get to work. Just because it's my first day does not mean I'm going to let you off easy, Ms. Palmer."

"Of course, Theo." I grin back, picking up on his teasing tone, and waltz out of his office.

The rest of our morning passes smoothly; even more smoothly than I could have wished for. Mr. Hurst and I review all the outstanding tasks that Mr. Peterson had left unfinished. We go over expectations of what Theo prefers I take care of and what things I can delegate to the others underneath me. So far, the transition is going flawlessly for day one.

As I watch him slowly fit into the role of CEO, all I can

think about is that first impression and the pink, leather note-book sitting on my desk at home. I try not to focus on how within a few minutes—*seconds*—he had checked the first thing off of that silly, "Perfect Man" list, but it's no use.

Number 10: Handsome as Sin

Theo sits me down and runs through his agenda of what he'd like to do with the company in the first year. I'm impressed that he's so prepared and has so many new fresh ideas. He aims to take the company to new heights, while still maintaining the integrity of the legacy that Mr. Peterson developed. As he outlines these things, I can't help but feel like he was exactly the right choice for this position.

He is exactly what this company needs to lead us into the future.

And as I get to spend more time with him today, a secret part of me can't help but wonder if he is exactly what *I* need, too.

3

___

THEO

"GOOD MORNING, MR. HURST," my assistant, Whitney, announces the minute I walk into her line of vision from the elevators. She's sitting behind her desk and giving me a wide smile that makes my stomach flip like I'm back in middle school, talking to a pretty girl for the first time.

My mind instantly flashes to the way that lacy bra of hers peeked through her soaked shirt on my first day. Jesus, what an entrance. I don't think that's something I'll be forgetting anytime soon.

Get it together, Hurst.

"Ms. Palmer," I greet her with a grin, unable to help myself at the way she rolls her eyes and smirks. We agreed on first names, but I can't seem to help myself from teasing her. I enjoy the way she beams at me when I get playful. "How are you doing this morning?"

I've only been here for a week, but we seem to have established our morning routine. I walk in, she greets me with a bright smile that always seems to give me a weird reaction, which I choose to ignore, I ask her how she's doing, playing it cool, and then we begin our day.

"Wonderful, as always," she chirps. I find it intriguing how she's always so energetic in the mornings. My last assistant at my old business was top-of-the-line, but it usually took her a few hours and at least three cups of coffee in the morning to find her groove. But not Whitney.

I think this woman wakes up ready and excited to work every morning. I find it a very attractive quality, since I, myself, tend to keep a motivated attitude. Or at least, I try to.

"Can I get you any coffee?" she asks just as I cross the threshold of my office. I stop and turn back to her, holding up the blue travel mug in my hand that she must not have seen.

"I'm all set, thank you," I tell her. She nods again and glances at her schedule.

"Don't forget, we have the board meeting today over lunch. I believe it's catered."

I look up at the ceiling. Oh yes, the wonderful board meeting. So far, they have been less than accommodating to me and very resistant to accept me as the new CEO. I'm guessing this meeting today is to discuss the next phase of transitioning over to my business model, and it will likely go less than perfectly.

I shoot Whitney a tight smile. "I can't wait." Her lips twitch, and I know she picks up on my sarcasm. Still slightly smirking, she goes back to tapping on her keyboard. I stare at her a moment longer before walking back into my office. I can't deny there is just something about Whitney Palmer that intrigues me.

Our day gets started without a hitch. I answer a few emails and hop on a phone conference call after Whitney lets me know the other participants are on the line. After I hang up, I start pouring over some of these reports, which is the perfect way to set off my irritation right from the get go.

The deeper and deeper I get into the financials and the past reports, the more I want to pull out my hair. There are too many things not adding up when I put two and two together. I hate to suspect the worst, but given the notebook of accounts I wanted to double-check or triple-check, it was hard to keep myself from veering in that direction. I'm not sure yet what scheme Vance Peterson was up to, but it wasn't good. I am going to figure it out, but I suspect it will still take a while until I have fully unearthed everything he had potentially buried. And that is a scary thought. My brother Chase will be eventually joining the company as the chief financial officer, and I can't wait to let him take over this issue. He's much better at numbers than I am and he'll get to the bottom of it.

When lunchtime rolls around and my nerve endings are fully frayed from staring at problems that don't make sense, I saunter out of my office towards Whitney's desk feeling a wave of ease settle over me when she comes into my line of vision.

She glances up at me and then looks back at her email. "Are you ready for your board meeting?" she asks.

I lean against the edge of her desk and stick my hands in my pockets. "Honestly, I've never been so excited to sit in a stuffy room full of old people in my life."

Her blue eyes fly up to me, and she laughs under her breath. "You've got jokes today."

"Gotta keep it interesting," I say with a wink. Her cheeks color, and she looks back to her computer.

Her fingers fly over the keys, and her eyes narrow in on something on her screen. Finally, she reaches for the mouse and then clicks into standby mode. Then, with a bright smile, she gathers the stack of notebooks and folders sitting on the edge of her desk, neatly organized.

"Shall we?" she asks, standing up and walking around the edge of her desk.

I dip my chin at her, letting her lead the way down to the boardroom, where I'll be leading my first Board of Directors meeting. "We shall. Wednesdays are for winning over Board members."

She chuckles, and I smile to myself too. This isn't my first rodeo. At my old job, the Board of Directors loved me. They thought I could do no wrong. Every meeting turned out to be a victory lap, going over my most recent stats and reports. For some reason, that's what I was expecting to be the case here too.

What I was not expecting was this board meeting to turn into a war zone.

Which it did.

Rapidly.

"You're making a laughingstock of our business, Mr. Hurst. When we hired you, you assured us you were capable of taking on a business such as this and promised to drive our numbers to heights our competitors would not be able to reach. Not to mention your goals of easing Nexus into the hotel division. But so far, you've been nothing but a disappointment."

I shift uncomfortably in my seat, feeling the weight of everyone's eyes falling on me expectantly. I clear my throat and go for a pragmatic response. "This is simply a transition period, Elena. I've been here for only a week. Surely you can't be gauging my performance already."

The aged woman, Elena, head of the Board of Directors, purses her lips as she looks down her nose at me. "I'm simply bringing it to the attention of the rest of the board. You promised us one thing, and we're not seeing the fruition of that yet."

"Elena makes a good point," one of the other board members—I haven't had a chance to learn his name—adds in.

He has a spreadsheet pulled up on his tablet. "I believe we should've at least seen some positive headway by now."

A few of the other board members mumble amongst themselves. The older man passes around the tablet, and they take a look at the spreadsheet before sharing grave looks with each other.

"It's only been a week," I protest again, pulling on my necktie. All of a sudden, it feels like it's strangling me. Is it hot in here? Sweat beads on my forehead. "I did send over my action plan to start in on acquiring some hotel properties. Did you not receive it?"

"We did. But after reviewing it, I am concerned that perhaps we made this decision too prematurely," Elena says, looking awfully pleased at herself with this ambush. "I believe we may need to take another look at your contract. We did say you would be hired with a ninety-day probation, correct? Don't get too comfortable here, Mr. Hurst. I don't believe this is the right fit for you."

Irritation, laced with a side of apprehension, travels down my spine and I find myself gritting my jaw maybe a bit too tightly. How could I be fucking this up so badly already? I want to do well in this position, and I *know* that I can. But I won't succeed if I'm not even given the chance.

"I think that's enough," Whitney says out of the blue, interrupting Elena in the middle of her rant. My attention snaps toward her, as does the rest of the Board.

"Excuse me?" Elena hisses. "It would be wise of you to know your place. Ms. Palmer, is it?"

I raise my eyebrows in surprise. From my understanding, Whitney has been a part of this company for years. I can't imagine Elena wouldn't know her name. Whitney straightens in her chair and meets Elena's gaze head-on, ignoring the obvious dig. "Yes, and you know that Mr. Peterson respected my opinion just as much as he did anyone else in this room."

I hope my jaw isn't hanging open in shock.

Whitney glances at me quickly before looking back at Elena and then staring down at everyone else at the table. "If Theo's contract says ninety days, then I think it's only fair that you give him ninety days to work through the transition period. That's what Mr. Peterson would have wanted—for his successor to succeed. Not be burned at the stake within his first week of employing the position."

The Board of Directors all watch her with grim expressions. Finally, Elena exhales and looks down at her wrinkly, manicured fingers. "I suppose you're right, Ms. Palmer. Alright. Theo, you have ninety days to present us with a report of your short-term and long-term goals with the company. This includes your operational and marketing reports, as well as a risk management evaluation."

"Of course," I say before I glance over to Whitney, sitting next to me. She furiously scribbles down every challenge Elena is laying down on the table.

"You have until the end of your probationary period, Theo," Elena says to me. I suddenly have the strongest urge to glower at the older woman sitting at the opposite head of the table. "If what you present to us is deemed not adequate, we will reevaluate."

I nod my head at Elena, who still stares down her nose at me. Her face is pinched like she smells something bad, and her eyes are narrowed as she sizes me up. Finally, she pushes her chair back and looks around the room. "I suppose we're finished for today."

With three large strides, Elena exits the boardroom, leaving the rest of us in her wake.

My lips press into a thin line as I say goodbye to the rest of the board members. When everyone but me and Whitney are gone, I look over to my assistant and give her a tight smile.

"Well, that was fun," I mutter.

She exhales sharply through her nose as she gathers up her folders and notepads. "I'm not sure that's the word I would use for that. I'm sorry, Elena shouldn't have jumped down your throat like that."

I push back my chair and button my suit jacket back up. Whitney, materials in hand, follows my lead, and we leave the boardroom side by side. My office and her desk are just down the hallway.

As we walk, I try my hardest not to gaze at her next to me.

The events of that board meeting aside, she amazes me.

Never have I met such a beautiful woman in my entire life. She is poised and determined to do well at her job, which is more of a turn-on than I would have guessed. I want to get to know her, unearth all her darkest secrets, and unwrap whatever she is hiding underneath that skin-tight pencil skirt.

It is the first time in a long time that I can openly admit that I might have a crush.

I am crushing on my personal assistant.

It is so cliché and so unprofessional—not to mention, completely against company policy—but I can't seem to help it. Every time she walks into a room, I feel like the world is just a little bit brighter; that everything has just a little bit more meaning to it.

Ever since I started last week, she has been all I can think about. There are obviously many more important things that I should be worried about in this transition phase, such as winning over the Board and accomplishing as much as I possibly can within these first ninety days. But all I can seem to focus on is Whitney Palmer.

And that, in and of itself, is alarming.

"I had some ideas on how we can get through all of these reports in the most efficient way possible," she says, pulling me out of my thoughts once we make it to my office. She looks up at me expectantly as we walk, her attention solely on me.

I stick my hands in my pockets. "I'm listening."

"Perhaps we can make a spreadsheet to—oh!" Whitney gasps as she stumbles over the threshold into my office, the toe of her shoe catching just right on the throw rug against the faux hardwood floor.

I step forward, reaching my arms out to catch her as the notepads and folders, which were in her arms, go everywhere. Her body sags against me, her own arms wrapping around my shoulders to catch her fall. When her momentum ceases, she's draped across my chest, her hands clutching me for dear life.

Time slows until all I can see is her, staring up at me with wide, unconfident eyes.

My chest constricts as we both try to catch our breath from the unexpected proximity.

Fuck, she's beautiful.

Before reality comes knocking, I take the chance to trace over every inch of her face, committing her to memory. If this is my only chance to hold her like this in my arms, I'm damn sure going to take advantage of it.

Whitney gradually gathers her wits about her and pushes off of my chest until she's standing straight again. She brushes her hands over her black pencil skirt, looking down at the floor, unwilling to meet my eyes.

"I'm so sorry," she stammers as she bends down to gather her items.

I follow right after her, crouching at the knees to help her collect the papers and notes that she's lost. "Don't be."

After getting everything together, we stand back up and I

pass over the papers I collected. She gives me a soft smile, and I try not to notice the flush staining her cheeks—but it's useless.

She's blushing.

Maybe I wasn't the only one basking in the feel of her body in my arms.

I stick my hands in my pockets so I don't try to reach for her again. "So, about that spreadsheet?" I ask.

And just like that, she's back in business mode. Ever the example of pure professionalism. The mask snaps back into place, and she nods before taking off in a series of sentences about how she thinks a spreadsheet will help organize the process of preparing my presentation for the next board meeting.

I do my best to listen to her because I know it's a good idea, but still when I look at her, all I can picture is the way her plump, red lips parted in a gasp as she fell into my arms.

For the rest of the day, that image haunts me, never giving me a reprieve.

When I get home and hit the weights at the gym in my building, I push myself a little harder than usual. Maybe it's to help clear my mind, or maybe it's punishment for the fact that I can't get Whitney out of my head.

I grunt and groan as I do set after set, relishing in the aching burn of my muscles. Finally, when I'm exhausted and sweaty, I call it a night.

With a wipe of my forehead, I go back upstairs to my apartment and head to the bathroom. When there is steam billowing out from behind the glass shower stall, I get in and do my best to rinse the day off.

But even in the protection and silence of my own home, my thoughts keep returning to Whitney. I can't get over the way her outfit hugged all her curves so perfectly today. She is a vision through and through. And those lips. *Fuck,* what I wouldn't give to know what they'd look like around my cock, or pressed to my skin.

I've only known her for a week, but in that entire week, she's consumed every waking thought. I've never crossed this line with an employee before, but when it comes to Whitney Palmer, I just can't seem to help myself.

With an exasperated sigh, I lean my forehead against the cool tiles of the shower. My hand wanders to my hardened cock, and I grip my length, moaning in relief from the pressure. My thoughts remain on Whitney, and I let myself imagine what it would be like if she were mine.

It's inappropriate beyond measure, I know, but I can't help it.

My hand rises and lowers over my cock, and I imagine that it's her dainty hand with her pink fingernails. I close my eyes and picture her on her knees in front of me, looking up at me through those thick eyelashes as she pleasures me.

I wonder how she'd react to praise. Even in the office, she's always aiming to please. I wouldn't be surprised if she'd get off to a *good girl* here or there.

I turn around and lean my back against the shower wall, my cock still in my death grip as I stroke it, all the while pretending it's her. My desire for her continues to climb until my body is trembling against the pleasure of my hand stroking up and down.

Fuck, Whitney, such a good girl for me.

With a loud grunt, I come, spilling down into the draining water of the shower. My chest rises and falls with pleasure, and I lean back against the shower wall again, cursing myself.

I take a deep breath and shake my head at myself. I can't be falling for an employee. It crosses every professional line and puts both of our jobs at risk. But I can't stop myself, either.

I am so fucked.

4

WHITNEY

"WHAT IS THIS?" I ask once I make it to my desk Thursday morning. For once, Theo is here before me. He looks up from whatever he's working on to see what I'm asking about. In a smooth movement, he pushes back his chair and walks out of the office.

In a way that is sexy enough to be sinful, he leans on his doorframe, slides his hands into his slack pockets, and hits me with an amused grin. "What is what?"

I point at the potted plant sitting on my desk. "*That.*"

"It's an orchid."

I roll my eyes. "Yes, I can see that. But *why* might be a better question."

"As a thank you for speaking out when the board started attacking me yesterday," Theo says. He gives me a soft smile. "I thought I would be a shoo-in, given my resume and the initial plan I had presented to them. I wasn't expecting the transition to be so...rough."

"Elena is an old bat," I explain, waving my hand. "She was

always riding Mr. Peterson about the stupidest things too. Every time she opens her mouth, something negative rolls out."

"Well, even still," Theo says, crossing his arms over his chest. The movement makes his biceps bulge, and though they're covered by his light gray work shirt, I can tell he puts a lot of time in at the gym. For whatever reason, that fact makes my palms sweaty. "I appreciate it. So, this is my thank you."

I look at the potted flower in front of me. The blossoms are wide open, each petal displaying its own intricate, violet pattern. The elegance of the flower is not lost on me, and I find myself staring at it, getting lost in the gesture.

"It really is beautiful," I whisper, still tracing over the purple streaks and dots weaving across the blossom with my gaze.

"A beautiful flower for a beautiful assistant," Theo says. His words finally draw my attention back to him, and I swallow thickly, noting that my cheeks are burning. He's watching me with an unreadable expression and a gleam in his eyes. My heart rate seems to pick up and my mouth goes dry as I clasp my fingers tightly in front of me.

We hold each other's gaze up until the point where it almost becomes uncomfortable. Finally, he pushes himself off the doorway. "Guess we better get to work. I've got a deadline to meet." He shoots me a wink and then disappears back into his office.

I look back to the flower as my computer boots up, still a little wonderstruck from the encounter. My mind is racing, wondering if there is any other hidden meaning to Theo's gift this morning. To distract my thoughts from straying too far, I do an internet search on the care and feeding of orchids, jot a few notes down on a sticky pad, and put it on the plant. It's not difficult. Surely, I can keep this thing alive.

I don't have the best track record when it comes to plants, but I am well and determined to do my best with this one.

No one has given me flowers before.

It's a sad fact at my tender age of twenty-seven, and yet, it's the truth.

Though I've had my fair share of relationships, I have yet to find a man who also noted the significance of simple gestures, such as gifting flowers.

Who knew I just needed to get a new boss to experience this life milestone?

For the rest of the day, my eyes keep being drawn toward the flower, and I catch myself smiling to myself one too many times. My thoughts stray to my little list *again,* thinking of the second thing that Theo's crossed off.

Number 5: Random Acts of Kindness

Two weeks go by, and surprisingly, I don't kill the orchid. Much to my satisfaction, the beautiful buds are still holding strong. As if acting as a beacon, it's one of the first things I see when I step out of the elevator on our floor, and it reminds me of the way he grinned at me as he called me beautiful. Every morning, it brings a smile to my face and I'm happy to have something to brighten up my day right away. Though, with the euphoric feeling comes a lingering curiosity, and I wonder if he feels a similar attraction to me as I feel to him. I try to reason with myself and play it off as Theo just being friendly, but still, the possibility is there.

Theo and I have fallen into a comfortable routine. He buries himself in work, and I try my best to support him where I can.

Nexus Realty Group, over the last few years, has really boomed into the corporate and commercial realty scene. Mr.

Peterson seemed to do a good job of setting up Theo for success without even realizing it. From last year's financial reports, which I've stolen a glimpse of while handing them over, Nexus is doing well financially—*really well.*

A sense of pride overtakes me when I realize that Theo really hit the jackpot with our business. As we get to know each other and spend more hours working together, I grow more and more impressed with the way he plans to improve Nexus. I sincerely hope that he can win over the Board of Directors and show them that they absolutely made the right choice by taking a chance on him.

"Whitney?" Theo's deep voice bellows from inside his office on a Thursday morning, about two weeks after the board meeting debacle.

"Yes?" I call back to him as I highlight another sentence in the contract I'm reading over on the computer. I just have to finish proofreading it for consistency before I send it over for him to sign.

"What is this on my schedule today?"

I peek up from my computer and in the direction of Theo's office. Pushing my chair back, I step away from my desk and slide into his doorway. I have to stifle a laugh at what I find, though it simultaneously sets my nerves on edge. His desk is a mess, with pens and sticky notes strewn everywhere. There's a stack of files off to one side, which I know he's supposed to be working through. I can't imagine having my workspace look like that.

Theo's deadline is still looming over both of us. We've both been working furiously, but he doesn't need to say it out loud for me to know that we're barely scratching the surface of what needs to be done.

Theo's sitting with his elbows on the desk and his head in his hands. His fingers are threaded through his dark, curly hair as though he wants to rip it out. When he finally registers my presence, he looks up at me, the epitome of overwhelmed.

"What is my appointment at one today?"

I cross my arms over my blue blouse and look at him, pretending to be stern. "That's your appointment with Chris Johnson, head of marketing. Remember, you specifically asked me to put that on the schedule today? Because we had a 'light' day?"

With a heavy sigh, Theo nods and then looks back down at the stack of papers in front of him. He scribbles something on a sticky note, slaps it on the top page, and then flips to the next.

I watch him with rapt curiosity. Being so used to how Mr. Peterson functioned, seeing someone else in the thick of it is fascinating. Mr. Peterson worked with gentle focus, making sure to give each task the appropriate time required before moving on to the next.

Theo seems to be a tornado in action. He's got a million things going on at once that all hold a small piece of his attention. Though he's only been here for a few weeks, he's gotten twice the amount of work done that Mr. Peterson could have finished in a month.

I suppose there is a method to his madness—quite literally. I'll never understand it, but if it works for him, so be it. It's not my place to force him to be more organized, even though the fact that he's not frustrates me to no end.

In the few weeks that Theo has been here, I've slowly started to learn his habits. He likes utter silence most of the time; any little noise or distraction seems to throw him off his game, and it takes him much longer to pick up back where he was. I've had to make some serious compromises—usually, I like to have some light piano music playing while I work, and a certain ringer set on my desktop phone.

I swear, the first time that thing rang, Theo had a full-blown meltdown. I answered it by the second ring, but not even a moment later, he was stomping out of his office and glowering at me from the doorway. After I had finished my call, he nipped this issue right in the bud. I was no longer allowed to have my ringer on my desk phone unless I was away from my desk or wearing a headset.

It was an adjustment for sure, and I had found myself getting annoyed with his strict expectations more often than not. But now, a few weeks in, I am starting to find the groove of working for him.

He is efficient, I'll give him that. I felt like a lot of the time, I had to keep Mr. Peterson on time with deadlines. His determination to give each task the proper attention tended to run us late. Not with Theo, though. Usually, if I handed him an invoice or something that needed a read-through and a signature, he'd have it back on my desk within the hour.

We are racing against a clock, which is where I think most of Theo's aggravation is coming from now. He has been reading through contracts, financial reports, budget analyses, and fiscal calendars—all the non-fun, housekeeping things that are involved when taking over a business.

And Nexus has been around a long time, which means there's only that much more to get through.

I can tell, though, Theo is committed. He wants to do well here and make a difference in this company's future, even with the Board of Directors breathing down his neck. It is an attractive quality—as if Theo needs any help in that department.

Number 4: Has the Ambition to Succeed

"I might need to reschedule," Theo mutters. "I feel like I'm still balls deep in these reports, with no end in sight. And the last thing I need is to push the deadline. I'm sure the Board of Directors would just *love* that."

I step further into his office. "Is there anything I can do to help?"

He looks at me wryly. "Yes, cancel that meeting. And maybe have lunch with me?"

My cheeks heat, despite myself. He's still been on this lunch thing, attempting to snag me for a lunch date ever since he first arrived. I've somehow managed to avoid it, though I know at some point, I'll have to cave and take him up on his offer. I'm secretly worried about how it will go. There is an undeniable attraction—at least on my part—and the last thing I need is to go to lunch with him and make a fool of myself.

"I'm sorry," I start, and Theo gives me an exasperated look. "I have a meeting I have to be at. Maybe another time?"

His lips pull into a sideways smirk. "You keep evading me, Whitney. One of these days, I'm going to catch you." My thighs clench at the sultry tone in his voice. Surely, I must be imagining the way his eyes heat as he stares at me from across the room.

He watches me as though he wants to have *me* for lunch, and it makes my body come alive with a mix of anticipation and dire need.

It seems that after my blunt outburst at the meeting, the dynamic between Theo and me has changed, despite how much we both try to keep it under control. Following that specific event, Theo seemed almost enthralled with me. I don't think I'll very quickly forget the way that he watched me as we walked out of that boardroom together. And, of course, that was only made worse by me, literally, tripping into his office and falling into his arms.

If I thought he was looking at me a certain way before, I quickly learned what it meant to have Theo Hurst *look* at me.

For the first time in maybe my whole life, right there in Theo's arms, I felt like I was finally being seen. And though I'm certain I was imagining it, there was a fire behind Theo's eyes that told me he liked what he saw. And even now, as I replay it, all I can think about is how he called me beautiful when he gave me that flower the following morning.

Perhaps there was more to that gift than just a friendly gesture.

Thankfully, we haven't had any more embarrassing events. Rather than wearing heels again and risking tripping over his threshold, I've opted for flats with only an inch heel at most.

Since that first week, our entire work life has been focused and driven by the need to check off the necessary requirements for the follow-up meeting in a few months.

Despite what my heart tells me, my brain agrees that this is for the best. Company policy at Nexus is no employee relationships.

Though Theo may be the most attractive man I've ever laid eyes on, he's not mine. He is my *boss*. Nothing more.

But even with that in mind, throughout the following days, I often catch myself admiring the way he tugs at his necktie when he gets too stressed or rolls up the sleeves of his dress shirt when he's frustrated.

It's all these little things that are drawing me away from seeing Theo as my boss, and instead, seeing him as a man.

A man I'm terribly attracted to.

And a man who might just be attracted to me too.

I just hope that I can keep reminding my heart to stay in line and listen to reason. Otherwise, I might just find myself in some treacherous waters.

5

THEO

AS I EMERGE from the confines of my work, I glance up at the time on my computer screen. My stomach rumbles the second I notice it's lunchtime. I forgot to pack something today, which means I'll have to fend for myself and either venture down into the lunchroom or go off-site to find somewhere to eat.

I'm buried deep in a mess that just seems to be getting bigger and bigger the more I dig. I'm not a numbers guy, but even I can tell when I look at these income reports that some things have been skewed.

If I had known what a battlefield I was walking into, I'm not sure I would've signed on the dotted line. I've overcome a lot of things within my career as an executive, but the premonition that this might be bigger than anything I've ever faced has me greatly concerned.

My goal coming into this company was to help lead it into a new avenue of commercial real estate, but if there's something bigger lurking here, I'm going to need to uncover it before I can even hope to start making any notable changes.

And with the Board breathing down my neck with their high expectations, I know it's going to have to happen soon.

A sneeze from outside my office breaks me out of my grim thought processes. *Whitney.*

I guess there have been some good things to come from taking over this company. If I hadn't made the deal, who knows if I would've had the pleasure of meeting my assistant.

A sly smirk forms on my face, and before I know it, I'm pushing away from my desk and sauntering out to Whitney's workspace. She looks up as soon as I'm standing in front of her, and my dick twitches at how her plump lips purse.

"Hi, Theo."

Damn. I could get used to the sound of my name on her lips. It takes every ounce of willpower to keep my gaze from falling back down to her mouth and wondering what those plump lips might feel like on mine.

"What can I help you with?" she asks as her fingers fly over her keyboard. She hits the *enter* key with her pinky and then turns her full attention to me.

I stick my hands in my pockets to act as some type of boundary between us. Not that I'd actually reach out for her, but the urge to be close to her pulls stronger and stronger every day. I'm fucked when it comes to her. No matter how hard I try to keep myself in line, even being in her presence has me balled up in knots. For the last few weeks, I've made valiant attempts to be professional, and so far, I haven't crossed the line, aside from when she fell into my arms. But each day, whatever this is between us seems to grow more and more pronounced.

I wonder if she can feel it too. I'm dying to know what's going through her head when she sees me. I suspect it's similar to how I'm feeling, based on the way her eyes dilate and her breath hitches when I roll up my sleeves. Or how her elegant tongue darts out and wets her lips when I catch her watching me chew on the cap of my pen. Or when our eyes meet and we don't look away from each other until a second longer than is generally customary.

"What's on your agenda today?" I ask her, forcing myself back into business-mode.

She looks down at her schedule, laying on her desk. "I have a meeting at two o'clock, but other than that, it's a light day. Anything you need me to do?"

"Yes," I say, and she perks up. *Fuck,* she's a dream. "Come to lunch with me." Her lips part slightly, and I smile victoriously, knowing I've finally got her. She can't say no now. "Please," I add, for good measure.

Her mouth purses off to the side as she watches me and considers my request. I'm surprised when she nods her head. Surprised, and then equal parts relieved, that I finally get to spend time with her outside of this office and concerned that we're making a terrible mistake in doing so. I know the stakes, and I'm sure she does too. But I just can't seem to help myself. "Okay, you win. Where do you want to go?"

I press my lips together in a tight smile. I hadn't thought that far ahead, sure that she would turn me down again. "Uh, wherever is fine. You pick."

She shoots me a conspiratorial smile, like she knows I don't know shit about what restaurants are around the building. "Okay, how about JT's?"

I shrug. "Sure. I don't know what that is."

Whitney laughs and reaches under her desk for her bag. Swinging it over her shoulder, she walks around the edge of the desk until she's standing next to me. "It's a pub. I'm sure there's something there that your refined tastes will like."

I can't help but grin at her as she leads us out of the building. I know we're getting a few questionable looks, but they can get over it. I'm just a CEO, having lunch with his assistant.

They can whisper about us all they want, but my day has gotten infinitely better now that I get to spend time with Whitney outside of our usual setting.

We walk just a few blocks from our building, over to the hole-in-the-wall pub. The minute we step inside, I know immediately that I'm going to like whatever food I order here. Since rising to the executive level, I hardly ever find myself in small joints like this. Nowadays, I'm more likely to be stuck in a stuffy boardroom with catered food. Which is fine, but every once in a while, I still have the urge to demolish a big, greasy burger.

Whitney leads us over to a high-top table in the bar area. A waiter comes over and sets down two coasters on the table before taking our drink order and handing us some menus.

Whitney doesn't even glance at it.

She still takes it gratefully, but lays the menu down flat on the table as soon as the waiter walks away.

I raise a brow at her. "Come here often?"

She gives me a sheepish smile and shrugs one shoulder. "Sometimes."

"So, what's good here?" I inquire, browsing over the menu and taking in all the options.

She laughs, and my eyes fly back up to her. "Pretty much everything. I don't think you could order anything bad from this place."

"Good to know," I mumble before snapping my menu shut, decided.

The waiter returns then with our drinks: a diet soda for Whitney and water for me.

"So, how's your day going?" Whitney asks, pulling the paper off her straw and sticking it into the ice and soda. She leans forward and wraps her lips around the straw, taking a sip of her drink.

I swallow thickly and pull my attention from her mouth. "Lots of financial reports today. So, in other words, terrible."

"Finances aren't your thing, huh?"

"No, that's more my brother's wheelhouse," I say.

"I heard he'll be joining us," she says, stirring her straw around. "Was that always the plan?"

I rest my elbows on the table, leaning toward her a little more. "Kind of. I pushed for him to be appointed as CFO, because I'm terrible at numbers. He's much better at it. We seem to balance each other well. I manage well, and he's good with numbers and statements."

I'm counting down the days until Chase gets to the office. I can't wait for him to see the mess I've uncovered—the mess that Vance Peterson seemed to go to great lengths to bury.

She nods as if that makes perfect sense. "Have you always done realty?"

"No, actually. Before this, we worked for a textile trading corporation over in London. When this opportunity presented itself, I knew we had to jump on it. My grandfather was great friends with Vance, and when he said he was looking to retire soon, my name got put into the ring. I worked hard to come up with a proposal that stood out enough to catch the attention of the Board. Hopefully, it pays off and they'll think I'm worth it in the long run."

She waves her hand, dismissing my negative thoughts. "They will. I know they will. So, your brother—what's his name?"

"Chase," I say. "He should be starting here in the next few weeks."

"Is he as apt for troublemaking as you are?" she says, her voice teasing.

I smirk and shake my head. "I'm sure I don't know what you're talking about."

She chuckles just as the waiter arrives again to take our orders. Whitney orders the chicken parmesan sandwich with a side salad. I follow through on my thoughts from earlier and order the thickest, juiciest cheeseburger they have—with added bacon.

"Now it's your turn on the hot seat," I say once we're alone again. "Tell me about you. We've been working together for a few weeks now, but I feel like I know hardly anything about you, other than that you're crazy about sticky notes and high-lighters."

I try to ignore the way pink blooms on her cheeks and how her eyes light up at the mention of her organizing habits. "There's not much to tell. I live a pretty boring life."

"Somehow, I doubt that," I say.

Whitney rolls her eyes. "Really. I come to work in the morning. Then I leave at the end of the day. I go home, scavenge something for dinner, and then go to bed, only to do it all over again." She glanced up to the ceiling, then back down to me. "Oh, and sometimes I hang out with my friend, Leila, on the weekends. She's a science teacher."

I nod my head but lean back in my chair. "There's got to be more. Come on, tell me. What's one of your deepest secrets?"

She gives me a look like she doesn't know if I'm joking or not. I'm not. I want to know her. When I don't budge from my expectant position, her shoulders depress with an exhale.

"My deepest secrets?" she questions. "Like, work wise or—"

I nod my head. "Anything. Your dreams, or ambitions, or whatever. Lay it on me. I want to know."

She's hesitant as she nibbles on her bottom lip. "Okay, fine. I guess I always dreamed that by this age, I'd be married and have a family. It's all I've ever really wanted. I never imagined I'd be stuck in the corporate world as an assistant still."

Something indescribable settles in my chest that she'd feel

comfortable admitting that out loud to her *boss*. And yet, I did ask for a secret. I feel honored that she felt safe enough to share that major aspect of herself with me.

"You want a family?" I ask her softly, even though she just said it out loud. She nods, and the way her face takes on a resigned expression eats at my heart. "Then why don't you have one?"

She plays with a strand of her sandy blonde hair and looks down, as if she's now embarrassed by this line of conversation. "I don't know. I guess I just never met the right person, and I got comfortable in my position with Nexus. And Mr. Peterson was a lot of wonderful things, but I doubt he would have been flexible enough to allow me to be a part-time mom and a part-time assistant at the same time. He'd love my children as if they were his own, but he'd need someone who could be there full-time for him."

"That's a shame," I say.

"I guess. I'm happy where I am, though."

I can't help the frown that forms on my face as I lean forward again. "Comfortable isn't always good, you know? Sometimes you have to get uncomfortable to grow into the best version of yourself. Sometimes you have to take risks to get what you want."

Whitney falls silent, and her eyes study my face intently like she's trying to find something that's not there. She blinks a few times, but then her lips twist into a smile. "You're right. Maybe someday."

"How'd you end up working for Peterson anyway?" I inquire.

A fond smile spreads across her face, though it's tinged with a hint of sadness and mourning. "It's kind of a long story." When I don't move, waiting expectantly, she inhales and then drops her shoulders. I suddenly have a spark of regret, knowing this is probably still a sore subject for her. But she surprises me when she jumps right into her story. "Okay, well. I grew up in a single-parent home. My father was never around, and then died when I was ten, anyway. So, it was just me and my mom. She died too, from an aggressive form of breast cancer, when I was eighteen. Mr. Peterson was a member at the church we went to, and he had always been a family friend. We spent a lot of holidays at their home. For pretty much my whole life, he was the only father figure I've ever had.

"When my mother died, he swooped in, kind of like a hero, and helped me get everything settled, and figure out what my next steps were. After everything, he offered me a position at his company to be his assistant, and I couldn't say no. At that time, I really had no home, and no money, so it was the obvious choice to say yes." She shrugs her shoulders like it makes perfect sense in her head. "And I've been here ever since."

My stomach twists with a sick realization that my predecessor was extremely important in Whitney's life. She can't possibly know that he was dealing in shady business, otherwise she wouldn't have such a fond expression on her face when she spoke of him.

It's hard to unite these two versions of Vance Peterson, knowing that he was such a good person in her eyes, yet possibly stealing large amounts of money from his company on the side. My mind and my heart are conflicted with the realization that at some point, she's going to have to accept that he wasn't the person she thought he was. And with that realization comes a sense of guilt, knowing that at some point, I'll have to ruin that perfect image she has of him.

"Why do you call him *Mr.* Peterson?" I ask, curious. "I'd think that if you were that close to him and his wife, you'd be more on a first name basis."

She shrugs her shoulder. "I don't know. I always called him

that as a child and for whatever reason, it carried into my adult-hood. The idea of calling him anything but that makes me feel weird." She tilts her head as she thinks it over. "I guess it's like if you ever had a favorite teacher in elementary school. I'm sure if you ran into them, even as an adult, you'd still refer to them as Mister or Missus whatever."

I chuckle and nod, catching on to what she's saying. Before I have the chance to ask her any further questions about her story, our food arrives, and we get distracted. Each of us digs into the plates in front of us. I try to ignore the way Whitney makes a satisfied noise when she takes the first bite of her chicken sandwich, but the sound cuts me straight to the core.

God, this woman.

She'll be the death of me, I swear it.

We make small talk while we eat our lunches, though we never get back to the subject of Peterson, which is probably by her design. I've just barely started telling her a story about when I was volunteering at a house build when she cuts me off with a raised hand.

"Wait. You *volunteer?*"

There's something about the way she asks the question that has me laughing. Like it's a fact that surprises her. "Yes. I work a lot with Habitat for Humanity. I donate to them annually, and I help out on their projects when I can."

She gives me that weird look again; her eyebrows knit together thoughtfully in the middle and her lips pull off to the side, and I'm not sure if I like it. It's almost as if she's gauging me against every other guy she's ever known. Yet, at the same time, there's a fire behind her gaze that tells me she likes what she's looking at. She likes what I'm telling her about myself.

There's something deep within me that wants to achieve Whitney's approval. She was so attached to her old boss that I feel like I have some high expectations to live up to, which, in the business world, is something I'm no stranger to. But in real life, struggling with feeling like I'm worthy has been something I've always had a hard time facing. Aside from the workplace, I just want her to like *me*.

It's been a long, long time since I've been this desperate for a woman's attention. Yet, every day, I feel like I'm pining after her for even the simplest lingering glance or, if I'm lucky, a smile.

"That's great, Theo," she says, and by the tone of her voice, I can tell she really means it. "I love that."

My chest puffs out a little at her praise, and my face morphs into a dopey smile. I can't help it. In our short time together, she's brought out a side of me that I had no idea existed.

I can't help but imagine what it would be like to please her like this all the time. I could easily see myself becoming addicted to the way her eyes light up with pleasure after hearing what I'm saying to her or seeing the look of awe morph over her features.

As we finish our lunches and walk back to the office, I know I'm in deep shit.

Already, I'm in way too deep. With each second that goes by, I feel our connection deepening and strengthening into a friendship, a partnership.

Which, at face value, may be fine, but I know those lines can easily be blurred.

How easy would it be for one of us to cross over into territory from which we can never come back?

As Whitney takes her seat at her desk, my chest pangs with regret. I shouldn't have pushed her so hard to have lunch with me. I should have accepted her excuses as a fact that she had no interest in getting to know me better. I should've kept the line between us drawn. But I just couldn't help myself.

The company policy is clear, and that fact lingers in the back of my mind, forcing self-doubt to rear its ugly head every so often as I go through the rest of the day.

I enjoyed my time with her. But we got the chance to know each other a little better now, differently from just boss and assistant roles.

But despite it all, when the day ends and she flashes me that pretty smile of hers before leaving, I know that even with the risks, I regret nothing.

I like her. I like Whitney Palmer, the woman, way more than I like Whitney Palmer, the assistant.

Which means I'm in trouble. We could *both* be in trouble.

Big time.

6

—————

WHITNEY

WHEN I HEAR the elevator door ding, announcing that someone is getting off on our floor, I hastily reach for my purse and pull out my powder compact. I feel silly as I open it and glance at my reflection, making sure that every hair is where it should be and that I don't have lip stain on my teeth, or mascara marks under my eyes.

Just as I'm snapping it closed, Theo walks around the corner and into the line of sight of my desk. He has a folder in his hands, but the minute he's in my vicinity, he looks up and gives me a wide smile. My heart skips a beat as my lips pull up.

His eyes quickly survey me sitting behind my desk, which sends my heart into overdrive. I don't think I'll ever get tired of how he looks at me as if I'm the most important person on Earth.

"How's the day looking?" he asks as he comes closer to my desk. He sets his folder down on top of some of my papers and then leans over the desk, into my personal space.

I catch a whiff of his clean scent, and my mouth goes dry with something I can only attribute to desire.

With every day that passes, my crush on my boss seems to deepen. And I don't know what to do about it.

Swallowing thickly, I turn my computer toward him so he can see his schedule. It's a somewhat light day because I know he still has a lot of headway to make on his reports. There are a few video calls scheduled with different agents whom Theo has yet to meet, but I did my best to cluster them together so he could use the rest of his time efficiently.

Theo hums low in his throat as he peruses his schedule. He points out a block that I manually put in there this morning. It's holding the spot right before our lunch hour. "What's that for?"

I grimace. "Elena asked to have a phone call with you today."

Theo looks as if I've just betrayed him. "You're kidding." I shake my head ruefully. "Did she say what about?"

Again, I shake my head. "No, she didn't. I'm sorry."

He groans and hangs his head, his dark curls flopping over his head. "You're killing me over here, Whit."

Whit.

That's the first time I've heard him shorten my name. Of course, my family and friends all call me Whit when they're joking around, but I like the sound of the nickname on his lips.

"Guess I better get to work then, huh?" he teases further.

I tilt my head and give him a smile. "I guess so, Mr. Boss-Man. Otherwise, I'll tell Elena you're wasting her payroll."

He narrows his eyes playfully. "You're mean. I like it."

I chuckle, and he winks at me before disappearing into his office. My face feels warm, and I press my hands to my cheeks, fighting off the blush that's already raging.

"Come on, Whitney, get a grip," I whisper to myself. I shake my head a few times and breathe sharply through my nose. I have to get a hold of whatever emotions are raging inside me.

Ever since we had lunch a few days ago, my interest in Theo has increased exponentially. The more I got to know about him, the more I liked what I saw.

I almost fell out of my chair at JTs when he told me that he volunteered and donated frequently to Habitat for Humanity. That was one of the most attractive qualities for me—willing to dedicate time and energy to those who need it most. And I could tell by the way his eyes lit up when he spoke about some of the projects he had worked on that this was something he was very passionate about.

It was almost too good to be true, that the new CEO of Nexus Realty Group had a focused goal in assisting Habitat for Humanity. Though our business focused more on commercial properties and selling realty for large businesses, there was something poetic about the fact that Theo was dedicated to improving what the word 'home' means to so many other people.

Theo would never know, but that small admission checked off the sixth item on my list, putting him at meeting four of my little requirements.

Number 6: Has a philanthropic passion

This was one quality that not very many of my previous love affairs had met. I live in a big city and often find myself attracted to many of the working upper class. Surprisingly—or maybe not—they are much more focused on helping them-selves, rather than helping others.

Which is why I wasn't too concerned when most of those relationships didn't work out.

I ignore the fact that Theo has already met four of my ten

list items. I think about the little notebook at home and fight off a smile. Though that seems insignificant, I have the feeling that Theo is going to surprise me in many more ways, the more I get to know him.

My morning passes uneventfully. I focus on responding to emails and other correspondence. Then I move on to filing and scanning essential paper documents into an e-file.

Lunch time comes up quickly; before I know it, my stomach rumbles in protest, letting me know it's time to take a break and get some food. As if on cue, the phone line rings, and I pick it up, placing the receiver to my ear. "Nexus Realty Group—Theo Hurst's office."

"Ms. Palmer," a frigid voice greets me from the other line.

I shoot an alarmed glance over at Theo's office. He's buried deep in paperwork, not paying attention to me out here. "Hello, Elena."

"Is Mr. Hurst available for our meeting?" she asks, though I know there's really only one acceptable answer to her question.

"I'll put you through."

I press the hold button and then dial Theo's line. I could just give him a holler, given that he's only a few yards from me, but I don't think he'd appreciate the rest of the floor knowing that Elena's likely going to rip him a new one—heaven knows what about, but that's her style.

Theo picks up on the second ring. "Yeah?" His voice is drained, and I instantly know he's not having a good time with his paperwork this morning.

"Elena's on the line for your meeting."

He sighs, thanks me, and says, "Can't wait to find out what this is about."

I bite my lip and press the buttons to send Elena to Theo's line. I hear him pick up from my desk when the phone rings, and he greets her with a fake, chipper attitude. I wheel my chair around so I can peek into his office a little better.

I roll my eyes dramatically when he sees me peering around the door frame. He grins and gives me a sarcastic thumbs-up before turning his attention to his computer. When he's deep into his phone call, I laugh to myself and grab my bag and other items, taking the opportunity while he's tied up to run downstairs and grab some lunch.

I can't put it off any longer. My rumbling stomach is a nuisance. I figure I'll grab something quick and bring it back up to my desk while I wait for Theo to finish his phone call. Roaming around the cafeteria, I find a pre-made turkey sandwich. I pick it up and then grab a package of chips and a cookie. To drink, I choose a glass bottle of Pellegrino sparkling water.

Once I check out, I'm ready to head back upstairs when someone calls my name.

I turn around to see some of the girls from accounting waving their hands at me. With a grin, I walk over to their table and set my stuff down.

"Hi there," I say with a smile. "How's it going?"

"Can't complain," one of the girls says—I think her name is Lucy. "Things have been pretty slow ever since Mr. Hurst took over. We've just been twiddling our thumbs, waiting for something to happen."

I frown a little at this information. "Are we not selling as many properties?"

Lucy shrugs and looks at the girl sitting next to her. "It's definitely declined."

My lips pull down even further. Does Theo know about that or not? "I'll have to look into that. It's not like our agents haven't been able to work since Theo took over."

Lucy stirs her salad around in her bowl. "Who knows? I

just work here. But like I said, you won't see me complaining about less to do."

My lips thin into a line, and I'm about to change the topic when I'm interrupted.

"Whitney," a deep voice that I've grown increasingly fond of mutters behind me. I can sense a tinge of amusement in his tone that has my palms breaking out in a sweat.

I turn around to face Theo, who is watching me and the girls with an amused grin on his face. "Hi, Mr. Hurst."

His eyebrow twitches at the formality, but he doesn't object. He wouldn't do so in front of his employees. "I thought we could debrief my phone call real quick before I have to run into my next meeting. Do you think you could come back upstairs in a few minutes?"

"Of course, I'll be right up."

He gives me a soft smile. "Thanks, Whit."

I already know my cheeks are heating up, just like they did this morning when he called me that. My skin prickles with the awareness of the other girls watching the interaction closely. Theo holds my gaze just long enough for it to be uncomfortable before he walks out of the cafeteria.

"Geez, just ask him to fuck you already," Lucy mutters under her breath, breaking me out of my spell as I watch him walk away.

I stare at her, slack-jawed, scandalized that she just said that. "Excuse me?"

"We all saw how he was looking at you," she muttered, stabbing at her salad with her fork.

I frown at her as I gather up my things. "He's my boss. Nothing more."

Some of the other girls share unconvinced glances, but I don't give them any more energy. I didn't lie. Theo *is* my boss and nothing more. There hasn't been anything further than a few awkward glances and a wink or two.

It doesn't matter that I turn to complete mush when he winks at me or gives me his sideways grin.

Definitely not.

Lucy rolls her eyes and goes back to her meal with a little smirk playing on her lips. "Whatever you've got to tell yourself, Whitney. Trust me, I don't think he'd be that opposed to it. Just be careful. I'd hate to see you get fired when you've worked here so many years over a stupid fling. Don't be stupid about it."

My face flames, and I can't find it in myself to fire anything back. Instead, I simply walk away, letting her words play on repeat.

As I walk back to our office, I'm gripping my glass bottle of sparkling water so tightly that I think the cap is making a permanent indent in my palm. The elevator dings to our floor, and I step off, still grumbling to myself about what she said. It was ridiculous. And inappropriate.

I find Theo in his office, tapping furiously on his keyboard. He looks up when I enter and folds his arms over his desk, giving me an amused glare. "I hope I didn't interrupt."

I wave him off with the hand holding my bottle of sparkling water, but then everything goes wrong.

"Shit!" I exclaim when the bottle flies out of my hand and smashes into a million pieces on the floor.

Theo hops up from his seat and rounds the desk, coming over to view the mess. His hands shoot out to stop mine when I crouch down and reach to pick up a few pieces with my fingers. "Stop, you'll cut yourself."

I pull my hands away before he can touch me, but the movement causes me to fall back. I stagger in my heels, off balance, but then fall backwards until I'm sitting on his floor. I cover my face with my hands and shake my head. Embarrassment burns on my cheeks.

"I'm so sorry."

"It's fine, Whitney. It was an accident." Theo's baritone voice has taken on a more soothing tone as if he can tell that I'm overwhelmed and frustrated. "I'll go find something to clean this up. Do we have a broom closet on this floor?"

I pull my hands away from my face and push myself into a standing position. "We do, but I can get it."

Before he has a chance to protest, I swiftly walk out of his office and down the hall to the broom closet. I hear his footsteps behind me, so I go quicker. When I make it to the closet, I swing open the door and step inside. He's right behind me, and I can feel his warm breath tickle the back of my neck as we both stand in the small space.

It's dark and smells like bleach and other disinfectants, mixed with the increasingly-familiar scent of his clean aftershave.

Before I can stop myself, I'm transported back to my dream on the night I woke up to the terrible phone call informing me that Mr. Peterson passed away.

Lips pressing against my skin, kissing, and nipping along every divot of my neck.

Sultry words and spoken promises that had my heart aching.

I pull myself out of it before I get too carried away.

"There's a dustpan," I say, and I curse myself for how my voice sounds. My normal tone comes across way more sultry than I intend it to, making me sound like being this close to him is turning me on. Theo's large body seems to tower over mine, though there's still a bit of distance between us.

That distance disappears as the two of us reach for the dustpan at the same time.

His fingers brush mine, and a white-hot shock of electricity travels from the tips of my fingers, all the way up my arm and into my chest.

I rip away from him with a gasp and lean back, trying to put as much distance between us as I possibly can. However, in that process, I bump into a mop handle, and it falls over onto a stack of other cleaning supplies, which tumble down with a crash.

Theo's hands quickly find their way around my waist, and he urges me out of the way. We both stare down at the floor. Once everything settles, he flexes his hands on my hips, holding me steady. Slowly, he raises his eyes to mine and my body heats under his gaze. His grip on me is unyielding as he pulls me closer to him.

As if time slows down, he brings me closer to him until I'm captivated by his gaze. My breathing shallows as his face inches toward mine.

His eyes are watching me for any possible sign of discomfort—waiting for me to tell him to stop.

But I don't.

I can't.

As he leans closer to me, I feel a magnetic pulse coursing through my body, urging me closer and allowing him to close the distance between us.

His mouth slowly lowers to mine until I feel the briefest brush of his lips against mine.

This is so wrong, so inappropriate.

And yet—

I close my eyes, tipping my jaw up and preparing for him to crash his mouth down on mine and claim me as his own.

But then my phone rings, shattering any type of illusion we are both living in.

Theo lets go of me as if he's been burned. My chest aches

as I reach for my phone in my waistband and pull it out. I frown down at the screen, seeing Leila's name flash across. I decline the call as Theo takes a few steps away until he's outside of the closet.

When I look back up at him, his face has morphed into stone. His hand rubs at the back of his neck, his fingers kneading deep into the muscles. His brows are furrowed, and his lips are drawn into a frown.

My eyes fall to the floor as I step out of the closet, dustpan in hand. Before I have a chance to apologize or even say anything, Theo is reaching for the dustpan and pulling it out of my grasp.

Without a word, he turns on his toe and walks away from me and into his office, where he closes the door.

The action is like a bucket of cold water washing over me.

In the few weeks that he's been here, he hasn't closed the door unless he's in an important meeting.

I go back to my desk and fall into the chair. My fingers flutter over my tingling lips, and I close my eyes, replaying back what just happened.

All I can think about as I recall the memory is that I may have lied to the girls at lunch. Sure, Theo is my boss, but there is *definitely* something more.

But now, the bigger question comes to mind. What am I going to do about this?

7

THEO

"THERE'S a call for you on line two," Whitney's smooth voice echoes through the intercom. This has been the only way we've been communicating today. I've been working with my door closed all day, which I hate to do, but it's a necessity right now.

I have work to do, and I simply can't do it knowing she's sitting outside my office at her desk, her perky little tits pressed so perfectly together in that tight, blue, low-cut blouse she's wearing today. My fascination with her has only worsened the longer I've been here, which is problematic at the very least.

I seem absolutely obsessed with how her cheeks turn a bright, rosy color when I call her *Whit*. Honestly, it was an accident the first time it happened, but the second time, and all the times I've done it after the fact, assuredly were not.

I feel compelled to sneak the nickname in as often as I possibly can so that I can see her slate blue eyes glitter and her cheeks flush in the sexiest way possible.

If I weren't drowning in reports and responsibilities, it would probably be fine.

Or if she weren't an employee under my payroll.

It may say a lot about me that the second detail was less important than the former. After all, if I didn't finish the tasks assigned to me by my deadline, she wouldn't be my employee anymore anyway, because I would no longer hold the position as her boss.

I dig my fingers in my hair and groan, giving the strands a slight tug and releasing some of the pent-up tension throughout my head. These financial reports are getting increasingly worse the longer I look at them. More and more evidence is piling up that there were some back door deals made somewhere and that Vance Peterson knew about them all along.

But I can't find the missing piece to tie it all together.

Numbers aren't my strong suit, and I think he was banking on that. Whatever he did, he wove it all together with a stealthy hand and hid it so effortlessly that you'd only catch it if you were looking at it.

But even though I've been looking at it for weeks now, I still can't put it all together.

And underneath all that frustration is a sense of guilt toward the fact that Whitney still knows none of this. I know I'll have to tell her at some point, but I'm going to wait for as long as I possibly can, and ensure that I am absolutely certain before ruining her opinion of the prior CEO.

Happy to have some kind of distraction, I pick up the phone and click the line two button, giving a quick greeting.

"Theo?"

I lean back in my chair as soon as my mother's familiar voice rings through the receiver. I lean back in my chair and fight off the affectionate smile that only my mother seems capable of bringing out of me. "Hi, Mom."

"I was just calling to check up on you, I haven't heard from you in weeks," she says. I can hear the sound of papers rustling on the other line, meaning my mother is probably at her own desk, sorting through her own piles of work. I wonder if her eyes are going as cross-eyed as mine have been.

"I've been busy," I tell her as I rub the back of my neck and turn my head to peer out the windows. It's full-blown autumn here in Chicago, though with every day, it seems to be leaning more and more toward winter. The skies have been a dreary, midwestern gray for most of the week. Having spent the last few years in London, I've grown accustomed to it, but I do miss the bright skies from the East Coast, where my family is from.

"How has everything been going?" Mom asks.

I exhale. "It could be better, could be worse."

She chuckles. "One of those situations, hm?"

I make a noise deep in my throat, acknowledging that it is *indeed* one of *those* situations.

"Listen, Honey, I was also calling to confirm that you'll still be in attendance for the gala at the end of the month."

I close my eyes slowly. I had *completely* forgotten about that, actually, with the amount of stress and work I've been doing. I don't say as such to my mother, though, putting on a cheerful tone and saying, "Of course. Wouldn't miss it!"

It just so happened that my mother was just as passionate about affordable housing and combating poverty as I was. She and my father held a charity gala every year for that specific purpose: to raise money for their foundation and many others who are dedicated to homing people who need it.

I've never missed a year.

Picking up a pen, I scribble the date of the gala on a sticky note and stick it right on the top of my computer so I don't forget it. As I stare at the date, I can only think about the mountains and mountains of reports and write-ups that I still need to get through.

"Chase has already told me he won't be able to make it, but I know I can always count on you. I have you down with a plus one," my mother continues, oblivious to the inner chaos I'm experiencing at the moment. "Do you know who you'll bring with you this year?"

"I haven't a clue," I tell her. Then my eyes fall on my closed office door, where I know Whitney is sitting right outside. "I'll work on it."

My mother makes a pleased sound. "Oh, wonderful. Alright, well, I've got to run. I'm having lunch today with Tippy Farthington, and I imagine Lauren will be there as well. Do you want me to give your regards to her? I'm sure she'd love to hear how you're doing."

The hairs on the back of my neck rise up, along with the dark feelings of worthlessness the name of my ex-girlfriend always seems to evoke in me.

"Mhmm," I respond noncommittally, hoping none of those feelings seep through in my tone. That ship containing Lauren Farthington had sailed a long time ago, with no hopes of ever being found again. Not that I ever wanted it to be either.

"They'll be at the gala too. Ah, well. Okay. Hope you have a wonderful day. I can't wait to see you at the end of the month." She makes a kissing noise on the other end of the phone, and then she hangs up.

With another long glance at the door, I try to bury myself in my work again, pushing all thoughts of my ex-girlfriend and my family aside, and trying to focus on the disaster brewing here underneath all the financial reports from last year. But, unfortunately, I end up just giving myself a headache. A knock on my office door has me looking up. I expect it to be Whitney, coming to keep me on track or bring me the lunch I ordered, but instead, I'm caught off guard when I first, catch sight of the time, realizing the workday is nearly over, and second, when I see my brother's familiar face peering in through the door frame.

I blink a few times, reorienting myself.

My brother steps into my office and slides his hands into his pockets, shooting me an amused grin. "Glad to see you too, brother. Thought I'd get a little warmer welcome than a confused smile. It looks like you're constipated, dude. Wipe that grin off your face."

That snaps me out of it. I shake my head and push away from my desk, closing the distance between Chase and myself. I hug my brother, glad to be seeing him for the first time in weeks.

He claps me on the back and then lets me go.

"'Bout time you showed up," I tease him. "These financials are killing me, man, I'm going to lose my mind any second."

My brother chuckles under his breath and pats me on the head. He loves the fact that he's a few inches taller than me. "You may be the oldest, but you're definitely not the smartest."

At that moment, Whitney peeks her head around the door frame and gives me a sheepish smile. "I'm sorry, Theo. He insisted that I let him in."

I wave her further into my office, still smiling widely. "Whitney, this is my brother, Chase. He'll be joining the company as the CFO."

Whitney, ever the professional, holds out her hand to Chase. My brother's eyes flare a bit as he takes her in, and I resist the urge to punch him in the throat for ogling her. I'm really on edge. Chase takes her hand, shakes it, but then holds on for just a moment too long.

"Pleasure to meet you, *Whitney*," he says. I don't like the sound of her name on his lips, and I have to bite my tongue.

She gives him a warm smile but pulls her hand back from his. "Glad to have you on board. Someone's got to keep your brother in line."

My brother laughs, but I eye her suspiciously, curious if

she's referring to our little rendezvous in the broom closet. We haven't had a chance to discuss what happened with that, with both of us choosing to sweep it under the rug and move on with business as usual. It's not as if we don't have plenty of other things to keep us occupied.

Honestly, I'm not sure I'd even have a valid excuse if we did end up discussing it. I shouldn't have leaned in. I shouldn't have brushed my lips against hers. I just shouldn't have.

End of story. Period.

But I did. And I'm itching to do it again.

Secretly, I'm dying to know how she's feeling about it. Is she yearning for another taste like I am? Is it all she can think about when she lays down in bed at night? Or was she uncomfortable with the whole thing? Does she want to pretend it never happened?

If she had been uncomfortable about it, I would want to know so I could solidify those boundaries. I wasn't about to make her job a place where she didn't feel safe coming to.

But if she felt the same as me?

Well, I'm not quite sure what I'd do with that information.

My animalistic side imagines that I'd grab her, pin her to the wall, and kiss her exactly how a woman should be kissed.

The more rational side of me thinks I'd nod slowly and internalize my relief that she had similar feelings to mine.

Either way, I don't believe that this conversation will be had in the near future, so it doesn't matter how I'd react.

"Yeah, my big brother, here, is the looks of the operation," Chase teases. "But I'm the real mastermind behind it all."

I roll my eyes. "Just because you're good at numbers."

"Among many other things," Chase says, shooting Whitney a wink. I grit my teeth so tightly my jaw starts to ache. Whitney looks amused but doesn't seem impressed by my brother's antics. Chase claps his hands together and looks between the two of us. "So, what's on the agenda for tonight? What special 'Welcome to Chicago' activities do you have planned for me?"

"Um, nothing," I say with a shrug.

"Come on, man. It's a Friday night in the big city," my brother whines. He then whips out his phone and rapidly taps on the screen. "Here, how about this place?"

He holds out his phone to show me the nightclub he just pulled up on a whim. I narrow my eyes at it. The Underground? I'd never heard of the place, but I'm also new to this city.

He shows it to Whitney, who peers at the screen but then grimaces a little. My stomach twists with her reaction. She's not into it.

"Maybe we should try something else," I suggest, thinking we could have a sit-down dinner at a fancy restaurant down town. Whitney would be much more comfortable with that. Maybe she'd even wear a nice cocktail dress.

"Aw, come on. This place has raving reviews. Have you ever been there, Whitney?"

She shakes her head. "No. I remember when it opened. It was a big deal. My friend, Leila, has been there many times, though."

"Oh yeah? You should invite her. Maybe she can show us the ropes," Chase says, winking at her again. A slow fire burns in my chest and my brother grins wickedly at me. I know he's ribbing me like this on purpose.

"I don't know," Whitney says, still unconvinced. I can practically see the wheels spinning in her head, and I wonder if she's mentally making a pros and cons list as we speak.

"*Please.* I need an expert to show me all the best places in this city. And my brother clearly needs an excuse to relax. I mean, his shoulders are up to his ears."

I stare daggers at my brother and he steps behind me,

squeezing the muscles of my shoulders and dragging them down to where they should be. I give nothing away, though now that he mentions it, I can feel the tension bound tight in my traps.

"Okay, okay," Whitney concedes, her lips curving up in a smile. "I'll see if Leila can tag along. Usually, she's always down for a night out, and she'd be your expert."

My brother looks enthralled. "Perfect! See, I knew we'd come up with something."

He looks at me expectantly. I stick my hands in my pockets and exhale. "Well, I guess this is happening, then."

Whitney gives me an amused look, her slate-blue eyes glittering. I can't help but smile when she's looking at me like that. I glance at my wristwatch and then announce, "Think it's time we call it a day, huh?"

Now Whitney's eyebrows arch up on her forehead. I suspect she's about to protest that we still are supposed to be here for another hour, but she doesn't. Maybe it's the sly look I give her or how my brother looks like the cat who got the cream, but Whitney plays along flawlessly.

"I'll go grab my things. We'll meet you there." Now it's her turn to wink, but she doesn't do it at Chase.

Fuck, no.

Good thing too, cause that might have been just the thing to set off the tension coiling inside of me like a tightly wound spring

No. She winks at *me*.

My slacks tighten as my cock hardens at the sight of her long eyelashes fluttering against her cheek.

I clear my throat and dip my chin. She wastes no more time before bouncing out of my office to grab her personal items from her desk.

When Chase and I finally leave the building half an hour

later, I can tell he's itching to razz me about the little interaction in my office.

Once we're in the car and the driver pulls away from the building, he turns on me.

"So, it's like that, *huh?*"

"Don't know what you're talking about."

"Sure. If you want me to back off Whitney, all you've got to do is say so," Chase says to me, still typing away at his phone.

I glower out the window. "I don't care what you do."

"Really? Because your jealousy would say otherwise. I think you're turning a little green."

"Fuck off," I mutter. "I'm not jealous."

My brother laughs. "Whatever you have to tell yourself to sleep at night."

I grumble under my breath, but don't say another word out loud. The last thing I need is for my brother to have more ammunition against me or to know exactly how deep my feelings for Whitney are beginning to run.

8

───────

WHITNEY

THE UNDERGROUND IS a popular nightclub right in the middle of downtown Chicago. I'm a little embarrassed to admit that I've never actually been here before, though I've heard great things about it.

My first impression when I initially saw photos from their opening night, was that it was loud, too busy, and potentially a cesspool for germs. Now that I'm officially here, I'm pleased to find I wasn't totally wrong.

Leila, though, is having the time of her life.

She pulls me through the doors after we are given clearance by the bouncer. Apparently, our names had been put on the list by one Mr. Theodore Hurst.

I never would have guessed that I'd be caught dead meeting my boss at a nightclub on a Friday night, but here we are. I wasn't convinced that Theo was actually into the idea, rather just going along with what his brother suggested.

Regardless, this will be a night for the books.

Leila weaves through the crowds of people until she spots the booth where Theo and Chase are already sitting.

Theo is nursing some kind of cocktail while his brother is already two empty glasses deep. Chase is lounging in his booth. His arms are spread out wide across the back, the epitome of relaxation, while Theo appears to sit uncomfortably in his seat.

I take in the two brothers sitting at the table and am impressed that they look so similar and yet, so different. They have the same build, similar height, broad shoulders, and a sharp jawline, but that's where the similarities end. Theo's dark, curly hair contrasts Chase's sandy blonde. Theo's eyes are calculating as he looks around the bar, and Chase seems to be completely at ease, enjoying the music.

Chase seems to spot us first, straightening up and grinning widely at us as we approach. His gaze instantly goes to Leila, while I'm subjected to the appreciative gaze of Theo Hurst.

My boss watches me with rapt attention as we stand beside the table. Leila looks between the two men, then shoots me an accusatory glare, as if she can't believe I've been holding out on her this entire time.

Chase scoots out of his seat and moves to sit next to Theo, giving us the entire bench to ourselves. I slide in first, sitting right across from Theo, and Leila moves in next to me.

I've never been in a VIP section anywhere, much less a nightclub. I look around and take in the bouncers standing by the entrance to the area, their arms crossed as they glower at the less fortunate. There are waiters and waitresses walking around to each booth, and then a private bar area for VIPs only at the end of the section.

"So, what are you ladies drinking tonight?" Chase asks the two of us once we're settled in our seats.

Leila flips her hair over her shoulder and looks Chase dead in the eye. "Depends on where my night's headed."

Chase's gaze grows dark as he traces her face.

I clear my throat and then glance at Theo, who appears to

be just as uncomfortable as I am. "I think I'll just stick with a vodka tonic tonight," I say.

Leila looks back at me and then grins. "She's boring, I think I want a Mojito."

I try to ignore how Chase and Leila stare at each other. I can only imagine the dirty things going through each of their heads at this exact moment.

"Alright, we'll go get those drinks for you," Theo says as he nudges Chase, pulling him out of the spell my friend seems to have him in. "I'll probably need your help."

Even though it takes great effort, Chase pulls his hungry gaze away from Leila and goes with Theo to the bar, leaving me and my best friend alone in the booth for now.

The minute they're a few feet away, Leila turns on me. Her hazel eyes spark with mischief and she flips her dark hair over her shoulder.

"*Whitney,*" Leila puts an emphasis on my name. I brace myself for the berating I already know is coming. "You didn't tell me that your new boss is an absolute dreamboat."

I pick at a hangnail on my thumb. "I don't know what you're talking about."

"Oh, come on. Don't feed me whatever lie you've convinced yourself. That man is into you! Did you see how his face lit up when we sat down?"

Despite my best efforts, I feel the familiar blush appear on my cheeks, and I curse my vascular system for being so reactive. "I think you're mistaken. That was *Chase* looking at you."

A satisfied smirk appears on Leila's lips, and she doesn't deny not noticing. "I'm definitely down for whatever happens with that tonight."

I bark a laugh. "Leila!"

She giggles as her eyes travel across the VIP section toward the bar, where Theo and Chase are standing with their backs to us. "I'm serious, Whit. That man is just as taken with you as Chase seems to be with me."

I also look at the bar, appreciating the way Theo's changed out of his work clothes and into a pair of dark wash jeans that do wondrous things for his backside. The two brothers are attracting all kinds of attention as they stand next to each other at the bar. The two of them are similar in brawn, though Chase has Theo beat. Chase's shoulders indicate lots of hours dedicated to the gym.

I chew on the inside of my lip as I drag my gaze away from the men. "Something did happen with Theo last week."

Leila's eyes sparkle as she leans in. "Tell me."

I fill her in on the broom closet incident, and Leila gets more and more excited as the story goes on, but her face falls when I tell her the ending.

"That's it?" she asks. "You didn't kiss him?"

"He almost kissed me, but then my phone rang and interrupted us."

Leila crosses her arms, looking unimpressed. "You left your ringer on?"

"Yes, and guess who was calling? *You!*"

She frowns at me now. "Well, consider this my apology. That's a bit anti-climactic, if you ask me."

"It felt anything but, though," I admit, remembering how Theo's hands felt on my waist as he steadied me in the supply closet. "You know how they say they feel a spark in all the romance books and movies when they touch? Well, I felt a freaking inferno."

Leila's eyes widen but she doesn't say anything for a moment, processing what I've just admitted to her. Finally, right as Theo and Chase turn from the bar to head back to our seats, she says, "Okay, well, we're going to have to do something about this."

I don't have the chance to question what she means by that before the guys return. Chase makes a big show of handing Leila her drink, falling to one knee and holding it out for her. Theo, however, rolls his eyes at his brother and slides my vodka tonic across the table toward me.

I give him an appreciative smile as I take a sip. Theo's eyes are on me the whole time, his expression soft and affectionate. It's doing stupid things to my insides. There's always a certain level of awkwardness to seeing people you work with outside their usual setting, but this is something completely different.

Theo looks more like a single, available man now than my boss. And that's a fact I can easily see myself falling victim to.

Boundaries have already been crossed, but I'm worried that we've barely begun to brush the surface.

We sit in our booth for a while more, making small talk. Eventually, Leila has enough of it, and when the music changes, she hops up and announces, "I love this song. Let's go dance!"

Before I have the chance to protest, she's pulling me out of the booth, out of the VIP section, and onto the dance floor.

I can't help but laugh when I'm dragged out into the middle of the floor, and Leila rounds on me, giving me a bright smile and urging me to dance with her. I have to admit, she did pick a great song to dance to.

Letting myself relax for a few minutes, I dance shamelessly with my friend, swaying my hips and raising my arms above my head as I move with the song's beat.

The flashing lights, the hum of alcohol in my system, and the thrum of the bass rattles through my body, and I really start to enjoy myself. It's been so long since I've let myself loose like this, unworried about my outward image or appearance. I dance like no one's watching and sing my favorite songs at the top of my lungs.

Time seems to blur together as the mix of songs continues endlessly. Out of my peripheral vision, I notice Theo and Chase have come down from the VIP section onto the floor to dance with us. I can feel Theo's eyes all over me as I dance, but I've had enough drinks already tonight that I don't seem to care.

When sweat starts to bead on my forehead, and my chest rises and falls with my breathing, the music changes to more of a slower pop song. Leila simultaneously grabs Chase's hand and then pushes me toward Theo with a wink and a "See you later," before disappearing with her man.

I watch the two of them walk away, and I'm a little bummed that Leila's left me. Then I remember Theo, who is standing right next to me.

My eyes travel over him, and maybe it's the headiness of the air around us or still the alcohol, but I boldly ask, "Want to dance?"

His eyes crinkle in the corners, and he closes the distance between us, not wasting any time in sweeping me up into his arms. His large hands circle my waist and pull me flush against him. I gasp at his brazenness but wrap my arms around his neck to hold myself steady.

Theo looks down at me. I shiver with the intensity of his gaze, feeling like I'm exposed from head to toe. But I like it.

I like being seen by Theo Hurst.

I've always been one to impress. It's something I always strive for, but Theo sees past all of that. He sees past the perfectionist side of me that always aims to please. Though I've been with plenty of men before him, they've never looked at me the way Theo looks at me. As though he's never seen anything quite like me before.

As if I'm extraordinary. As if I'm exactly what he's been waiting for.

He holds me close, and I'm overrun with his presence. His body feels solid, pressed up against mine, and my own body thrums with awareness at how we seem to fit perfectly together. Theo watches me with his warm eyes. His tongue darts out to wet his lower lip, and my belly clenches.

We dance together for a few songs, lost in the feel of each other's body. As I stare into his eyes, I let my mind wander and imagine what it would be like to have this be my life. To be held in Theo's arms all the time, rather than just occasionally.

"You look beautiful tonight," he whispers, his voice laced with desire.

I look down at my skin-tight, black dress, and my body heats up. I turn my gaze back up to Theo, watching him from under my eyelashes. "Thank you." And maybe it's the effects of the alcohol tonight, or maybe how the way he's looking at me seems to make me brave, but I steel myself and say, "You look handsome tonight too."

Even in the dark, I can see how his eyes flare appreciatively. A low sound grumbles from deep in his chest, and he takes a deep breath.

"I don't like how Chase was looking at you today," he admits begrudgingly. His hands flex possessively on my lower back; for the first time in a long time, I feel wanted. "And I apparently don't like seeing you flirt with other people either."

I look up at his face, trying to dampen the anticipation welling in my chest. "No one was flirting with anyone."

He laughs under his breath and turns his gaze away. "I know I shouldn't be having these feelings of having any type of possession over you, much less expressing them. It's inappropriate. Unprofessional."

My head spins but I blink it away, trying to make my eyes focus on Theo standing in front of me. I'm not sure if the dizziness is from the euphoric setting of the club, the heat of the dancing, or the quick change of direction our conversation is going.

"I think me choosing to dance with my boss at a nightclub is just as bad as admitting you don't like your brother hitting on me," I tease back, trying to ease some of whatever inner guilt he's working through right now.

Theo's eyes find mine again, and he draws me closer to him. His neck bends forward until he's leaning his forehead against mine. The length of his nose presses along mine. His eyelids flutter closed, and he breathes deeply, as if reveling in our closeness.

"I just don't know what to do with how I'm feeling," he says, his voice low. He pulls away so he can look into my eyes. "When I'm with you, I feel like I'm spinning out of control, and I can't stop it."

My breath hitches, and I nod my head. "I think I feel the same way."

"How long do you think we can pretend that there isn't anything between us?" he asks. "Because there is, Whitney. There's something between us, you know it. I know it."

"I don't—"

"Hey, lovebirds!" The sound of my best friend's voice breaks us out of the trance we were falling into. Theo's hands immediately fall from my waist, and he takes a few steps away from me. I snap my head around to see Leila standing a few feet away, attached to Chase's hip. "We're heading out. Just in case you were wondering where we went when you decide to look for us."

The two of them don't stick around for a response, but their interruption was like a bucket of cold water dropping over my head. I cross my arms over my chest and look at Theo warily. His brow furrows like he's about to protest, and he reaches for me again, but I skitter away.

I go back to our booth and take a long drink of water. His presence is evident behind me, my body hyperaware of his, but I don't turn around, still drinking and rehydrating myself— coming back down from the high of being held in his arms.

When I set the cup down on the table, I finally turn to him. "I think I should go too. I'll see you Monday." He looks like he's about to protest but I tear my gaze away from him, avoiding eye contact so I don't give into my need for him.

I walk away from him again before he has the chance to say otherwise. I quickly make my way out of the club, ignoring the few catcalls or appreciative glances as I go. My fingers fly across my phone screen as I order a rideshare to come to pick me up.

The minute I'm outside on the sidewalk, I take a big gulp of fresh air, glad to be out of the mixture of sweat and pheromones.

But still, I'm not entirely on my own.

I sense him as he walks up next to me. Theo watches me warily as he comes to stand right by my side.

"Well," he says, looking around at the sidewalk. It must have rained while we were in there. The streets have a glisten of moisture covering them, and the earthy scent of a storm lingers in the air. "Need a ride?"

I fold my hands together in front of me and shake my head. "No, I'll get an Uber."

Theo's lips turn down at this. "Whitney, I don't think—"

"It's fine. I do it all the time. I've already ordered one anyway."

He exhales, defeated. "Fine. How far are they?"

I pull out my phone and check the app. "Two minutes."

Theo nods. "I'll wait with you."

I don't protest, knowing it would fall on deaf ears. Theo sidesteps so he's closer to me. I can feel the warmth radiating off of him in the cool night and I want to press myself up against his side, even though I know I should be going the other way. He seems to give anyone who walks even remotely too close to me the stink eye, silently warning them to keep their distance.

I chew on the inside of my lip, feeling awkward. I wish this damn Uber would hurry up. Too many things happened tonight, and I need to be home—away from Theo—to fully process them.

I can't seem to think straight when he's standing this close to me. Maybe it's the way his cologne makes my head spin or the apparent attraction between us. Either way, I feel like I completely lose my brain whenever I seem to need it most, which is when he's right next to me.

After what feels like an eternity, my Uber pulls up next to the curb. I give Theo a wane smile, which he doesn't return, and then quickly shuffle myself into the vehicle. The driver greets me, and I politely say hello back.

As he pulls away from the nightclub, I turn around to see Theo standing on the curb, looking after me.

I watch him closely until we round the corner, and he's out of sight. Then I fall back in my seat and close my eyes, leaning my head back against the rest.

Theo may feel like he's the one spinning out of control, but I sometimes feel even worse off. At least he can put meaning into the way he's feeling. I'm just over here, silently falling harder and harder for the one person I can't have—my boss. Maybe in a different reality, we'd find each other and we wouldn't work together at a company that had a strict no dating policy.

I don't know what I'm going to do about this. When I think about having to ignore everything I'm feeling for him, it makes my chest hurt. My heart is telling me to take the risk and make a move, but my mind is convincing me I can't. I could quit

Nexus, but I love this company, and I'd hate to let Mr. Peterson down, despite the fact that he's not here to witness it.

I wonder what he'd say if he could see this mess I've made. I'm sure he'd be disappointed in my lack of professionalism, yet at the same time, I wonder if he'd urge me forward, telling me to listen to my heart instead of my brain for once.

But for now, my brain is still in control. Before I even get home, I decide to go into self-preservation mode. There's no time for any of this heart business right now. All that matters is that I do my job and help Theo succeed at his.

Surely, that's the best course of action, right?

I suppose only time will tell.

9

———

THEO

THE SMELL of coffee hits my nose, urging me into a more-awake state as I pour it into my mug. It's one of my main habits in the morning—roll out of bed, straight to the coffee machine. My head is throbbing from our night out.

I didn't drink that much, but I think the combination of the little alcohol I did have plus the tailspin dancing with Whitney threw me into was too much for one night.

My hands flex, and I can still feel how she fits into my grip perfectly.

Dancing with her was like something right out of a dream. With her in my arms, I never wanted the night to end. Something about holding her so close to me felt so *right*. As if the two of us were exactly where we were meant to be.

The disappointment still stings a bit from when the moment ended.

If I could have frozen time right there, I think I would've.

But as all good things tend to do, the special moment came to an end, and she left me standing on a wet curbside, watching her peek out at me from the rear windshield of the car.

Even after I came home last night, all I could think about was her and how her body moved against mine.

I was a man addicted, and she was my vice.

I wasn't sure what I was going to do about this, but I figured at some point, something had to give.

"What are you brooding about?" My brother's voice calls me out of my thoughts of my stunning assistant.

With a shake of my head, I say, "Nothing."

"Sure didn't look like nothing."

I laugh under my breath. "Nope, I'm sure it didn't."

My brother leans his elbows on the breakfast bar, leaning forward like he's stretching his lower back out. He and Leila had been locked in my guest bedroom last night when I got back, and they hadn't emerged for the rest of the evening.

I take another sip of coffee. "You and Leila?"

Chase narrows his eyes at me. "Like you're one to talk. I was pretty sure you were going to rip Whitney's dress off of her right there in the middle of the dance floor before we interrupted you two."

I grimace. "I most certainly was not going to do that."

"Whatever, man, I'm just saying. At least I closed on the deal."

"I'm guessing you had a good night."

"Good? Try the greatest night of my life *ever*. I think Leila and I were meant to be."

The sound of the bedroom door clicking open has Chase standing up straight and looking around the kitchen frantically. He picks up a dirty washcloth and throws it into the sink after wiping off some crumbs from the counter. I smirk at my brother in amusement.

"Whatever that face is, cut it out," he grumbles, still skittering around the kitchen, trying to tidy the already tidy space. "Just play it cool, man."

"Sure," I respond as his bedmate from last night—and Whitney's best friend—rounds the corner.

She only hesitates a moment when she sees the two of us standing there. "Good morning."

Chase and I mumble the greeting back to her. She slides into the barstool next to where Chase was standing just a moment ago and gives me a shy smile. This version of her is entirely different than the one that seduced my brother just last night.

"Coffee?" I ask her, trying to fill the room's newly acquired silence.

She wrinkles her nose. "No, thank you. I'll take a cup of hot water with a lemon if you have it."

I stare at her blankly, wondering if she's joking.

"You heard the lady," Chase snaps at me. I glare at him but go for an extra coffee mug, filling it up with water from the tap before popping it into the microwave.

"I don't have lemons."

Leila gives me a tight smile. "That's okay."

When it's finished, I hand her the cup of hot water, and she takes it appreciatively, wrapping her hands around the warm, ceramic mug and breathing in the steam emanating from the contents.

"Need anything to eat?" I ask her, trying to be as hospitable as possible, even though she's not *my* guest.

My brother is staying with me for the time being, until he can rent a place of his own. I have the space in my penthouse, so it's not a big deal. Thankfully, once the deal with Peterson had been confirmed, I went ahead and got the apartment. It had been sitting pretty much empty until it was time for me to move here.

I'm only a five-minute drive from the office, which is convenient for those early mornings and late evenings.

"Do you have any cereal?" Leila asks, and I pause again. I was thinking along the lines of bacon or eggs.

"I do—it's just Cheerios, though," I tell her.

"That's perfect."

Chase is giving me a look like he's warning me not to make a big deal of his lady's little quirks, and I do my best. I grab a bowl and then collect the milk from the fridge and the cereal from the pantry. I leave it to Leila to serve herself. She pours herself a heaping bowl of Cheerios and then douses the cereal in milk.

"What?" I ask when she gives me another strange look.

Her eyebrow twitches, and it appears as though she's fighting off a smile. "Got a spoon?"

"I got it," Chase interjects as he pulls open my utensil drawer, and then hands Leila one.

She beams at him and then digs into her cereal. She says between bites, "I had such a fun time last night. We'll definitely have to go back to that club sometime."

"Agreed," Chase says, giving her a wicked smile.

"Did you have a good time, Theo?" Leila asks. Somehow, I suspect she's trying to ask me something completely different.

I lean my hip against the counter and nod slowly. "I did."

"Yeah, it looked like you did," Leila says with a smile. "You and Whitney both."

I clear my throat, but don't respond. Leila goes back to her cereal, eyeing me suspiciously while she eats. When she's finished, Chase swoops in and collects her dishes before rinsing them out in the sink.

I want to roll my eyes, but I don't. I'm not sure I've ever seen my brother act so gentlemanly before toward a woman he brought home.

"I'm going to go hop in the shower, babe," Chase says to Leila before leaning down and kissing her on the cheek. She beams at the gesture, looking up at Chase like he is the star that lights up her sky.

Leila reads his hidden request and nods her head. "Give me just a minute."

Chase's lips pull into a smirk before he saunters out of the kitchen and down the hallway to the bathroom. Once he's entirely out of earshot, Leila turns to me.

"So, you like Whitney, huh?"

I nearly spit out my coffee and look over to the woman sitting at my bar. She's blowing gently on her steaming cup of *water*, looking awfully pleased with herself.

"Don't give me that look. I'm letting you know I approve, but don't hurt her. She might come off as uptight and have some ridiculous expectations, but she's really vulnerable on the inside. Just take care of her."

Ridiculous expectations? I had no idea what the hell that meant. Whitney had never given me any indication that she had expectations of any sort. Thankfully. I'm not sure what I'd do if I found myself in another relationship where I never felt like I was up to par. Going through one of those already was one too many for my tastes.

I nod my head. "Noted."

"Thanks, Theo. This was a great talk. Hopefully, I'll see you around." She gives me a wide smile before sliding out of the barstool and floating down the hallway with a mug of hot water. I try to ignore the fact that I hear the bathroom door opening and my brother's appreciative groan when she clearly joins him in the shower.

I'm left standing there, coffee mug in hand, wondering if Leila just unexpectedly gave me her blessing.

Having her permission or not, there's still the inner turmoil of whether or not I can or should pursue Whitney further.

I want to scream *yes* and convince Whitney that there is no other man she should be with besides me, but still, my reason knows that wouldn't be the best course of action at this time.

So, with a resigned sigh, I shuffle into my living room and reach for my briefcase next to the couch. I pull out my laptop and power it on, clicking on my email icon. I mouse over to the *new* option and pause when a blank email draft pops onto the screen. My fingers hover over my keyboard, and I hesitate, running over all potential outcomes.

Of course, I could just text her this, but perhaps creating this professional boundary right from the get-go would be the best decision.

Finally, I shake my head and begin typing.

TO: Whitney Palmer
From: Theodore Hurst
Subject: Monday

MS. PALMER,

We should discuss our conversation from yesterday. I'm not satisfied with how we left it. Unfortunately, I believe we may need to go in a different direction than what was initially implied.

Let's schedule a time to meet and go over the details of this matter sometime Monday.

SINCERELY,
Theo Hurst.

. . .

I SEND it before I can change my mind. My eyes fly over the completed—and sent—email. Obviously, email inboxes are monitored by IT, and while I may be the CEO, it doesn't hurt to be as discreet as possible. In my opinion, the email comes across as an email from a boss to his assistant about any old matter. Nothing more, nothing less.

I fall back into the cushions of my sofa and stare blankly at my screen. This will work. Whitney and I will have a chance to sit down and talk about this. We'll have a heart to heart, lay it all out on the table, and then hopefully nip whatever this is in the bud before it has the chance to bloom into anything further.

We both have an attraction for each other, so what? We're both adults, I imagine we will be capable of putting feelings aside during work hours.

But what about after *work hours?* My traitorous thoughts feel the need to make themselves known.

It's not an option, I think back to myself, then shake my head. This woman really has me so twisted up that I'm having conversations with myself.

When I don't get an emailed response right away, I distract myself. Again, I reach into my briefcase and pull out a stack of reports that I'm right in the middle of going through. Might as well distract myself from work with more work.

I grab a highlighter and pull off the cap with my teeth. From down the hallway, I hear my brother and Leila laugh together. Gritting my teeth, I try my hardest to block it out.

The last thing I need right now is to hear my brother head-over-heels for a woman. My chest aches as I think about Whitney. I make the resolve then and there that we will end whatever this is on Monday.

Even still, there's a twinge of regret for not seeing the

potential of what we could be together. But I know this is the right thing to do.

No matter how badly my heart tells me I'm wrong.

10

WHITNEY

"MORNING," I chirp as soon as Theo walks into the office. I don't bother looking up when he comes closer, though I can feel his presence.

"Whitney," he says my name when I refuse to look up at him after he's been standing there for a solid minute.

"Yes?" I ask, still staring at my computer screen.

He doesn't respond immediately, letting the tension between us build. I never responded to the email he sent me on Saturday, and I know he is well aware of that fact. Based on the slight irritation I can feel rolling off of him, he's not too happy about it either. From my guesses, Theo Hurst is a man not often ignored.

Finally, I can't take it anymore, and I give in, drawing my eyes away from my work and up to him. He's frowning at me, unamused with the apparent cold shoulder this morning.

"Did you get my email Saturday?" he asks me.

I turn to my screen and tap my keys to finish my sentence. "I did."

Somehow, his frown grows even more profound. "You didn't respond."

"I didn't think I needed to."

"I asked you a direct question," he says, his tone raising slightly. My eyes flash down the hall where our secretary, Charlotte, sits at her desk. Not to mention the HR department just down the other hallway.

"It wasn't about work," I say with a slight shrug. "I didn't think it warranted a response."

"I see."

Something about how he finishes the sentence so bluntly has me looking up at him again. His face is etched in stone, and I can't pick up a single thought or emotion in his expression. I swallow thickly, wondering if I made the right decision to ignore him.

I clear my throat and point at my planner on my desk. "Your day is packed. You have a status review meeting with some Board members later this afternoon, including Elena. And then a few other meetings here and there leading up to that. And all of those things are much more important."

He exhales sharply through his nose. "I'm sure they are. I guess we better get to work then. Just give me a call if you need anything. Otherwise, I'll see you when we need to head down for our meeting."

Despite myself, I frown as he walks away from me and into his office. The way he closes his door behind him almost feels personal.

I purse my lips to the side but get to work anyway. The minutes tick by and I cross things off my to-do list. Eventually, the time comes for us to head down to the conference room. I collect my items off my desk and hesitantly knock on Theo's door. I hear a muffled 'Come In' from the other side and I twist the handle, peeking my head into his office.

"Ready?" Theo asks me, his voice still devoid of any type of emotion that I had grown accustomed to being there.

I nod my head and Theo pushes back from his desk. He stretches his arms high over his head in a movement that makes his arms bulge through the white button down he's wearing. I avert my eyes, and stare down at the floor, ignoring the way my blood hums in my ears. Theo finally grabs his laptop and other things needed for the meeting and we walk down to the conference room silently. Though I walk next to him, my stride is stiff, and my brain is on overdrive as I try not to overthink everything.

Theo was on my mind all weekend. Even the night after dancing with him at the club, I couldn't get him out of my thoughts. His email the following morning only made things worse. I had been fretting over what to do with his request for the rest of Saturday and into Sunday. Finally, I decided it might be best for us to go on as if none of this happened.

We could do that. Right?

I'm fully resolved that we can when we stop at the doors to the conference room. Theo looks down at me, and finally, I see that icy demeanor he's been wearing all day crack just a little. He's nervous.

That fact seems to crumble down the walls I have started to build. I give him an encouraging smile, and we go inside.

"Good to see you both," Elena says when we enter the conference room. She stands to greet us but quickly sits again in her seat, scooting closer to the table and folding her hands over the finished oak. "I hope you have brought evidence of good progress."

Theo unbuttons his jacket and then sits down. I sit next to him, open my laptop, pull up the presentation he prepared and emailed to me, and then get the copies of some of his reports he had me print for Elena and the other Board members to review.

While my laptop is loading the presentation, I hand out the packets and then retake my seat. Theo catches my attention again, and his eyes flare as if trying to convey something to me. Again, I give him a small smile and a nod.

The room is so quiet, I can hear everyone's breathing. Each of the present members of the Board is raptly flipping through pages, their eyes scanning over the words and figures that Theo has meticulously put together since the last Board meeting.

My laptop pings with an incoming message in the middle of a tranquil moment. I click on my email icon and read the newest email in my inbox.

TO: Whitney Palmer
   From: Theodore Hurst
   Subject: Following Up

WHITNEY,

We can find an alternate time to discuss the matter mentioned in my prior email. We must work past this roadblock as a team. So, let's find a time to chat, okay? Looking forward to hearing from you.

SINCERELY,
   Theo

I READ the email and then give Theo the side-eye, hoping to convey that I'm not amused with his note in the middle of an important meeting. Theo simply sets down his phone on the table. He crosses his arms over his chest in response, leaning back in his chair so he's out of my eyesight unless I turn my head entirely toward him.

"Well, looks like you've made decent headway," Elena says as she finishes her last page of Theo's strategic goals report. "I think these are all very reasonable, attainable goals for the company."

I can feel Theo's shoulders deflate from his position next to me in relief. He has been running himself ragged for the last few days, ensuring that everything in this report is exactly as it should be. With Elena and Maxwell both breathing down his neck, the pressure has been on.

"I'm glad you think so," Theo says, his voice even, though I catch sight of his hands shaking as he folds them into his lap.

My chest aches. Theo came into this position thinking he would be welcomed warmly as part of the team. Still, his experience thus far has been nothing but. So far, the Board is out to get him or, at the very least, make his transition as difficult as possible.

"Shall we begin to run through the financials presentation you've prepared?" Elena asks as she picks up a pen to scribble something down on her copy of the report.

"Absolutely," Theo agrees. He pushes out of his chair and straightens his jacket before walking up to the presentation screen at the head of the room. I click over to my presentation app and mirror the slides onto the screen so Theo can begin his spiel.

"So, on page four, you'll have the projected numbers for this quarter," Theo says. I hear pages turning in the room.

"Those are significantly lower than the financials from this quarter last year," one of the Board members observes. "How do you expect us to be able to make the leap for hotels with numbers like this? This is much different than what you originally proposed."

Theo clears his throat and his eyes flash to me. My eyebrows furrow and I tilt my head, waiting to hear his explanation.

"Yes, well I had to make some changes when I had the opportunity to scour through the financial reports in greater detail. You'll notice on page nine that I have made additional proposals and listed out some solutions to bridge the gap for the difference in the projection."

A few of the Board members murmur to each other but they flip to page nine and nod their heads after reading his suggestions. Elena's expression is stony as she watches Theo, her eyes tracking his every movement. It's something I find odd for her, that she's watching him so closely, but I suppose she's just waiting to see how he goes about explaining his solution. Feeling more confident now that he avoided the conflict, Theo continues his presentation flawlessly.

Watching him explain everything he's working on and his plans for the next phase feels like poetry. I find myself getting lost in how he articulates and forms his words, so professional and yet, casual. I hang off every word he says. Theo catches my eye a few times as he speaks, and his lips tilt up a little at the corner before he can re-school his features. Each time this happens, my heart seems to skip a beat.

When he concludes his presentation, he saunters to sit beside me again. I nudge his arm with mine, silently telling him he did well.

Elena folds her hands again on top of the table. She exchanges glances with the other Board members and then nods her head. "I think you're on the right track for now. I look forward to seeing everything else you come up with in your following review."

Again, I can feel the relief rolling off Theo's shoulders. He thanks Elena and the rest of the Board profusely, maybe even a little too much. I grin to myself as I gather up my things.

We walk back to our own workspace when we leave the conference room. Theo isn't saying a word. Occasionally, his arm brushes mine when our steps align, and it's enough to drive me mad. With every little touch of his forearm against my skin, my breathing becomes more and more rapid.

All the thoughts I tried desperately to quell this weekend come roaring back with his touch. I try my hardest to get a grip on myself and not get lost in the memories of the way he held me while we danced on Friday night.

"I'll be back in my office if you need me," Theo says when we get to my desk. His voice is low, almost defeated, which is a shame given the win he just achieved in the conference room.

I fall into my chair and purse my lips to the side. Theo disappears into his office before I can say anything, again closing the door behind him.

I feel out of sorts, even though I know he's respecting the boundary I created and trying to give me space. I've grown so used to our friendly work relationship that everything feels empty now that it's gone.

Running my fingers through my hair a few times, I rub my fingernails against my scalp, trying to ease some tension before returning to work. After a few good deep breaths, I feel ready to tackle the rest of my to-do list over the next few hours. I bury myself in my tasks, only stopping to refill my water cup or to use the bathroom.

Fifteen minutes before the end of the workday, I'm finalizing a document when I hear the intercom on my phone buzz.

"Whitney?" Theo says my name.

He has barely talked to me all day, and then he waits untilI'm almost finished to summon me? With a frustrated look toward the ceiling, I push my chair back and walk into his office, not bothering to knock at the closed door as I push it open and saunter in. "Yes?"

Theo holds out a piece of paper in response. I narrow my eyes but cross the floor to his desk and accept the paper he's offering me. I scan over the details and then look at him in confusion.

"What is this?"

"An itinerary. I will need you to block off those dates on the note attached. My mother is hosting a charity gala, and I'll need to attend."

"Okay," I say when I accept it. "Why the itinerary, though?"

Theo hits me with his warm eyes, and my insides melt. "I was hoping you'd be able to come with me. My mother told me to bring a plus one."

"As your assistant?"

"Of course."

I'm glad I'm not wearing my workout watch today. If I were, I think I'd be getting an alert about an irregular heart rate right about now. "For the whole weekend?" Theo nods slowly as he watches me, gauging my reaction. I swallow thickly and then glance down at the dates. "I should be able to make these work."

It's a Friday through Sunday trip, which would be a quick turnaround for the following week. I have no idea what kind of charity gala this is or what to expect. I've never been to anything fancier than a wedding at the botanical garden. Mr. Peterson always attended his work events alone, and I never received an invite.

"Excellent," Theo says, then picks up his phone before typing a message. I stand there and wait, still confused about the whole thing.

"Theo?"

"Hmm?" he murmurs, still looking at his phone.

My heart feels like it's in my throat when I say, "I was thinking we could talk...about the thing you emailed about."

Theo pauses and then slowly sets his phone down on the desk. "Okay." He takes a deep breath and then presses his lips into a line thoughtfully before saying, "I want to apologize."

"For what?" I ask, my voice coming out a little breathy.

"For—" He hesitates and narrows his eyes as he thinks about it, darting his gaze to his office door, which I stupidly left open, before landing back on me. I don't imagine anyone will walk in, but we're not the only people on this floor. "Everything, I suppose."

I blink at him. "What if I don't want you to be sorry?"

Theo tilts his chin up and looks at me curiously. "What does that mean?"

I shrug up one shoulder but then shake my head. "I don't know."

"Whitney." He draws out my name so that it sounds much sexier than it should. "I need you to be honest with me. Tell me exactly what's going through your head right now."

I stay silent for another minute, processing what I want to say to him. Finally, I settle on, "I missed talking with you today. I don't like it when your door is closed."

Theo dips his chin. "Okay, noted."

"And I don't want you to email me on the weekends because then you seem to consume my every waking thought, and I just work myself up overthinking everything until I get to see you on Monday," I blurt out, though I keep my voice soft so I know only he can hear me. It's been weighing on me all day, and I might as well put it out there. "Because I think I feel the same way you do, even though I don't know what that is."

Theo's watching me, his expression is apprehensive, but I

can tell he is soaking up every word that comes from my mouth.

"I have never been this—" I pause, trying to find the right word. "Conflicted about anyone before. We both obviously know the boundaries we'd be pushing if we pursue anything together, but at the same time, I can't imagine us not."

Theo pushes himself out of his chair, rounds his desk, and saunters up to me until I have to crane my neck to see him. His brown eyes seem to trace every feature of my face. Slowly, his hand rises to cup my cheek, and I can't help but lean into his touch.

He looks deep in thought as he gazes down at me. His thumb strokes my cheek tenderly, and I want to cry at how intimate this moment is. "We should probably stop this while we're ahead," he says, his voice low too. "That's what I was going to say when I emailed you that we should talk."

My throat feels sick as I nod. "Okay. That's probably for the best."

"That's what I *was* going to say," he corrects, emphasizing the past. "But now, I don't know. I think I'm just as conflicted as you are."

"What do we do?"

"I don't know," he says. "I like working with you. I like you being the first person I get to see in the mornings."

"Except for Charlotte," I tease.

He breathes a laugh. "Except for Charlotte. But we both know the policy. No work relationships."

"So maybe we just...see what happens? Outside of work?" I suggest hesitantly, unsure if this will be enough of a gray area that he'll be on board with.

He nods twice. "I think that might work. As long as you are okay with that."

A weight feels like it lifts off my chest, and I exhale like I can finally breathe again. Theo's still holding my cheek so tenderly that I never want to move from this position. "I like that idea," I whisper, looking at him through my eyelashes.

Theo's eyes darken ever so slightly, and he steps closer to me. "Whitney," he begins, saying my name in the way that only he can. "I want to kiss you right now. If you don't want this tonight, I need you to tell me. There will be no repercussions. We can end whatever this is right here, right now, or slow it down. You hold the reins."

I swallow thickly as I stare into his warm eyes. He means it; I know he does. He's giving me an out, a chance to back out before we both fall in too deep too quickly. Maybe if I were smarter, I'd take his offer, slow this down, and ease into it a little more.

But I don't. My heart wants to step on the gas and go full throttle.

"The door is open," I whisper.

Theo raises an eyebrow and a wicked smile appears on his lips. "Yeah?" he asks in challenge. "Tell me what you want me to do, Whitney."

My lips part with a gasp as if I'm shocked I willingly agree to this, but I give a slight nod of my head. "I want you to kiss me."

Theo's eyes dilate, and then he closes the distance between us, not wasting any more time. He captures my lips in a wild, controlling kiss. The kind of kiss that only comes from desire which has been dampened for too long.

My back arches the minute his mouth is on mine, and I make a wanton sound low in my throat. Any other time, I'd be embarrassed at the sound, but currently? My mind is too focused on how Theo feels about me to care.

I wrap my arms around his neck and press myself against

him, trying to get closer. He groans low in his throat as I kiss him back with just as much fervor.

This is so wrong. So out of pocket and against the rules. But it's driving me mad. My body lights up within seconds and all I want is to be closer to him. I want his arms to wrap around me tighter and hold me to him like he never wants to let me go.

Too quickly, he's putting space between us and breaking our lips apart. "Okay," he says before pecking my lips again. "Okay. Let's slow down a bit, baby."

I can't help the whimper that escapes me. Theo's hands cup my face, brushing away the stray hairs lingering on my forehead.

"I don't want to get too ahead of ourselves," he whispers. I force myself to nod in agreement. I know he's making the right decision here, no matter how much I dislike it.

I step away from him and straighten my shirt. Theo clears his throat and watches me appreciatively. My cheeks burn, but this time it is more from desire than embarrassment. If Theo hadn't stopped me, I don't know how far I would've taken things.

Kissing him was more than I could've ever imagined. Like a million shooting stars traveling across the night sky. Magical. Enchanting. Everything.

And now that I know what it's like to kiss Theo Hurst, I can easily see myself not wanting to ever stop.

We each share a quiet smile and then slide back into our business modes without mentioning the explosive kiss we shared. I go back to my desk and gather my things. When I'm ready to leave, Theo has his stuff and is waiting for me.

Together, we walk down the hallway toward the elevator. I can still feel the electricity sparking between us, though we stand on opposite sides of the cab as it takes us down to the ground level. We don't push the limits again today.

Theo gives me one last lingering look when we're in the lobby. "I'll see you tomorrow, Whitney."

God, I want to kiss him again. Already, I'm counting down the moments until I can feel his lips against mine. "I'll see you tomorrow," I say back.

Theo winks at me, sending my heart into a sporadic rhythm, before walking out the front doors of the building and sliding into the backseat of the black sedan waiting for him. This time I watch *him* drive off. When he's gone, I go to the parking garage and get in my car.

That night, when I snuggle up in bed, I can't help but smile as I remember the weight of Theo's lips against mine. He's all I can think about as I fall asleep.

We may be making a big mistake not drawing the line, but right now, I just can't find it within myself to care.

11

THEO

MY EYES BURN as I stare at the computer screen before me. I've been trying to write this email for far too long, but the words don't seem to be coming to me. This week has seemed to drag on. It's only Wednesday, yet I feel we've been stuck in a perpetual warp.

Distantly, I hear Whitney's phone ring. She picks it up and runs through her spiel, then pauses, listening to whoever is on the other line.

I finish writing up my email and then click send. Reaching for a pad of sticky notes, I scribble a note down and then saunter out of my office and to her desk. Whitney looks up at me briefly when I approach her, but her attention quickly falls back to her phone call.

Slowly, I place the sticky note on her desk so she can see it. Whitney's blue-gray eyes scan over the message and then flash to me, asking a silent question. I give her a grin and motion with my chin at the note I've passed her.

Meet me tonight? 7:00 Gino's?

Whitney's eyes study my face for a moment before she nods and then crumbles up the note, tossing it in her waste basket.

I wait there for a few more minutes while she finishes up. While I wait, I admire the orchid I gifted her, still holding strong. The purple blossoms are still wide open with no signs of deterioration.

Even if they do end up dying, I figure I'll just buy her a new one.

The flower delivers a nice pop of color to Whitney's desk, even though she has many different colored accessories, like a purple, tie-dye mouse pad and other colored pens. In the short time we've worked together, she always keeps her workspace clean and orderly. Though there may be stacks of different things for her to work on, every note and document is precisely where she wants it to be.

It's a stark difference from my own desk, where I have an exorbitant amount of reports piled upon one another, that I'm slowly working through, one at a time.

A part of me wonders if it bothers her that I'm not as orderly as she is. Does she notice my clutter like I see her lack of clutter?

Finally, she finishes her call and swivels in her chair to look at me. "Why Gino's?"

I glance back at her. "Don't you like pizza?"

"Of course, I do," she says with an eye roll. "But *why?*"

Because I want to spend time with you, I want to say. Instead, I stick with my cover story. "I figured it would be a good idea to review the itinerary I gave you last week. The trip is coming soon, and I want to ensure all the details are smoothed out."

Whitney nods her head as if this makes perfect sense. "I think I've got everything booked. The hotel had rooms blocked off, so I booked us two conjoined king rooms. Then you mentioned you could get us flights? That should be it."

"Yeah, we'll take my jet."

"What else do you need to go over? I'll run through everything before our meeting to have it ready." She reaches for a pen and a paper pad and scribbles *Gala Notes* on the top before drawing a squiggly line underneath.

"Whitney," I say her name slowly. She looks up at me expectantly, like she's waiting for me to dictate more tasks for her to work on this afternoon.

"What?"

"Just..." I pause and run my fingers through my hair. I'm about due for a haircut. I should probably do that before the gala. I glance up the hall, where I know Charlotte is sitting at her desk. I wonder just how much of our conversation she can hear. "I'm sure you have everything in perfect order. Just come to dinner with me."

Her eyes widen for a second before she finally catches on. "Okay," she whispers. "That sounds great."

At the end of the day, I find myself waiting outside Gino's East, looking at my watch and hoping Whitney didn't decide to back out. As I reach for my phone to shoot her a text, someone approaches me and places a gentle hand on my shoulder.

I turn around and face the woman who seems to haunt my every waking thought. My face splits into a grin as I take her in. After we left, she changed out of her work clothes. Though her usual everyday attire compliments her immensely, I wasn't prepared for how attractive Whitney could be in a pair of dark wash jeans and a silky, flowy top.

"You look great," I say, my voice breathy as my gaze returns to her eyes.

She ducks her head as though my compliment embarrassed her. "Thank you."

I'm dressed similarly, in my nicer pair of jeans and a blue, button-down shirt. It is a relief sometimes to have more casual events. Though professional, wearing a suit and tie can be highly uncomfortable day after day.

After finishing the rest of our pleasantries, I motion to the door. "Shall we?"

We walk into the restaurant and up to the podium, where the hostess watches us approach. I had arrived about ten minutes early to put my name on the list so we'd have a table ready for us right when Whitney arrived. I give her my name, and she grabs some menus, leading us back to a corner table in the restaurant.

As soon as we're seated, someone swings by, dropping off glasses of water and getting our orders for any other type of beverage. Between getting our drinks and ordering our dinner, Whitney and I briefly discuss the day's events and our weekend plans.

Finally, once our pizza is ordered, I ask, "Have you always lived in Chicago?"

Her eyes fly to mine in surprise, but she nods. "Yes, all my life."

"Have you ever wanted to go somewhere else?"

Her eyebrows furrow just a bit, but she shakes her head. "No, I have no plans to leave. I mean...why do you ask?"

"I've lived lots of places. I find it interesting that someone would just choose to stay in one place when there's a whole world to be explored."

"I can respect that," she says with a smile and a shrug. "I

love that you got to experience all of that. But for me, I don't even know where I'd go. All I have is here. Leila, my job."

There's something that bothers me about how short that list is, but I don't make a big deal of it. "This job really means a lot to you, doesn't it?" I muse.

"It does. Especially now, I feel like it's the last piece of Mr. Peterson that I have, besides pictures or memories. I want to see the company do well, for him."

Anxiety bubbles in my stomach at the knowledge that her hero wasn't all that he said he was. I still haven't given her any indication that there may be something amiss with him and his books. I stomp down the worry, saving it for another day.

"Are you still happy, with the job?" I ask. I hope she's still happy working under me. I know how much the old CEO meant to her, and I sometimes feel like a consolation prize. All my life, I've felt like I've been running up hill, trying to be the best version of myself for everyone else. And now, sitting here, staring into Whitney's alluring eyes, I want to be enough for her more than ever.

"Of course," she says, her voice going soft. "I've loved working with you."

I note how she says *working with* and not *working for*. Something about that minute detail makes me happy. Technically, on paper, she does work *for* me, but I've always strived for more of a team-like environment.

"I've enjoyed working with you, too," I tell her. "Honestly, I think it's one of the best things about taking over this position."

"Really?" Her eyes glitter in the low lighting of the restaurant.

I nod my head. I'm about to say something further when the waitress swings by, delivering a pan to our table, along with utensils and many napkins. We both give her our gratitude and then look down at our dinner.

"This is it?" I ask, trying to fight off the disgust lacing my tone as I observe the massive pie smothered in sauce before me.

Whitney laughs and reaches for the spatula they delivered with this monstrosity. "Yes, haven't you ever had deep dish before?"

"Apparently not," I mutter. I grimace when she cuts into the pizza and pulls out a slice. Gallons of cheese ooze from the middle and coagulate onto the plate the second the piece settles. Whitney hands it to me, and I look at my dinner warily. Perhaps I've made a mistake.

"Come on. You've got to at least try deep dish if you're going to live in Chicago," she teases.

"Maybe I should just turn in my resignation. I'm not sure how I will stomach all of this."

"Oh, you're being dramatic."

I give her a wary look but then reach for my fork and knife, opting for bravery. I cut off a piece and ignore how my stomach is already rejecting the dairy before I've eaten it. I pop the piece into my mouth and chew. Whitney is watching me, pure amusement etched on her features. After I force myself to swallow, I reach for my beer and take a big gulp to wash it down.

"So?" she asks and arches her eyebrow, almost like a challenge.

I look her square in the eye and say, "That was disgusting. That's not even pizza."

Whitney tosses her head back and laughs, her wavy curls bouncing around her shoulders as she does so. My chest constricts at how beautiful she looks right now, so carefree and happy. She seems completely unfazed by the deep-dish pizza, taking bite after bite.

"So, about this gala," Whitney begins, trailing off her sentence.

I wipe my mouth with a napkin and swallow thickly. Fuck, this pizza is going to rip up my stomach. This was a terrible idea. I've made it about halfway through my serving and regret it immensely. "Yes. You've already seen the gist of it from the itinerary I gave you, but I just wanted to run through everything."

She bobs her head and pulls a notebook out of her bag. Of course, she came prepared. I fight off the smirk that wants to pull on my lips.

"So, we'll leave early Friday morning, and the actual event is Friday night. Then Saturday we can take as long as we need to. I believe there will be a luncheon if you want to attend. I'll have my jet on standby so we can leave whenever necessary."

"And I'm assuming this is a black-tie event?" she asks as she scribbles something in her notebook. She's writing in some kind of cursive that I can't make out from my position across the table. I am curious as to what she's jotting down.

"Yes, I'll be in a tux," I tell her, winking when she looks up at me.

She smiles and then writes something in her book again. "I'll have to find something to wear. I don't think my prom dresses from high school will fit me anymore."

"I can have—" I stop mid-sentence when she holds her hand up, halting my train of thought.

"Do not offer to buy it or have one bought for me," she says. She's still smiling softly, but now I can see the resolve in her eyes. She means what she says. "This is not going to be one of those relationships where the measly, middle-class girl dates the big bad CEO and lets him buy everything for her."

I lean my elbows on the table. "They make relationships like that?"

Finally, the gleam is back in her eye. "Oh, yes."

I laugh. "Noted."

"You said your mother hosts it?" she asks. I nod my head, and her expression morphs into something thoughtful. "So, your mother will be there?"

"She will. We'll likely be seated at her table."

"Does she, um—" Whitney hesitates, unsure how to ask her question. "Does she have any indication that I'm *more* to you than just an assistant?"

I tilt my head and observe her, trying to figure out why she's asking me this.

She quickly says, "You know, just for my sake. I need to know how I'm supposed to act. If it's going to be as your assistant or your date." She whispers the last word and looks up through her eyelashes. I catch a sliver of hope in her blue-gray eyes and blink a few times, wondering if I just imagined it.

"You'll be coming as my date," I confirm. Now that we're out of the office, I can drop all pretenses. If Whitney is going to be by my side, on my arm, in some knockout dress, she is damn well going be referred to as my date.

"So I shouldn't bring my notebooks and color-coding system?" she asks, teasing me again, though now I notice her shoulders relaxing into her seat.

"Not unless you really want to. I won't stop you," I say fondly. "There won't be much to work on, though. It's really just for leisure, more than business."

She bobs her head. "Good to know. I don't think I'll have much to protest about then."

"I hope not," I say playfully.

We finish our meal on a light-hearted note. There never seemed to be a lull in conversation between us and each topic flowed seamlessly onto the next. As I hand the waitress our paid check, I can't help but feel content. I don't think I'll ever grow tired of getting to spend one-on-one time with this beautiful woman in front of me.

Now that she's agreed to come with me to the gala, I'm sure it's all I'll be able to think about for the next few weeks.

As we're on our way out, something catches my eye. I grab Whitney's hand before she can get too far ahead of me and hold her back. She whips around and gives me a questioning look. I tilt my head toward the wall with names and quotes scattered all over it.

"You got a permanent marker?" I ask.

She stares at me blankly before sighing. "Of course, I do."

After digging around in her purse, she produces a black permanent marker. I frown at it. "That's not going to work. The walls are black."

"Oh, for the love of—" She stops mid-sentence, then goes over to the maitre d' and whispers to them. Whitney returns to me with a white paint pen and slaps it in my palm a little too forcefully. I give her a grin.

"Thank you."

Walking over to the wall, I uncap the pen and start scribbling. Whitney stands at my side, peeking over my shoulder to see what I'm writing. When I'm finished, I recap the pen and look at her, waiting for her approval.

W + T

First Date at Gino's

"You didn't tell me you were such a sap," Whitney says, nudging my shoulder. She's teasing me, but I can see how my little note makes her eyes glitter in a way they haven't before.

My chest feels full as I wrap my arms around her shoulder. We drop off the pen before walking outside of the busy restaurant.

"How do you know we're meant to be?" she asks as she wraps her arm around my waist, holding onto me just as tightly as I am to her. We stop in the middle of the sidewalk outside the front doors. "Maybe this is just a fling."

"Maybe," I say, though I don't believe that one bit. "But even then, I think we were meant to find each other. I don't think people who aren't meant to be around each other feel this way."

Whitney stares thoughtfully at me, and I'd give anything to know what she's thinking right now. Finally, she stands up on her tiptoes and kisses the side of my mouth. I catch her around her waist with one hand and hold her close to me.

When she pulls away from me, her eyes are glassy. Her full lips rise into a smile, and she whispers, "I think you're right."

12

WHITNEY

MY ALARM BLARES, waking me up from my dream. I blink a few times before shutting it off and checking the time.

Shit.

It's already five o'clock. I meant to get up at four-thirty, but I must've hit the snooze button one too many times.

Tossing the covers back, I fly out of bed and into my bathroom. My hands grapple with the shower handle, turning it to the exact spot where I know the water will be perfect. I shower quickly, hop out, and dress in the clothes I set out last night.

I give my hair a quick blow-dry and dab on some light makeup. I'll be in Theo's jet most of the morning, so I don't spend too much time on my outward appearance. Hopefully, we'll have plenty of time to rest and freshen up in the hotel before appearing at the gala. I'll worry about the smaller details of my makeup routine then.

Thankfully, I packed just about everything I needed for our short trip last night. Tossing the final things in—like my toothbrush and retainers—I grab my overnight bag and hurry down to the lobby of my apartment building.

I immediately catch sight of the car waiting for me and curse under my breath. Running my hands over my hair to smooth any potential strays, I walk out the front doors and onto the sidewalk.

"Hey, you ready?" Theo asks when I step outside. Of course, he's got his phone in his hand, but his attention is only on me. Those warm, brown eyes widen as soon as I'm in front of him, and he looks me over appreciatively.

I can't deny that that fact makes my stomach flutter a little. I've never seen someone's face light up the way his does when he sees me. It's something I've always dreamed I'd get to experience, that utter joy in having me around. I know Leila loves hanging out with me, and Mr. Peterson always liked my presence. But with Theo, everything feels amplified. Every day it seems that he is just as happy to see me as the last.

"Ready, Freddy," I respond and instantly regret it. Why, oh, why did I say that?

A smirk forms on his face, and he laughs under his breath before exiting the car and reaching for my suitcase. We'll only be gone for the weekend, but we have a few important events, so I had to pack a few extra things so I'll be presentable.

"You make me laugh, Whit," he says, winking. "I got this. Go ahead and get settled."

I do what he says and slide into the back seat of his car. His driver catches my eye in the rearview window and greets me. I've never met this driver before. Maybe since it's so early and outside his usual business hours, Theo had to get someone other than his regular driver, Tod.

The trunk slams shut, and then Theo slides in next to me. He gives me a wide grin before instructing the driver that we're all set. Theo taps at his phone screen as soon as the car is in motion.

I peek out of my peripheral vision to watch him sign off on

an email and tap send. The familiar *wooshing* sound of the email app goes off, then Theo clicks the lock button on his phone and turns his attention back to me.

"Kinda early, huh?" he says, like an icebreaker. "Have you eaten?"

"No, I accidentally slept through my first alarm, so I didn't have time to grab anything."

"The jet should have full service, so we can get you some coffee and breakfast once we board," Theo says, offering me a polite smile. "Thank you again for coming with me. I can't imagine anyone else I'd like next to me tonight."

My chest flutters at his meaningful words, but instead of saying something just as nice back, I blurt, "Of course, that's what assistants are for." Instantly, I want to eat my words, but I give him a tight smile.

He doesn't smile back, instead choosing to study my face intently, something unreadable in his expression. I think back through our dinner at Gino's last week, how Theo explicitly answered my question that I was not attending the gala tonight as his assistant but rather as his date. At first, I had thought he was just saying that, but now, based on the intensity of his gaze, I think he meant every word.

"Do you have much to do on the plane?" I ask him, hoping for a quick change of subject.

"I just have to run through my speech one more time. I can't believe my mother waited until yesterday to tell me about this," he grumbles. Then he adds, "Maybe send a few emails, too, but nothing massively urgent."

I nod my head pensively. "Well, let me know if you need my help."

He gives me a wry smile. "You're not working this weekend."

I shrug a shoulder and then turn away from him, looking

out the window. We pull up to O'Hare, driving around to a private access entrance. We get out of the car, and a few attendants come to pick up our bags. Just like if we were flying commercial, we have to go through security checks before we're allowed through.

Finally, we load into a golf-cart-like vehicle that takes us through the airport and onto the tarmac. The jet awaits us; the white metal glints off the rising sun. Already I can hear the hum of the engines warming up. I hope my jaw hasn't gone completely slack out of shock. I don't think I've ever seen such a beautiful plane in my life. An attendant is waiting for us at the stairs, who bows his head once we pull up.

"Pleasure to see you, Mr. Hurst," the attendant says once Theo steps out of the golf cart.

Theo gives him a wide smile and holds his hand for a shake. We're then ushered up the stairs onto the plane. When we settle in our seats, I look around, leaning my head forward and back to try and get a good view of the entire layout. Theo places his hand on my leg, drawing my attention back to him.

He's watching me in amusement. "Do you need a tour?"

I settle back in my seat and feel my cheeks flush. "Sorry, no. I've just never been on a private plane before."

Theo stands before I can say anything else and holds his hand out. "Let me show you all the bells and whistles."

I slide my hand into his and let him pull me up and out of my seat. He shows me the main cabin of the plane and all the special features. There is a large table where he could hold meetings in the air if needed. There's even a large TV that he could connect his tablet or laptop to wirelessly if he needed to view his screen on a larger scale.

He shows me all the hidden compartments and secret nooks. He also points out the lavatory, so I know where to find it.

"And now, the best part," he says, waggling his eyebrows. Theo pushes open one final door at the back of the plane, revealing a large, queen-size bed and a private bathroom.

I let go of his hand and step into the private room, walking in a small circle and taking it all in. "This is insane," I mutter. "I can't imagine this being my life."

Theo slides his hands into his pockets. "Trust me, things lose their magic appeal once you live it."

I nod, understanding where he's coming from. "Yeah, I can see that happening." I walk over to the bed and run my hand along the pristine satin duvet. "I bet I could take some pretty incredible naps in this bed, though."

Theo laughs and shakes his head. "Well, if you get tired during our flight, feel free to come on back here."

"Really?" I ask him a little too eagerly.

He chuckles again and then holds a hand out for me again. "Absolutely. Let's stick with our seats for now though."

When we're settled back in our seats, a flight attendant swings by to take food and drink orders. I ask for some French Toast and coffee. Theo orders an omelet and two mimosas to go with our breakfasts.

The attendant writes our orders down and informs us she'll get these for us when we're in the air. Our flight to New York isn't long—a little longer than two hours—but a little breakfast sounds perfect.

Theo pulls out his phone again and scrolls through his notes app, reviewing the speech his mother apparently bestowed upon him for this evening. Theo was kind enough to let me take the window seat to watch us take off. I'm peering out the window and watching the crew down on the ground get everything ready for takeoff.

Before too long, the plane starts moving down the runway. As soon as we start accelerating for takeoff, my hand flies to

Theo's forearm, gripping it. He glances over at me, but rather than look back at him, I clench my eyes shut, preparing to no longer be on the ground.

Theo removes my hand from his arm but then winds our fingers together. He gives me a reassuring squeeze. Then I feel his lips on my ear, and he whispers, "Relax, Whitney."

"I can't."

"Are you afraid of flying?"

"Apparently."

He laughs under his breath and gives my hand another squeeze. "It's okay. I'm here right next to you."

His words are surprisingly reassuring, but he doesn't say anything else. I keep my eyes shut until my equilibrium feels the plane level out in the air. As soon as everything feels right again, I let out a large breath of air and open my eyes.

Theo is watching me, his lips curled into a sideways smile. "You going to make it?"

I press my lips together, slightly embarrassed, but nod my head. "I think so."

He gives me a long look. "Glad to hear it."

Finally feeling brave enough, I look out the window, watching the plane steadily rise over the earth below us. After a while, the attendant brings us our breakfasts. The smell of the hot French toast fills my nose, and my mouth instantly waters. I pour the syrup over the toast and am about to dig in when Theo halts me.

I look up at him, ready to attack him for keeping me from my breakfast, when I see him holding out a champagne flute. "Mimosa?" he asks, handing mine over. He holds his out in a toast when it's in my hand. "Here's to a lovely weekend with the loveliest woman I know."

My cheeks warm, and I clink my glass against his before taking a sip. My lips curl into a smile as the bubbly orange drink hits my taste buds. Turning from me, Theo digs into his breakfast, and I take his lead, cutting a huge piece off and sticking it in my mouth. I nearly moan from the flavor that explodes on my tongue. This has got to be the best French toast I've ever had.

Who knew I had to get on a private jet to experience it?

I scarf down the rest in record time, then lean back in my seat, fully satisfied.

And sleepy.

"You can nap if you want," Theo offers. He doesn't look up at me, but somehow, he can tell I'm getting increasingly tired as the minutes tick by.

Swiveling around in my chair, I find a comfortable position, propping my elbow on the armrest and resting my chin in my hand. "No, that's okay," I murmur before yawning. "I'm good right here."

My eyes feel heavy, and I can't help but close them. Theo says something else from far away, but I'm already too far gone to hear it.

The next thing I know, I'm being jolted awake, and an arm wraps around me tightly, holding me in place. I blink my eyes a few times, trying to get rid of the sleep still clouding them. My cheek is pressed against something warm, and my hands are knotted tightly in front of me.

I realize I'm resting against Theo's chest, and his arm is placed protectively around my waist. I pull away and wipe at my mouth to make sure I wasn't drooling all over him.

Theo gazes at me warmly once I'm sitting up. "What happened?" I ask. "How long was I out?"

"A little over an hour," he says before reaching up and brushing a few strands of hair off my forehead. "We just hit some rough turbulence. But you were out like a light."

"Sorry I fell asleep all over you," I say with a timid laugh.

"Trust me, it was no inconvenience," Theo says, his tone hinting that there's an underlying meaning to his statement.

"How much longer do we have?"

Theo checks his wristwatch. "Probably half an hour, forty-five minutes or so?" Looking back at me, he shrugs a shoulder. "I'm not entirely sure."

I settle back in my seat and look out the window. The rest of the flight passes with very few encounters of turbulence. When we land, we're escorted off the plane and into another cart, which takes us to a black car waiting for us.

The attendants load our luggage into the trunk, and Theo opens the back door, motioning for me to get in first. I slide across the seat, leaving room for Theo to join me. He lands beside me with a soft *oomph* and then leans forward to say something to the driver.

When we pull away from the airport, Theo asks, "Have you been to New York?"

"Once, when I was little, you?" Then I laugh at myself. "That was probably a dumb question, considering this is an *annual* gala we're attending this weekend."

Theo smirks at me. "Not a dumb question. But yes, the gala is held here every year. Growing up, we traveled to New York often for my father's work. My mom would take us around the city while my dad was in business meetings."

"What does your dad do?"

"He's retired now and mostly helps with my mom's charity. But before, he was a freelance financial advisor. I think that's where Chase got his love of numbers from," Theo says with a fond chuckle for his brother.

"Is it just the two of you?" I ask.

Theo shakes his head. "No, we have a sister, Kelsey. She's the youngest out of the three of us. She works as an agent for a record label in LA."

"Will she be here tonight?"

"Doubtful. Usually, my siblings leave it to me to be the tribute. I suppose I could have dealt with many worse things as the oldest."

I laugh. "I don't know, going to a fancy gala with an open bar seems a pretty difficult endeavor."

His eyebrow twitches, and he fights off a smile. "I'm unsure how I would have gotten through it without you tonight."

Though I know he's teasing, I can't help the flush that appears on my cheeks. I give him one more amused smile and then turn to look out the window, watching as the streets of New York pass us by.

After a bit of a drive, we pull up in front of our hotel doors. Theo and I enter as a bellhop waits beside the car to unload our luggage.

"Hello," I say eagerly to the concierge at the hotel's front desk. I place my bag on the counter and dig around in my wallet, pulling out the black Amex business card Theo gave me. "We have a reservation for two king rooms under the last name Hurst."

The woman behind the desk gives us a warm smile and then types on her keyboard, her eyes flying across the screen as she browses her bookings. Slowly her smile falls, and my stomach knots.

"Oh, I'm so sorry, it appears I only have one king suite booked for you tonight under that name."

I frown at her, and Theo shifts on his feet behind me. "That can't be right. I have the confirmation email. Can you check again?"

She gives me an apologetic nod and scrolls her mouse. Finding my phone, I pull up my email and type in a keyword to pull up my confirmation email.

There.

I show the clerk my phone screen where it clearly says *two conjoined king rooms.*

Her face pales, and she rolls her lips together. "I'm so sorry; there must have been some mix-up on our end. Perhaps seeing the same last name on the rooms, someone thought it was a mistake." She clicks a few times on the screen and then grimaces. "We are all booked up this weekend. We have a major charity event tonight and also two weddings this weekend. Unfortunately, I have no other rooms available."

My eyes widen, and I spin around to look at Theo, silently asking him, *"Can you believe this?"* He shrugs and then looks back at his phone.

Taking a deep breath, I calmly fold my hands on the counter. "How can we fix this?"

The woman gives me a tight smile. "I'm sorry, there are just no other rooms to switch you to at this time."

Frustration starts to bloom in my chest. "But I booked us for two rooms. I paid for two rooms."

"I'll issue a refund for the second room."

"That doesn't change the fact that I now only have *one* room," I say. Pinching the bridge of my nose, I exhale sharply. "I'm sorry."

"Don't apologize. This is our mistake. Unfortunately, as I said, I don't have any way to upgrade you or get you another room. The suite you booked has a pullout couch and the king bed if you need another sleeping space." She looks between Theo and me, as if unsure of our dynamic. Can't really blame her. Sometimes *I'm* still unsure of our dynamic.

At that moment, Theo decides to join the conversation. He steps up next to me and rests one of his large hands on my lower back. I momentarily look up at him to meet his gaze before he turns to the concierge. "That will be fine. Can you just make sure to refund us for the extra room?"

The woman looks a little starstruck by the intensity of Theo's stare. "Of course, sir."

"Thank you," Theo says, effectively ending all discussion of the one room vs. two rooms.

We get our hotel keys, and then, with his hand still on my lower back, Theo guides me toward the elevators and presses the button to call the car. When the doors close behind us, I cross my arms and huff out a breath.

"I promise I booked us two rooms. I even have the confirmation email!" I shout, about to reach for my phone, before Theo grabs my hand and threads his fingers through mine.

"It's not a big deal, Whitney. It's for one night."

I close my eyes and breathe through my nose, letting Theo's hand be my grounding force. "You're right. I'm just sorry for the inconvenience. I can take the pullout bed."

He scoffs. "Don't be absurd."

"There's no way I'm letting *you* sleep in it," I fire back. "I doubt you've ever slept on anything but the finest mattress with the highest thread count sheets."

He gives me an amused smirk. "Oh, yeah?"

I glower at him. "Am I wrong?"

He nods once but is still smiling. "Yeah, you're wrong."

I turn away and glare at the doors to the elevator. I wouldn't be surprised if he's lying just to make a point. "We'll see. Good luck getting me into that bed."

Now Theo barks out a laugh. "Is that a challenge, Whit?"

I glare at him but don't deign to respond. We make it to the hotel room, and I swipe the key over the door to gain entry. The room is nice. Immediately after walking in, we find the lounge area with the couch that I assume is the pullout bed.

Walking right over to the couch, I drop my purse onto it, effectively claiming it as my own. Theo watches me, unamused, with his hands shoved in his pockets. Thankfully, he doesn't press the issue and walks further into the room toward the bedroom.

I follow him, mostly out of curiosity, just to check if the rest of the room is as nice as the lounge area. Right in the middle, against a side wall, is the king bed and a TV hangs directly across it on the other wall. The bed is immaculately made with several colorful throw pillows and a beautifully stitched bed scarf right at the end.

I hate to admit it, but that bed looks incredibly comfortable. Maybe I should've let him be the gentleman and take the king bed for myself.

But I've planted my flag. I can't go back solely based on principle. But that's a problem for later tonight. Surely there's no harm in claiming it for myself until then, right?

Glancing at the time on my phone I ask, "What time is the event?"

"Not until seven this evening. We've got plenty of time to do whatever. I've got to check some emails and catch up on a few other things, but then we can maybe get lunch and walk around the city if you'd like."

"Mind if I take a nap?" I suggest. Theo nods, tilting his head off to the side as if gesturing for me to go ahead.

Wasting no more time, I launch myself onto the bed, landing right in the center of the squishy mattress and heavenly pillows. Theo's eyes are wide, clearly not expecting me to have done that. I shoot him a sardonic smile as I wiggle under the covers and get settled. Theo's expression turns from surprised to amused. He shakes his head and smirks at me before switching the lights out and closing the bedroom door behind him.

I smile, pleased that I could stake a claim for now. As I get more and more comfortable, I start to regret making such a big deal out of me taking the pullout. Going from this five-star bed to a likely lumpy and squeaky roll-out mattress will be hard.

Once I'm settled, I reach for my phone and send a quick text to Leila, letting her know we made it. After she found out I'd be attending this gala with Theo this weekend she was all in, begging me to send her every little detail. I had no doubt she would've been able to attend had Chase made it this weekend as his date, but he was busy moving himself out of Theo's apartment and into his own.

After I put my phone down, I close my eyes and try to relax. The minutes tick by, and I'm frustrated I'm not asleep yet. My mind is too jittery with thoughts of how tonight's event will go. Aside from the fact that I've never been to such a fancy event before, Theo's parents will be there, and that knowledge is making me over think everything. I want to make a good impression on them. I want them to know that their son is important to me, and I hope they'll appreciate that fact. I'm terrified that I won't know how to act or make a fool of myself and that will somehow prove to them that I'm not worthy of Theo's attention.

But at the same time, I know Theo will never let that happen. He's the one who asked me to come with him after all, as his *date*. He'd never put me in a situation where he wasn't confident I belonged.

Thoughts of how he stared at me on the airplane flood my mind now, putting the anxious thoughts to ease. His warm, brown eyes become all I can think about.

Eventually, my body starts to feel heavy, and suddenly, I can't find it inside myself to care. Slowly, I fall into a deep sleep and dream of ballgowns, castles, and beds fit for a king.

13

———

THEO

WITH ONE LAST look in the hotel room mirror, I'm satisfied that this is a good look for tonight. I settled on my black slacks and a white shirt. Whitney ordered me a dinner jacket specifically for this event, and I'd be lying if I wasn't impressed with her style. She picked a slim-fit charcoal gray jacket with a subtle embroidered floral pattern. I paired it with a black tie and silver cufflinks.

I'm still fiddling with my tie, unsure I have the knot correct. We're already pushing the time too close, so this will have to do. I rap my knuckles against the bathroom door to let Whitney know we've got to hurry up, and step back into the living area in our hotel room to wait for her.

Only a few minutes pass before Whitney throws open the bathroom door and enters the main room to greet me. The minute my eyes fall on her, my mouth goes dry.

She's an absolute vision.

Adorned in a long, royal purple formal dress, she seems to have stepped out of a dream. The shape of the dress does amazing things for her figure, the neckline dipping low and showing off the exquisite swell of her breasts. And to make matters worse, her dress has a long slit running up the side of her leg.

I swallow thickly, attempting to get ahold of myself as she turns to me with a wide smile. "How do I look?" she asks.

"Stunning," I choke out and then clear my throat. "You look great, Whitney."

Her cheeks heat, and her eyes fall down to the matching purple clutch she holds in both hands. She tucks a strand of her silky hair back behind her ear and then looks up at me again shyly. "Shall we?"

I offer her my arm and try not to let myself get too carried away with ideas when she loops her own arm through. We go downstairs to the ballroom, where the gala is being held. This isn't the first time I've attended this event with a plus one, but none of those others were Whitney. As we walk into the ornately decorated room, Whitney draws all the attention to herself. She receives gazes of adoration from the women and desirous looks from the men.

As we walk across the floor, my chest swells with pride as she catches everyone's attention. She is easily the most beautiful woman here, and she's here with *me*. I can't keep my eyes off her, just as much as everyone else here.

"Theo!" a deep voice booms across the ballroom. I tear my gaze away from Whitney to catch sight of my father ambling toward us. He's dressed in a navy suit with a silky, cream-colored tie, which perfectly complements my mother's cream ballgown. I have no doubt that my mom coordinated their apparel for tonight meticulously. My mother has her arm looped through his but is staring at my date appreciatively. However, her dark eyes gleam in a way that raises my suspicions.

When they approach us, I give quick introductions. "Whitney, this is my mother and my father."

My mother removes herself from my father's side and steps closer, eyeing Whitney intently. "Oh, it's so nice to meet you, dear."

Whitney nods to my mother, and the motion is a bit stiff, but she still plasters on a bright smile. "Pleasure to meet you too, Mrs. Hurst."

My mother eyes Whitney again, and doesn't correct her in her greeting. The hair on the back of my neck stands on edge, wondering why my mother is being standoffish towards my date this evening. My father extends a hand to her, warmly, and Whitney takes it, giving him a brisk handshake. My father looks pleased. "I'm Robert. We're so glad you two could make it tonight."

I step up next to Whitney again, my arm sliding around her waist and pulling her closer. She gives me an appreciative glance, as if grateful that I had taken my place beside her again. "Glad to be here," I respond.

"Oh, Theo, I believe I just saw Lauren across the room," my mother informs me. Right away, I grit my teeth together, wishing she would have just left well enough alone. That must have been that suspicious gleam I noted in her eye just a moment ago. "Perhaps you can make an effort to go say hello to her."

I can feel Whitney's eyes burning through me like laser beams. "We'll see," I say noncommittally.

"Have you prepared your speech for tonight?" my mom asks me, changing the topic again and clasping her hands together in front of her.

"I believe so. Hopefully, it's good."

Whitney laughs. "He's been working on it nonstop all

week. I have no doubt that you'll be impressed. Theo is going to knock the socks off everyone."

My mother gives Whitney a sideways glance, as if she's unimpressed by the praise my date has for me. "I'm sure he will. Well, we have a few other people to greet. We'll see you two back at the table. Whitney, I'm so glad you were able to attend. I can't wait to get to know you more."

With a final, meaningful look at me—which I suspect is her silently telling me she approves of my date—my parents excuse themselves to make their rounds.

As we walk to our assigned table, I note Whitney's sudden silence. I swallow thickly, my throat feeling tight as I think of the best way to trouble-shoot the can of worms my mother unintentionally brought up.

"Lauren is a family friend," I say, my voice even.

"That's nice," she says, but her hand tightens around mine.

I clench my jaw again, ignoring the way my muscles protest. "We did date for a few years, but she wanted more than I was apparently capable of giving her."

The tightness in my chest reminds me just how much she reminded me that I wasn't enough for her. How I seemed to be deficient in every possible aspect for her.

"Theo," Whitney says my name softly, squeezing my hand again and banishing those darker thoughts of worthlessness. "It's really none of my business."

"It kind of is though, don't you think? You're here as my date, my mother shouldn't have mentioned anything about Lauren or any type of history we once had. I can't believe how rude that was."

"It's okay. I'm sure she meant nothing by it."

I make a noise in the back of my throat, knowing despite Whitney's protests, I'll be having a discussion with my mother about this at some point. I can't figure out why she'd make such a pointed comment unless she had some ulterior motive. But that wasn't at all like my mother.

"You have your mother's eyes," Whitney whispers to me as we continue to make our way across the ballroom floor.

"I suppose I do." She hums next to me, and I look down at her to get a better look at her face. She's grinning from ear to ear at me. The pressure in my chest lightens from the delighted look on her face, no longer bothered by some sideways comment from my mother. "What?"

"I don't know," she shrugs, still beaming. "I just really like that fact about you."

I laugh under my breath. "I'm glad I'm living up to your expectations."

Whitney's smile falls off her face, her eyes narrow slightly, and her brow furrows like she's unsure of what I mean. I study her face, trying to figure out what I said that caused her confusion. "What is it?" I finally ask, when I continue to come up blank as to why she'd be so bothered.

Snapping out of whatever stupor I unintentionally threw her into, she shakes her head, and her smile returns in full force. "Nothing. Let's go find our seats."

I'll ask her about it later, willing to let her brush it away for now. This is neither the time nor the place to dig into whatever that was. Together, we walk to the table my parents have assigned us. It's the same number every year—number six. My mother does this intentionally, so some more prominent patrons can sit at the higher-numbered tables and feel infinitely more important.

After pulling out Whitney's chair for her to sit, I sit right next to her, scooting my chair a little closer so her arm brushes against mine. Over the next few minutes, I point out some familiar faces I know from past years. Most people in attendance tonight are intimately involved in my mother's organization, focusing on creating affordable housing for everyone.

My parents return to our table a little while later and take their seats. A few of my parents' friends join them, and soon, our table of eight is full. We all make small talk as the waitstaff arrives and delivers house salads to each of us.

We make it through all of the dinner courses before the MC for the night is summoning me up to the stage to give my speech. After dabbing at my mouth with my napkin, I excuse myself from the table and walk up, smiling and nodding politely as the attendees clap for me.

Once up at the podium, I focus on the words I've practiced all night. The spotlight on me is blinding, and I squint through, searching for one familiar face. Finally, I find her back at the table, beaming up at me with pride shining through her expression. My eyes lock on Whitney, and though everyone in the room watches me with rapt attention, I only look at her.

As I finish my speech, the room erupts in applause. I bow my head slightly before stepping off the podium. My mother and father are both waiting for me at the end of the stage. My dad pats me on the shoulder, and my mother hugs me. "That was excellent, honey."

"Thanks," I tell them both with a smile. They each give me one more fond smile before they take the stage.

Walking back to our table, I get stopped a few times to receive congratulations on my talk. I thank them quickly each time, itching to get back to Whitney and out of the spotlight.

She's watching for me, and her full lips turn up at the corners when she sees me. My heart seems to skip a beat, and I find myself walking faster, increasing my pace to get to her as soon as possible.

"You did great," Whitney says, leaning toward me. "I think you had this whole room hanging off your every word."

I settle in my seat again. "That was the goal. I didn't come across too pompous, did I?"

"Of course not. I thought it was very tasteful. Your mother's foundation will see an uptick in donations after that. It was very convincing."

"Theo!" a twinkling voice calls my name and the high I was riding from the applause quickly disappears.

I turn my head to glower at the blonde I know is standing right behind me. Having no sense of boundaries, or consideration for the woman sitting next to me, Lauren Farthington bends down right next to me, making sure to show off her cleavage in her low cut dress to anyone willing to see. She wraps her arms around my neck and then presses a kiss to each of my cheeks.

"Oh, I've missed you so much? How long has it been?"

"Not long enough," I mutter low enough that only she can hear it.

I have no desire to play into her trap tonight. Lauren can be manipulative, but I'm not falling for it anymore. After undergoing years of verbal abuse by her, repetitively telling me that I was cheap and worthless, it finally took me walking into our home to find her sprawled out on the couch with another man to see the truth of her ways. I won't let her make a fool of me again.

Now that I'm away from her, I've gone to great lengths to keep those reminders at bay. Hours of therapy have been spent convincing myself that I am more than what she tried to convince me of. Though she still acts as a reminder; a beacon for those darker thoughts.

When she pulls away from her one-sided embrace, her cosmetically enhanced lips are puckered into a pout and she crosses her arms over her chest—again, showing off her low-cut dress line.

"Theo, I've missed you. Can't you at least be a little happy to see me?"

I stare at her blankly for a moment before turning to Whitney, who is watching the entire exchange with wide eyes. "Do you need some fresh air? It's feeling awfully stuffy in here all of a sudden."

Lauren scoffs behind me. Whitney doesn't get the chance to respond before more chaos is added to this show.

"Oh, Lauren!" my mother exclaims once she makes it back to the table, my father in tow. "I'm so glad you were able to stop by this evening."

My mother wraps her arms around Lauren's thin body, pulling her into a hug. Lauren returns the gesture, closing her eyes and rubbing my mother's back fondly, playing into the part exceedingly well. Just as she's always done. She always put on a good show for our parents, saving her vindictive insults for when we were alone. "I wouldn't have missed it. You know I look forward to this event every year! It's always so good to see you both, and to catch up with you, Theo. You really shouldn't be such a stranger."

I give her a tight smile and reach for my wine glass. Rather than gauge Lauren's reaction to my less-than warm response, I turn to Whitney. She's still watching the whole interaction with wary eyes, but doesn't intervene, letting it play out.

My mother and Lauren talk for a little while longer, like they are old friends. Which I guess they are, given that my mother routinely will meet up with Lauren and her mother for lunch. My mother is not fully aware of the terms of our breakup. I can't imagine that if she were she'd be putting on a show like this. But I don't have it in me to drag Lauren through the mud anymore. Losing control of me and my family's inheritance was enough of a punishment for her.

Finally, after what feels like an eternity, Lauren excuses

herself back to her table. My mother looks after her fondly, but then turns back to the table once she's out of eyeline.

I place my hand on Whitney's leg in an attempt to soothe any type of turmoil she might be feeling. She turns to me and gives me an affectionate look. I can't help but smile at her softly. She's so lovely tonight, and for the first time, I don't feel the pressure of anyone looking over my shoulder. I can't seem to keep my hands off of her.

"So, Whitney," my mother begins as she picks up her wine glass and swirls it a bit. "Tell us a little about yourself."

Whitney nods her head, turning her attention to my mother. She rattles off a few things about her, how she worked under Vance Peterson and helped him lead the company to where it is now. I know she's trying to make an impression after having been unwittingly compared to Lauren. It's shameful to say, but I tune her out a bit, choosing to focus on how her toned thigh feels beneath my hand.

Finally, satisfied that she provided a thorough investigation, my mother sniffs and looks down her nose at Whitney. She gives the two of us one more long look before excusing herself for her speech for the evening. My father goes with her, leaving just the two of us at the table.

Whitney turns to me and exhales. "How do you think that went?"

I offer her an encouraging smile. "It was just fine. Relax."

She takes another deep breath in through her nose and turns toward the stage where my mother is now standing behind the podium. The lights in the ballroom dim a bit, the spotlight centering on my mother as she jumps into thanking everyone for attending.

My hand is still on Whitney's leg, and my fingers stroke the smooth, creamy skin of her thigh rhythmically. She takes another deep breath and I notice she relaxes further into her chair. I can't imagine what's running through her mind right now, but I want to make sure that she knows she's the only woman in this room who I give a damn about tonight.

As the minutes tick by, the blood traveling through my body seems to run just a bit faster, and I'm compelled to move my hand slightly, dipping under the silky seam of her dress. It just so happened that the side of her gown with the slit up her leg is the side closest to me, and I'm unable to ignore that.

Arousal explodes through my body when my fingers touch the smooth spans of her thigh. Her breath hitches when she realizes what I'm doing and shoots me a warning glance. I give her an innocent shrug.

Any second, I expect her to swat at my hand, effectively ruining any fun we could have here. However, I'm surprised when she keeps her expression level, staring up at the stage as if nothing is amiss.

I'm even more surprised when she spreads those sexy legs wider for me, allowing my hand to continue to travel higher.

As my mother continues her speech at the podium, Whitney's eyes seem to turn a bit glassy and her breath hitches. I move closer to the apex of her thighs, and her chest rises and falls with anticipation. Enamored with the way she responds to me, I do it again.

And again.

The third time, I move all the way up. My middle finger brushes over the fabric of her panties, and I have to swallow down a noise when I realize just how damp they are. Slowly, my finger circles over the nub of her clit through the material, and her breath hitches. Whitney squirms in her seat a little in an attempt to find the best position for me to access the most forbidden parts of her. She gives me the side-eye, and I give her a wicked grin.

All it would take is for her to tell me to stop, and I'd keep my hands to myself.

But I love that she doesn't almost as much as I love how her cheeks are already starting to flush as my finger swirls over her.

Things heat up even more when I move my finger to the side, finding the seam of her panties and swiftly moving underneath them. Whitney hums a little the minute my fingers graze her pussy, and I bite my lip, entranced by how soaked with desire she is.

Whitney moves closer to the table, simultaneously pushing my hand farther up against her but making it so my arm doesn't have to stretch so far to reach her. Thankfully, the tablecloth is pooled around her lap, so the person sitting across her cannot see me having my way with her under her dress. That paired with the dim lighting, and we're perfectly shielded.

I'm impressed the longer this goes on. She seems to be able to handle herself well, giving nothing away. I, however, am getting more and more worked up by the moment. She loses a fraction of control when I slide my middle finger deep inside of her.

A gasp escapes her lips, but she quickly covers it, reaching for her glass and taking a sip of water. She shoots me a scandalized look, but I only lean toward her and whisper, "You look a little flushed."

"Do I?" she whispers back, maybe too harshly. If it weren't for how she repeatedly tilts her hips against my hand, I might suspect she isn't digging the way I was torturing her. But she continues to surreptitiously move her pelvis, searching for the spot that feels the best for her, taking her pleasure from me.

We continue on this way, me fingering her under the table and her keeping up pretenses as if everything is as it should be. My need for her continues to mount to immeasurable lengths. But I continue our game, wondering how far I can take her before she gives in. With each minute that passes, I become just as wound up as she is. Her pussy clenches around my fingers, and finally, I know she's had enough.

"Theo," Whitney whispers to me when she seems unable to take anymore. Her voice is low enough that anyone else at the table can't hear her. I turn my head to look at her and catch my breath when I set eyes on her beautiful face.

Her cheeks are flushed bright red, and her eyes are blown wide. I don't know how it's possible, but I grow even harder against the zipper of my dress pants. This entire time I've been fingering her, I've kept my arousal at bay, but now? With her coming all over my fingers in front of everyone here?

Fuck me.

"What is it, baby?" I ask her, though I know what she needs from me without her saying anything. Languidly, I pull my fingers out of her soaked pussy, and she shivers from the sensation. "You need something?"

Slowly she dips her chin and gives me what I can only describe as bedroom eyes. Her blue-gray eyes are darkened with desire, and her eyelids are hooded as she looks up at me through her eyelashes. My cock throbs. "Can we go back up to the room?"

"You not feeling well?" I ask, a little bit louder for the people sitting nearby. I get a few curious glances from the other donors as they overhear our conversation. My mother is still up on the stage, speaking about the goals of the organization for the coming year.

Whitney's cheeks turn an even darker rose color, and she nods. "I think I need to go lie down."

Fuck yes, you do, preferably on my cock.

"Alright, let's get you upstairs," I say as I push my chair back and offer her the hand whose fingers were inside her not long ago. Without another word to anyone, I whisk Whitney out of the ballroom and to the elevator.

She's practically panting when the elevators close behind us, and I don't waste any more time. I close the distance between us.

My girl needs taking care of, and I'm sure as fuck going to be the one to do it.

14

———

WHITNEY

THEO'S LIPS are on mine before the elevator doors shut all the way. He crowds me against the wall, his hands and strong arms framing me.

In between feverish kisses, I manage to say, "I can't believe you did that with your parents sitting right *there*."

"Can you blame me? You are so fucking sexy, Whitney," he whispers. One hand peels off the wall and traces the outline of my body, starting just below my breast and trailing over the curve of my hip down to my dress's skirt. "I can't wait to get you out of this dress. How does that sound? Would you like that?"

"Yes, of course," I say back, breathless. "But—"

He groans against my neck and presses his lips against my pulse point. "But what?"

I hesitate, unsure if I should give into my insecurities or not. I'd be lying if I said that seeing Theo's ex-lover didn't affect me in some way, even though it shouldn't have. She was tall, and blonde, and beautiful. She was the kind of woman who was made for a man like Theo. She had all the qualities, all the good habits, the proper etiquette to be on the arm of a powerful man.

And I didn't.

"Do you think we should talk about what happened earlier? With *Lauren?*" Her name tastes sour in my mouth, and I hate myself for it. I barely know the woman, yet I can't help but feel an unnatural jealousy toward her.

Theo finally pulls away from me and his face turns down into a frown. Before I can say otherwise, he's reaching behind him and pulling the emergency stop button on the elevator. The car comes to a screeching halt, and I look at him in alarm.

"What are you doing?"

He leans against the door and crosses his arms over his chest. "We're going to settle this right here and now."

"Settle *what?*"

"Who did I ask to be my date here tonight?" Theo questions.

I nibble the inside of my cheek twice before answering, "Me."

"And who was I fingering underneath the table just now because I couldn't stand to keep my hands to myself?"

I breathe in sharply and let it out in a *whoosh*. "Me."

"Precisely," he says. He pushes off the wall of the elevator and stalks toward me until he's right in front of me again. His hair raises to cup my jaw and he tilts my face up to meet him. "So, I'd greatly appreciate it if we'd keep any mention of my ex-girlfriend at bay. Because she's my *ex* for a reason, do you understand?"

I nod, my head spinning with the possessive way Theo is looking down at me, as if he's seconds away from losing control and ravishing me right here in the elevator.

"I assure you, I am not harboring any type of feelings toward her other than indifference and maybe even a little disdain. She is my past, and I don't like to dwell in the past."

His lips find my neck again and he presses a kiss to my flushed skin. "Okay?"

"Okay," I agree, my voice breathy.

Theo spends a few more minutes giving plenty attention to the side of my neck and the divot of my ear. When he pulls away and presses the button to make the elevator start running again, my heart is hammering in my chest and his eyes are darkened with need.

"God, I can't wait until you're falling apart around me again," he says as he leans in and rubs the length of his nose against mine. I can smell the remaining hint of his whiskey from the gala on his breath, and it's doing weird things to me. I never thought I'd care for the smell of alcohol on a man's breath, but all bets are off with Theo.

"Such a dirty girl, letting me finger you at the table," he continues his bedroom talk, turning me into a melted puddle right before him. "In front of all those people. Did you like that? Coming around my fingers in front of everyone?"

I mewl and nod my head, all thoughts of any insecurity now long forgotten. Theo's hand is gripping the edge of my skirt, and he slowly starts to drag it up. I wonder if he'll have time to dip his fingers into my panties again before the elevator arrives at our floor.

I get my answer when the doors ding as his finger grazes my clit over my panties. Theo drops my skirt and pushes himself up until he's standing straight. He grabs my hand and escorts me off the elevator car and into the deserted hallway.

I trail after him as he struts to our conjoined hotel rooms with a purpose. He holds his phone to the sensor, and the door immediately unlocks. He pushes it open and drags me behind him. Once the door closes, his mouth is on mine again, and his hands wrap possessively around my waist.

"Fuck, baby," he mutters against my lips in-between kisses. "God, you've been driving me crazy all night in this dress."

"I was hoping you'd like it."

"I fucking *love* it," he growls. "But I might lose my mind if I don't get it off of you in the next few minutes."

Without further prompting, I turn away from him and drape my hair over my shoulder. Theo picks up on the nonverbal cue, and his fingers come to the back of my neck to grasp my zipper. Slowly, he unzips me tortuously. His fingertips trail along my spine as the dress slowly opens across my back. Goosebumps erupt over my skin as he gently caresses me all the way down.

When it's fully lowered, his hands come back up to my shoulders, and he sensuously pushes the straps of my long dress down my arms. The dress slips down my body and pools into a silky puddle at my feet. Theo grips my waist to steady me as I step out of it. I turn to face him as my fingers go to unclasp my strapless bra. That soon joins the dress, discarded on the floor.

Theo's eyes turn molten as he takes in my bare body. "You are perfect," he whispers, the deepness in his voice going straight to my core.

His hands cup my breasts, and he claims my mouth again. Distracted by his tongue doing wondrous things with mine, I barely notice him leading me through the room until the back of my knees hit the edge of the mattress.

I break away as I fall flat against the bed. Theo stands over me, his eyes roving over every inch of my body, spread out for him.

His hand goes to the belt on his dress pants, and he unclasps it with one hand. The sight makes my core clench in anticipation. As he undoes the buttons on his shirt, I wiggle out of my panties and start to unclasp my high heels, but Theo stops me.

"Leave them," he commands as his hand covers mine on one of my ankles. I nod and then fall back on the mattress again.

Theo walks toward me, his eyes wild as he takes me in, lying before him, ready to be ravaged.

"Look how pretty you are, baby," he says as he spreads my legs to see me. His eyes heat as they trail over the seam of my thighs before traveling back up to my face. "You're a mess."

My cheeks heat, and I writhe against the bed. "Theo, please."

"Please, what, babe? What do you need."

"I need you."

"Do you want me to play with that pretty pussy of yours?" he whispers as he leans down to press his lips to mine. "You want me to make you come again?"

I whimper as I nod fervently. My lower body bucks against his, desperate for friction, for any type of release.

"Okay, okay," he soothes me. He kisses me one more time before trailing his lips down my body. With one hand on each of my knees, he spreads me wide open for him. In any other circumstance, I would be embarrassed to be so exposed, but I'm so turned on now; all I care about is Theo's touch. "Poor girl," he mutters as his finger trails between my legs and circles my clit. "You need to come so bad, don't you?"

My inner muscles clench around nothing as he toys with my clit relentlessly. I grow wetter and wetter, making a mess of the bedding underneath me, but that doesn't seem to faze Theo. Whenever I open my eyes and peek at him, his attention is rapt on the space between my legs. He's propped up on one shoulder, playing me perfectly with his other hand.

I jolt when his lips suddenly enclose my pussy. His tongue traces the seam, from top to bottom, before dipping inside me and swirling.

"Oh, *fuck*," I wail as he fucks me with his tongue.

"That's right, baby, let me hear you," he says before diving right back into eating me.

I lose myself to the sensation, and before I fully know what's happening, my body is tensing with a glorious release. He doesn't let up as he licks and sucks at my sensitive clit. One of his thick fingers slides inside me and begins gentle thrusts, similar to how he worked me down in the ballroom. My muscles clench tightly around him, but he continues his onslaught.

"Come on, baby, give me one more," he says, his lips above my clit. The vibration of his voice hits me and sends me close to the edge once more. His finger inside of me hooks toward my G-spot and works it rhythmically. "Come on, Whitney, come for me again."

I let out a scream as stars explode behind my eyes. My body clenches around his fingers, and I feel tingles down to my toes. Theo works me through it, his movements with his fingers only slowing to a steady pace as I come down from my high.

Number 8: Attentive in the Bedroom

"Come here," he says as he pulls his mouth away from my core, after kissing my clit one last time. My body trembles intermittently from the aftershocks of the orgasm. He has to help me, because my muscles don't respond.

His strong arms snake under my pelvis, and he flips me onto my belly, grabbing my hip bones and raising them until I'm on my knees.

I know what's coming, and my body aches for it.

Theo guides himself into me, and I moan the minute his cock pushes inside my body. He growls lowly as soon as he's seated deep inside me. I am so deliciously *full* of him in this position, and already I feel like I could come, though he hasn't even started to move yet.

As if trying to get a handle on himself, Theo folds his body over my back until his lips are next to my ear. One of his hands wraps around my waist until his fingers find my clit again. He begins to strum it back and forth, and I moan into the pillows.

"I'm going to fuck you so good, Whitney," he says. "Do you want that?"

"Yes, Theo, Yes!" I shout, though it's muffled by the bedding.

He draws his hips back slowly before thrusting in deep. I lurch forward and let out a feral sound I didn't know I could make.

"Let it out, Whitney," Theo rumbles in my ear. "Scream for me. Let everyone know who's making you feel this good."

"I'm going to come!" I shout.

"Yeah? Are you gonna come for me again? That's a good girl; give it to me now." His thrusts grow rapidly and he hits every possible erogenous zone deep inside me. "Come now, Whitney. Come."

I can't hold on anymore—I shatter around him.

For this moment, I'm just a woman, and Theo is just a man. He's not the CEO of the company or the boss I'll have to report to again come Monday. Right now, he's the man bringing me undeniable levels of pleasure, and I'm the woman driving him crazy.

My body floats into nothingness as euphoria overtakes me. The walls of my pussy clench around him, and he grunts as he fucks me. The noises he makes as he moves deep within me bring me to new heights that I've never experienced before. I've never been with a man as vocal as Theo during sex, but now that I know just how much it heightens my pleasure, I'm not sure I'll ever be able to go back. I'm obsessed with hearing just how appreciative Theo is of me, and my body seems to come alive with every moan and grunt that escapes his lips.

With a roar, Theo thrusts deep inside me, and then he stills as he comes. His body drapes over mine again, and he holds me tightly. His breathing is ragged, and his heart thumps against my back. His body twitches a few more times, and then he pulls out of me before slumping onto the mattress at my side.

The minutes pass, and finally, when I feel I've caught my breath, I roll onto my other side to face him. Theo's got one arm draped over his forehead, and the arm closest to me spread out wide. I curl up at his side and lean my cheek against his chest. His arm falls around my waist, and he pulls me into his body before turning his head to press a kiss to my forehead.

"You were perfect," he says against my skin. I preen against his praise and snuggle in deeper. He sighs, breathing me in, and then swears, "We didn't use a condom."

"I'm on the pill. Have been for a long time," I say to reassure him. I have no intentions of getting pregnant anytime soon. This isn't my first rodeo.

He hums against me. "We should get you cleaned up."

"Just a minute longer," I say and hold him tighter, breathing in his scent—remnants of his cologne mixed with his sweat from fucking me. I've never experienced pheromones, but I would assume this is what they're like. He's irresistible.

My inner muscles clench again, the remaining soreness reminding me that I'm not quite ready to go again.

When I agreed to come on this trip with Theo, I never would have thought this was where we'd end up. The attraction between us has been palpable for weeks, but both of us were toeing the line as best as we could. I suppose being away from home, and the office, was just enough to push us both over the edge.

Satisfaction settles through me, and though I know that we'll have to deal with the aftermath of this one way or another, I feel perfectly content with staying like this for as long as we can.

15

THEO

MOVEMENT in the bed is what jostles me awake. I roll over on my side to see the outline of Whitney's body scurry into the hotel bathroom. My chest expands with a long, deep breath as I slowly wake myself up more.

When I hear the toilet flush and then the sink turn on, I move again, so I'm lying on my back. Propping my arm up under my head, I wait for her to finish. Finally, the bathroom door opens and she steps out into the room.

"Is that my shirt?" I ask her, unable to keep the grin off my face.

Whitney's fingers play with the hem of my blue dress shirt, which is way too big for her. She has the three buttons done up, covering herself from my view, but she's still flawless in every aspect of the term. She gives me a shy smile as though my face wasn't buried between her legs last night. "Maybe. I couldn't find my clothes."

I extend my arm out to her. "Come back to bed."

She hustles back to the mattress and settles in against my side, nestling her head against my chest. I wrap my arm around her tightly, pulling her into me. Leaning my nose against her forehead, I breathe her in, appreciating her scent and how much being this close to her seems to comfort me.

"Did you have a nice night?" I ask her eventually, breaking the comfortable silence we fell into.

Whitney pulls away slightly so she can meet my eyes. I note a mischievous gleam hiding in her gaze. "At the gala or after?"

I chuckle and lean forward to press a kiss to her lips. "Either," I murmur against her mouth.

"Well, I definitely had a good time at the gala," she says, pecking my lips again. "And I guess the activities afterward weren't too bad either."

Playing along, I hum low in my chest. I move us around until I'm hovering above her on the mattress. "Not too bad, hm? I guess I have to up my game then."

Whitney's hands thread through my hair, and she pulls the strands, bringing my face down to hers. I press my lips against hers again, this time tracing my tongue over the seam of her lips, and begging for her to open for me. When she does, I waste no time in pushing deeper and ravaging her so completely that we're both left breathless when I finally pull away. I run my fingers down her face until I'm cupping her jaw. She looks deep into my eyes with an intensity that makes my chest hurt.

"You're—" I pause, unable to find the right words. "I'm enraptured with you, Whitney Palmer."

She beams at me, preening under the praise. I roll back over onto my back but pull her with me, drawing her in as close to my body as possible, not wanting there to be any distance between us. Whitney hitches one of her legs over my hips and wraps an arm tightly around my middle.

We lay there together, soaking in each other's presence. My

fingers stroke over her hair methodically until she melts against me.

A thought dawns on me, and I blurt it out before I can stop myself. "I never officially asked if you were seeing anyone. That was pretty shitty of me to just assume."

She chuckles and runs her fingers over my pectorals. "Well, if last night wasn't indication enough, you can put your mind at ease. I'm definitely not with anyone, other than you."

Whitney had never given me any other indication that she wasn't single, but still, I should've asked her long ago before we obliterated any and every boundary between us. I suppose I had been far too caught up in her to keep my wits about me. But still, that was a conversation that should have been had right away.

I close my eyes and curse myself. "I'm sorry."

She pulls away and props herself up on her elbow, looking down at me. "For what?"

"I don't know. I should've asked you if you were available before pursuing you."

"Theo," she draws out my name. "Do you think I would've let you get away with all that you did if I wasn't interested in you too? If I had been with someone, I absolutely would have let you know. Immediately."

I run my hand over my face, feeling overrun with guilt. "It should've been the first thing I asked you when we had lunch that first time."

"You kept that lunch very professional," she says. "I think it would've been a little too much, too fast, if you had come out directly and asked if I was single."

"Maybe," I acknowledge.

"Hey," she says as she cups my jaw with her hand, pulling my face toward hers. She looks me square in the eyes and continues, "Everything that happened last night, and everything leading up to that, was *consensual.* You did not do anything that I didn't want you to do, do you hear me?"

I nod my head.

"If anything, *I* took advantage of *you,*" she teases as she lets go of my face.

"How so?" I ask her, raising a brow.

"Well, as we found out, your defenses were not nearly strong enough to withstand me in that ballgown last night. It was inappropriate of me to assume that you'd be strong enough to resist me."

"I see," I respond, playing along now. "You're probably right. You were simply irresistible in that dress. I was your victim all along."

She grins at me. "Indeed, you were. So, can we stop with this pity party now? I'd really prefer you do something else with your mouth than complain that you're a terrible man who abused authority over his assistant. Because I assure you, you're one of the best men I know, and I was much too willing to let you have your wicked way with me."

"Oh yeah? What is this something else you speak of?"

She sits up, and my body instantly goes cold from where she was lying against me. Slowly, her nimble fingers find the buttons of my shirt, and she undoes them, one-by-one. When the third button is released, she rolls her shoulders back, allowing the material to slide down her arms, exposing her lovely breasts to me. Her nipples are pebbled and standing proudly at attention. My mouth waters simply at the sight of her baring herself to me.

Taking her cue, I sit up, too, leaning my head down and capturing one of her perfect nipples in my mouth. I run my tongue across her hardened peak, over and over, as my other hand rises to cup the other one. Carefully, I guide her until she's lying down again. She watches me with hooded eyes, her gaze filled with desire as I put her in the position that I want her in.

Slowly, I place my hands on her knees, drawing her legs apart until she's bared to me. I bend forward and kiss one nipple before moving to the other. My lips then pave a trail down her sternum and to her belly. I spend some time nuzzling and kissing along the curves of her hip before continuing lower. Whitney writhes below me, arching her back and guiding me exactly where she wants me.

"Is this what you were wanting?" I ask her as I press a kiss right over her pubic bone.

"Yes!" She gasps as my tongue dips lower and slides over her core. "Don't stop!"

I chuckle as I do it again. "Would never dream of it, sweetheart."

With another swipe of my tongue, we fall into our urges, spending the rest of the morning getting lost in the pleasure we can bring each other.

Later in the day, when we're on the plane heading home, Whitney turns to me and purses her lips. I give her a quizzical look, waiting for her to say what's on her mind.

"What happens when we get back?" she asks.

"You mean—"

"With us," she clarifies. "What happens with us? Was this a one-and-done situation?"

I scoff. "Absolutely not. Did you not hear me last night when we were discussing how I don't even put you in the same category as all my past girlfriends? You're in a category of your own, Whitney. And I don't say that lightly. I have no intentions of letting you go anytime soon."

The corners of her lips twitch up. "Then what?"

"What do you want to happen?" I turn the question back to her.

She shrugs a shoulder. "I just want to be with you. I want more of what we had this weekend."

I smile at her. "I do too."

Relief pours over her features. "You do?"

I nod my head, more sure about this than anything else in a long time.

"Do you think we should officially report a relationship between us? Talk to HR and inform the Board?"

Everything comes to a screeching halt in my mind. The thought of approaching the Board with this has my heart rate skyrocketing. I already have Elena breathing down my neck. Would it really be the best decision to come out and say I'm dating my assistant while there's already so many things piled up against me? The company has a strict no dating policy. Even if we hid it, if we were found out, I could get fired for the nondisclosure and the simple act of dating my assistant itself. On top of that, Whitney could get fired.

The thought of termination from this job is concerning, but not as much as the potential of having to leave Whitney just when we were getting started. And I don't know if I'd be able to live with myself if she were to lose her position at the company which means so much to her.

"What if we just...wait?" I suggest, and she frowns. "Maybe we don't make it official yet—to the Board," I add on quickly.

I can see the wheels in her head spinning though they don't gain any traction. "You want to keep it a secret?"

"Just when it comes to work," I tell her. "Until I can get through that ninety-day review with the Board of Directors, then I'll have more leeway with them and I'll be able to make more changes to policy. After that, we can officially report our relationship to anyone you want. We can scream it from the rooftop if you want to."

Whitney is still not sold, her expression grim as she tries to work through my reasoning. "Why?"

I reach over and take her hand, winding our fingers together and giving her a reassuring squeeze. "I promise it's nothing to do with you or wanting to be with you. You know the employee relationship policy as well as I do. And right now, still being so new to the CEO position, I don't have the ability or the power to make any changes or really do anything about it. Does that make sense?"

Finally, Whitney nods her head. "Yes."

My hand moves to the side of her face, and I brush my thumb over her full, heart-shaped lips. Her eyes glisten, and it stabs at my heart. "Whitney," I whisper. "I don't want to lose you yet, not when I think I've finally gotten you. But I think the right move for now is to wait to make things official with HR or the Board."

"Okay," she whispers and nods her head gently against my hand. "I trust you, so if you think this is the best course of action, I'll go along with it."

I lean over and kiss her, grateful she's being so flexible. I'd never want to put her in a situation where she was uncomfortable, so knowing that she's willing to let me guide us through our relationship this way so early takes some pressure off of my shoulders.

When we land, Whitney and I are escorted off the jet and down onto the tarmac. We both slide into the backseat of the car waiting for us. Whitney is quiet the entire drive to her apartment, responding only when I ask her something directly. I'd be suspicious that she was upset about our agreement if not for the way she kept looking over at me and giving me that secret smile, and reassuring me that I am still on her mind like she is on mine.

As soon as we arrive in front of her apartment building, I

get out of the car and round to open her door for her. Together, we walk over to the sidewalk while my driver gets her bags out of the trunk of the car.

When we're standing face to face, my hands rise to frame her cheeks. She looks up at me, her eyes sparkling with affection. My chest feels full as I gaze back down at her. Without needing to say anything, I bend my neck and capture her lips with mine, doing my best to convey everything I'm feeling through my kiss rather than with words.

Whitney grips my suit jacket with her fingers and holds me tightly to her. When we break apart, we're both breathless and flushed.

I tuck a strand of stray hair behind her ear, my fingers lingering maybe a second too long. "I'll see you Monday," I whisper.

"See you Monday," she says back before standing up on her tiptoes and kissing me again.

Finally, she untangles herself from my arms and grabs her bags, hurrying into the lobby of her building. I stand there for a moment longer, waiting to see if she'll return. When she doesn't, I breathe in deeply through my nose and get back into the car.

As we drive further and further away, I find myself counting down the minutes until I get to see her again. Even though I'll have to try my hardest to make sure my desires for her are hidden, I'm looking forward to being near her again. We are playing a dangerous game together, exploring this new relationship. Anyone could find out and bring it to HR or the Board of Directors before I'm ready for them to know about it, and that would be bad news for both of us. But even with that risk, I can't seem to stay away from her.

For the first time in what feels like an eternity, I'm excited for Monday to come.

16

WHITNEY

"SORRY, MISS, THIS ENTRANCE IS CLOSED." I'm halted in my tracks by a man in a neon-yellow vest and a bright orange hard hat. Frowning, I peek around his shoulder just to make sure. He doesn't seem to like that. Gruffly, he mutters, "You can take the side entrance."

I frown but don't protest any further. Gripping my bag in my hand, I strut down the sidewalk, around the building, and to one of the side entrances. This is not how I saw this morning going. After the amazing weekend I had with Theo, I had grand dreams about how we'd greet each other first thing this morning.

As I was lying in bed last night thinking about it, my romantic heart conjured up all types of scenarios. Maybe Theo would beat me to the office, greeting me at the elevator with a soul-searing kiss. Or maybe he'd be waiting for me at my desk with a coffee and a muffin he picked up, especially for me.

I'm still holding out hope.

After I finally make it into the building, I go to the elevator and click the button for our floor. My anticipation rises as the floors tick by. When the doors finally open, I'm dismayed to see all the lights on our floor still turned off. With a defeated sigh, I step off the elevator and find the light switch, squinting a bit when light floods the floor.

I make my way to my desk and fall into my chair. Going about the rest of my early morning routine, I boot up my computer, check my messages, and run over the schedule for the day. When I hear the elevator again, my ears tune in, but then my shoulders deflate when I realize it's Charlotte, our secretary, getting settled in.

I watch the time tick by, wondering when Theo will get here. We barely spoke after he dropped me off at my apartment, though I was stalking my phone like a hawk, waiting for a text message or even an email. But nothing happened.

I feel pathetic, waiting for him with bated breath, but I can't seem to help myself. In between waiting for a message from him and finding ways to distract myself, I'd get lost in the memory of our time together this weekend.

Never before had I been with a man so attentive to my needs or so tuned into how I was feeling. Theo rocked my world, and the second we were both finished and sated, I wanted to go again. I'd be lying if I said I wasn't a little disheartened by his wishes to keep this quiet for now. I wanted to stake my claim on him and lock him down so no one would steal him from me.

Yet, at the same time, I understood where he was coming from, so I agreed.

But that doesn't mean I have to be happy about it.

After what feels like an eternity of watching the clock and fiddling with my fingers, the elevator door dings, and this time, I know it's him. I sit up straighter in my seat, waiting for Theo to walk off. I hear his shoes hit the floor with strong, powerful strides. With each step that brings him closer, my pulse increases with impatience.

Finally, he rounds the corner, and my breath catches in my throat. Though it's only been a day since I've seen him, I feel like I'm setting eyes on him for the very first time.

Theo's got his usual uniform on—a white collared shirt, black slacks, and a suit jacket. His jacket is slung over one arm, and his other hand is occupied holding his cell phone to his ear. He looks like he just stepped out of an Armani ad, the way he's so perfectly put together. The buckle of his black belt gleams at me, and my fingers itch to undo it.

His brown eyes find mine as soon as I'm in eyeshot, and, though he's deep in whatever conversation he's having, his lips tilt up at the corners, and he shoots me a wink. I'm scooting my chair back as he gets closer to greet him, but instead of stopping at my desk, he breezes by, into his own office.

I blink a few times before turning my head to look after him. All of a sudden, I feel foolish for thinking that anything out of the ordinary would happen this morning. That was his whole point, wasn't it? We would continue with whatever *this* was outside of the workplace, but go back to our usual roles as boss and assistant inside these walls.

I had agreed to his proposition, but I suppose I hadn't realized what he truly meant by that.

With a longing sigh, I go back to my work, choosing to focus on striking things off my to-do list rather than wasting my energy on being disappointed with the predicament I'm in.

The morning goes slowly. When I've finally checked off the last thing I need to complete today, I look up to see it's barely lunchtime yet. I scowl at the clock on my computer, cursing it for moving at such a snail's pace today.

I lean back in my chair and flip through the schedule for

the week, hoping that something will come up to keep me busy and keep my mind off of these traitorous thoughts of my boss.

As if the universe is paying attention right at this moment, the building's alarm system goes off, and the emergency lights flash on. The alarm blares loudly across the floor, the sound so sharp that I have to cover my ears.

Theo's door flies open before I have a chance to figure out what's happening. His eyes find mine, and he reaches for me, his hand wrapping around my bicep and pulling me up.

"Come on, Whitney."

"What's happening?" I ask though I know it's a stupid question.

Theo takes a second to respond as he leads me over to the stairwell. He pushes the door open, and we start our descent. "I have no idea. But I'm going to find out."

We're on the eleventh floor, so normally, the stairs would be out of the question, but in this case, it's all we have. Same with the rest of the building. Nexus Group still owns the entire building, though our employees only inhabit the top three floors. Theo clearly takes that very seriously.

With each level we get to, more and more of our coworkers and members of some of the other companies within the building crowd the stairwell. Though it's loud, Theo's got his phone plastered to his ear, making call after call to figure out what's happened. He gains a few questioning glances as though our coworkers are amazed to see him slumming it in the stairwell with the rest of them. If it were any other situation, I'd find it amusing.

I suppose to most of the lower floor workers, Theo is still a bit of an enigma. He hasn't been with the company for very long yet, so many of them haven't gotten a chance to meet him, much less get familiar with him.

When we get to the third floor, he finally slides his phone

back into his pocket. I give him a questioning glance, never faltering my stride. "So?"

His face is stuck in a frown as he watches where he's stepping. "Someone was heating up their lunch on the sixth floor and didn't realize the takeout box was made of aluminum. Lit the whole kitchenette on fire."

"Oh my gosh," I gasp, as well as a few of our other coworkers who are close enough to hear.

"The sixth floor has been evacuated; so far, no known injuries and the fire department is on its way. We'll have to figure out what to do with that workspace if it's unsafe for them to return," Theo says, and I wonder if he's still talking to me or thinking out loud. The sixth floor is not a part of Nexus, but it's still our responsibility as the owners of the building. "I'll have to call whoever is in charge of their lease."

His eyes are downcast still, and I can't see his expression well enough to determine what he's thinking. Theo doesn't say another word, though, until we make it down to the ground level. There's already a large mass of people waiting in the lobby as if they're unsure where to go. A few groups of people leave the lobby to go wait outside.

Theo pauses one second, taking everyone in, and then he steps into the crowd, cupping his hands over his mouth and shouting to get everyone's attention. Slowly, the room quiets, and Theo can speak to everyone.

In a loud, booming voice—which I have never heard from him before—he instructs everyone to slowly exit the lobby and go to the parking garage to wait for further instructions. A few people from our company have questions about how long it's going to take, or if we'll take a half-day. He answers as best as he can in this moment and helps filter everyone through the doors.

I stand by his side, trying and failing not to be impressed

with the way he's handling the situation. I'd never had to go through a potential emergency with Mr. Peterson, yet somehow, I imagine even if I had, he wouldn't have handled it as smoothly as Theo is right now.

Number 7: Good Leader

Theo approaches me after talking with the fire chief, looking exhausted. Though it's a breezy autumn day, Theo has sweat beading on his forehead from running around and taking care of everything.

"I think I'm going to send everyone home," he says to me. "They cleared the other floors so everyone can go get their personal items, but it's been a shit show. Might as well start fresh tomorrow."

I nod my head. It's barely noon, but we've been out here for nearly an hour. "Okay. How's the sixth floor?"

Theo looks dismayed as he says, "Well, the microwave didn't make it. But I think once we get the kitchenette remodeled, we can find a good replacement."

I stare at him, trying to decide if he's being serious, and then I laugh. His eyes glint, and finally, I see the Theo I've known all along—*my* Theo.

"They're running through the floor again right now, double-checking everything in the kitchen and break room. It should still be fine to work in, though."

"Thank goodness," I say.

"Indeed," Theo agrees. "That would've been a nightmare."

It would have. We have about a hundred people working on each floor, and it would've been tricky finding new work spots for them. We probably would've had to have them work remotely until the floor was remodeled.

"So, half day?" I tease.

He chuckles and pulls out his phone. "Yes, I'll send the email out now."

"Do I get to have a half day too?"

He's staring down at his phone, typing the message out on the screen. "Yes, of course."

"What about you?"

Finally, once he's hit *send*, he looks up and gives me a wry grin. "I never get a half day. I'll probably work from home. I still feel like I'm drowning in paperwork."

I rock on the balls of my feet as I consider my impending offer. I should just take the half day and run, but I'm still unsatisfied with the way today has gone with Theo, given everything that happened over the weekend. Biting the inside of my cheek, I finally decide to offer. "Do you want me to come with you and help?"

Theo's eyes flash with something indescribable, and he trails them over me. My body heats up under his gaze, and I nearly shiver when he visibly swallows. His voice is gravelly as he says, "Only if you want to."

I nod my head fervently. I think I would do anything for this man if he asked me in that tone of voice. "I do."

Theo nods his head and then looks out at our coworkers, who are slowly getting the memo that work is canceled for the day. "Let me make sure everyone gets out of here okay, and then I'll call a car." Then he shoots me a glance. "Unless you want to drive yourself over to my place."

My stomach tightens when I realize the implications of me leaving my car here overnight. If I do that, then I'll have no way home or back to work in the morning—unless I spend the night and ride with him. Desire courses through me, and I tell him, "I'll just ride with you."

Theo's eyes darken as he studies me again. "Okay then." I want to do a happy dance when his eyes trail over the length of my body, and he licks his lips as if, all of a sudden, he wants me just as badly as I want him. "Do you need to get anything inside?"

I nod, and he tells me to go ahead and go get it and that he'll be along shortly. I do as he says, saying *thank you* to the firefighters still lingering in the lobby. They tell me I can use the elevators, much to my relief. I think I might've died of a heart attack if I had to climb eleven flights of stairs just to get my planner and laptop.

Once I'm on our floor, I grab what I need and then scurry into Theo's office, packing up the folders he has strewn across his desk into his briefcase as well as his laptop before going back downstairs.

Theo's waiting in the lobby, talking to the fire chief. He looks up when the elevator opens, catching my gaze. His eyes fall to his briefcase in my hands, and he nods appreciatively before going back to his conversation.

Within fifteen minutes, we're sliding into the backseat of his car and driving to his home. My body is hyperaware of his next to mine. He keeps sneaking glances over at me, and I wonder if he knows I can see him out of my peripheral vision.

We arrive at his building, and he leads me into the elevator, pressing the button for the penthouse level. My mouth goes dry with anticipation. I haven't been to his home yet, much less a *penthouse*.

It's everything I imagined it would be and somehow more. Theo's home has all of the latest interior design trends and finest appliances to date. I try my hardest to keep my jaw from falling open the second I step inside his home, but I'm unsuccessful.

Theo watches me in amusement as I take everything in. I brush my hands over the sofas in the living room, loving the expensive texture of the upholstery. I wander over to the large, floor-to-ceiling windows and stare out over downtown Chicago.

"I think I can see my house from here," I whisper, talking to myself.

"I'm sure you can," Theo agrees, startling me as he comes up behind me.

"This is amazing."

"I'm glad you like it," he says, placing his hand on my lower back as we stare out the window for a while longer.

Finally, we agree that it's time to go back to work. Theo shows me around and asks where I'd prefer to do my work. I decide to set up shop at his kitchen island, which he seems slightly surprised about, though he doesn't protest. I don't tell him it's because I can appreciate the view from his windows from there, but I imagine he suspects my reasoning.

I get comfortable on the stool and pull out my laptop and planner. I was able to get my to-do list done this morning before the fiasco, but I still have a number of important emails to attend to. Theo disappears into his home office, and I don't see him for the rest of the afternoon.

After a solid few hours of work, I close my laptop, call it a day, and swivel around on my chair. The sun is starting to set, turning the sky a fiery orange color and reflecting off the clouds in an ethereal way.

I lean against the back of the chair and sigh happily. I could definitely get used to a view like this. My mind is quiet as I watch the sky slowly turn from orange into a mixture of deep violets and blues once the sun disappears beneath the horizon.

Finally, then, I hop off the stool and go in search of Theo. Surely, he must be about finished with his work for the day. My heels click against his hardwood floors as I wander down the hallway until I get to his office.

My knuckles rap against his open door twice, and I wait for his attention.

"Hey," he says, glancing up at me quickly before looking back at his screen. He's squinting through his thick-rimmed glasses at whatever it is he's reading.

I stand on the threshold of his office, unsure if I should approach him or not. My fingers knot together in front of me as I deliberate my small dilemma. As if sensing that something's not quite right, Theo looks up again at me and frowns.

"Everything going okay?" His voice is deep, solid, and sure. When I hear his voice, all I can think about are the filthy things he said to me over the weekend as he coaxed me to climax over and over again. He must notice something on my face because he reaches for his glasses and pulls them off his face, dropping them on the desk.

"Yeah, would you mind calling the car to come pick me up?"

"What's wrong?" he asks, eyeing me closely. I hate that he knows me well enough already to know when something's on my mind. "I thought you'd be staying over tonight?"

"I—" I pause, taken off guard by his bluntness. But then I gather my wits and do my best to be bold and tell him how I'm feeling. "I feel stupid for even bringing this up after everything that happened today, but I'm a little heartbroken there wasn't *more* today."

"More," he repeats, almost like a question.

I nod my head. "It's just, this morning, before everything happened with the fire, you acted like nothing over the weekend ever happened."

He blinks at me, his chin rising ever so slightly as he observes me. "Isn't that what we agreed?"

"It is," I admit and then run my tongue over my lower lip. "So I know I'm being unfair and all, it's just—"

Theo stands from his position and crosses the room until he's in front of me. He lifts my chin with two fingers until I'm staring straight into his eyes. He studies me for a moment before bending down and kissing me gently on the lips.

"I'm sorry I made you feel that way," he breathes against my mouth when he puts a bit of distance between us. Embarrassment courses through me, and my belly knots together.

I shake my head. "No, don't be sorry. I shouldn't have brought it up."

Theo frowns. "I'm glad you did. I don't want you to keep things bottled up."

"But we're not in a relationship," I protest. "So I have no room to say things like this."

Somehow, his frown grows even deeper. "Aren't we?"

My shoulders deflate. "Not officially."

He hums and moves his hand from my chin, over my hair, and down to cup my neck. "I think you misunderstand. We may not be official where it concerns the Board of Directors or Human Resources, but I assure you, Whitney, you're mine, and the minute I can make that known to everyone, I will."

A full-body shiver erupts at the top of my head and travels down to my toes.

You're mine.

I've always yearned for a man to say that to me in such a possessive manner, and Theo did not disappoint. Pleased with his declaration—though private as it may be—I lean up on my tiptoes and press my lips to his. He hums again, this time appreciatively, as he kisses me back and wraps his arms tightly around me.

"I'm yours, huh?" I whisper against his lips.

"Damn fucking straight you are," he mutters back, kissing me deeply. My body comes alive under his touch, and I want more. My breasts feel swollen in my bra, and I long to take my clothes off and let his fingers ease every ache in my body.

I lean back, and his eyes move straight to my lips; I wonder if they're swollen and if he likes that. Feeling emboldened, I sink my teeth into my lower lip, hoping it comes across as seductive. I think it works because his eyes flare, and he swallows thickly.

Then, I say the words I've always wanted to say. "If I'm yours, then prove it."

17

______

THEO

"IF I'M YOURS, then prove it."

White hot need courses through my body, and I don't waste any more time before crashing my lips to Whitney's and proving to her that I mean every word I say.

My hands grip her waist, pulling at the fabric of her blouse until it's released from the high waistband of her pencil skirt. My fingers travel underneath her shirt until I find the smooth skin of her hips and belly.

Her skin breaks out in goosebumps as my hands explore the sides of her abdomen. She's trim, and my hands look large against her waist. I can't help the appreciative rumble that emanates deep in my chest, and I press her even further back against the wall and slide my knee between her legs. I nearly groan when I find her center already wet for me. Whitney whimpers against the pressure between her legs, and she undulates her hips, gasping in pleasure when she finds just the right rhythm and angle to rub her steadily swelling clit against my thigh.

I lean down and capture her mouth, breaking through the

seam of her lips and kissing her deeply. My hands grip her waist, and I guide her in the rhythm that I want her to move. Whitney's gasps and mewls with every upstroke have me thickening in my pants, and I can't wait to be buried deep inside of her.

Pulling away from her mouth, I waste no time before trailing kisses along her jaw, down her neck, and into the divot of her collarbone. She shivers against me, and I suspect she's seconds away from losing complete control. Her fingers bury themselves in my hair, and she tugs at the strands, still grinding herself against the firm muscle of my thigh. By the desperate way she's moving and the noises she's making, I know she's about to come.

I move her up and down my leg harder, encouraging her to tilt her pelvis a certain way so she's hitting all the right spots. "That's it, baby."

Her head falls back against the wall, and her swollen lips open with a gasp. I release one side of her hip, only to trail it under her shirt, up the middle of her torso, and over one breast. My fingers dip into the cup of her bra, and I find her nipple, strumming it at a steady pace and watching the way it drives her wild.

"*Theo*," she moans, squeezing her eyes shut.

"Eyes open, baby," I mutter as I lean forward and press my lips right next to her ear. "Look at me when you come all over my leg."

More goosebumps erupt across her arms as if the sound of my voice is just what she needs to push her all the way. Whitney convulses in my arms, but I don't stop. I continue to guide her hips with one hand and tweak her nipple with the other. She shatters around me with a strangled cry.

I groan appreciatively in my throat at the sight of her falling apart against me. She sighs at the sound of my voice. I wrap my arms around her, under her arms, and haul her up against me, capturing her lips again.

I need to be inside of her. Right. Fucking. Now.

As if reading my mind, Whitney wraps her legs around my waist, holding onto me tightly. I walk us out of my home office, down the hall, and into my bedroom. I kick the door closed behind us.

Thankfully, Chase finally found an apartment of his own and moved out over the weekend while we were at the gala. Even still, I like the idea of the door being closed while I do unspeakable things to my beautiful girl.

Shuffling across the floor, I let Whitney down just a few feet from my bed. I take a step back from her and gaze over her body appreciatively. She's wearing far too much clothing, but she still looks stunning.

"Take your clothes off," I instruct her.

Whitney holds my eyes boldly as she reaches behind her back and unzips her skirt. It falls around her hips, pooling around her ankles. She steps out of the material and then kicks off her shoes before reaching for the hem of her blouse and tugging it over her head.

I lick my lips, desperate for a taste of her as she's standing in front of me in only her underwear. She doesn't hesitate before reaching behind her back again and unclipping her bra. The undergarment slides off her arms, and she flings it to the floor before shimmying out of her underwear.

Her breasts are swollen and heavy, aching for me to taste and suck on those perky nipples. I become impossibly hard as I reach for her. She walks seductively over where I'm sitting on the edge of the bed. Her nipples are at exactly the right height where I can dart my tongue out and taste them.

So I do.

Whitney throws her head back and sighs blissfully as my

tongue wreaks havoc on her pretty little nipples. She maneuvers her hips against me, searching for more friction.

My hand slides up the side of her thigh and to the apex of her legs. Whitney spreads her legs open for me, giving me access to her wet center. I play with her expertly, running my fingers along her slit before delving deeper inside of her, paying close attention to the way she responds to my touch.

It doesn't take long before she's coming on my fingers, soaking them with her arousal and clenching around me so tightly. While she's still in the throes of her pleasure, I grab her hips and maneuver her onto the bed. She's pliable, completely blissed out from her orgasm. While she's staring up at me with dazed eyes, I remove the rest of my clothes, tossing them to the side to be worried about later.

I seat myself between her legs and slide home, groaning in relief from the feel of her tight heat around me. Whitney wraps her legs around my back, holding me tightly to her as I move deep inside her body.

This is heaven.

My thrusts gradually grow more and more rapid, and I feel the familiar tingle in the base of my spine, telling me I'm close to finishing. When Whitney's pussy clenches rhythmically around me, I know I'm done for.

With a guttural groan, I thrust in one last time and seat myself as deeply as I can as I come hard. Whitney's legs fall from around my waist and land limply on the bed. When I finally pull from her, she whimpers but then kisses me passionately on the lips before scurrying off to the bathroom to clean up.

I twist and fall back on the mattress, draping my arm over my eyes as I try to catch my breath. Whitney pads out of the bathroom a while later and snuggles into my side, resting her head against my chest.

We lay together for a little while, basking in the afterglow of our sex. Finally, my stomach rumbles, and Whitney's head pops up, a wry grin twisting on her face.

"Hungry?" She teases me.

"Famished, actually," I say back with a smile of my own.

We decided to go out for dinner to a small restaurant at the corner of my block. Whitney dresses back into her clothes from the day, and I find myself some dark-wash jeans and a button-down.

Luckily, the restaurant isn't too busy, and we're seated right away. The waiter comes by to take our drink orders and then our food orders shortly after.

While we wait, Whitney chatters on about the events of the day and how there had never been a kind of emergency like that before. I nod my head, listening to her tell me more about her time working under Peterson. Somehow, the conversation morphs into something more light-hearted once our food comes, but that doesn't slow her down.

I find myself watching her with rapt attention, loving this chatty side of her that I only get to witness when we're outside of the workplace—when we're just us, Theo and Whitney.

"So *then*," Whitney enunciates as she sets her fork down on the table and steels me with a steady gaze. I really shouldn't be this invested in hearing about her worst dating experiences, but here we are, on one of our first official dates together following a series of mind-blowing orgasms, and she's regaling all of the worst possible scenarios. "He looked at me, said he had a great time, and then gave me a *high five* before walking away and leaving me right in front of the restaurant."

I laugh as I run my finger over the cool rim of my wine glass. "You're kidding."

Whitney leans back and gives me a solemn shake of her head. "I swear, I'm not."

"Where do you find these guys?" I ask, curious as to how such a beautiful woman like her could possibly attract such losers as she's describing.

"I don't know, anywhere? That one I met at the grocery store."

"Well, there's your first problem," I mutter. "Let me guess, you found him in the frozen vegetable aisle?"

"Worse," she says, her voice tinged with amusement. "Gluten-free."

I glance down at the now-empty plate that once held a heaping serving of spaghetti. If Whitney is anything, it's definitely not gluten-free. "What were you doing in that aisle?"

"I was trying to make a recipe I found online, and it called for almond flour. But instead of picking up the almond flour, I picked up this guy instead."

"Was it an even trade?" I question, raising an eyebrow.

She laughs and shakes her head. "No, definitely not."

I can't help but chuckle at her as my eyes take her in. She looks so happy this evening. Her skin is still glowing from the pleasure I gave her earlier, her cheeks maintaining the rosy remnants of a blush. Her slate blue eyes are twinkling at me as she takes me in, too.

My chest aches as I realize just how lucky I am that I found her. To date, I've not been with one woman where I feel so content to sit and listen to her talk about anything and everything. Sitting there gazing at her, I realize that I never want these moments to end. I want to have evenings like this with her every night. I want to have a nice dinner out, knowing that I get to take her home to my bed afterward, and then I want to wake up with her being the first thing I see every morning.

Then, the intensity of my thoughts takes me a bit by surprise, though they're not unwelcome. I continue to ponder these thoughts, still actively engaging with her in conversation. I pay the tab, and then we go back home to my penthouse.

As if she's lived here all her life, the minute Whitney crosses the threshold of my bedroom, she starts undressing, dropping her clothes all over the floor, and then crawling up on my mattress. She turns to face me, giving me a hooded stare that makes my cock thicken in my pants.

I follow her lead, and then the next thing I know, we're repeating the events from earlier this evening.

And there's no better way I'd rather spend the rest of the night than buried deep in the woman that I'm slowly starting to fall for.

***

"HEY, WHITNEY," the familiar sound of my brother's voice echoes from out by my girlfriend's desk a few days following the incident with the sixth-floor fire. "Theo in?"

Whitney's delicate voice confirms his question. I look up just in time to see Chase crossing the threshold of my office. He swings around and closes the door behind him, effectively shutting everyone else out. Frowning at him, I sit up straighter. "What's going on?"

My brother exhales sharply and digs his fingers through his hair. "You know how you told me there was something about these financial statements that just wasn't sitting right with you?"

"Yeah," I draw out the word, hoping he'll get to his point sooner rather than later.

Chase takes a few steps forward and drops a stack of papers on my desk. He falls into one of the chairs and then glowers at me. "I think I finally figured it out."

My fingers hesitantly grab hold of the papers he dropped

for me, and I begin to thumb through them, unsure what I'm looking at. I catch sight of many different strategic marketing evaluations and other invoices from sales and leases.

"What is all of this?"

Chase shakes his head. "He was sneaky about it. But that mother fucker was pocketing hundreds of thousands of dollars every year."

I nearly drop the stack of papers as my hands go numb. "You're kidding."

"No. It took me ages to figure it out," he says, leaning forward and resting his elbows on his knees. "But I finally found a trend."

I brace myself to continue going through the stack he's delivered, gearing up for the worst. Chase watches me as I try to put two and two together. My brows furrow when I come to one specific property—a lakefront view, tons of space, and fully renovated.

"You're telling me this is the cost that this went for?"

My brother's lips pull into an unamused smirk. "According to *our* books and everywhere else? Yes. But in actuality, it went for about two hundred thousand more than that."

"How'd you discover this?"

"By doing exactly what you're doing. I picked a date and went through every single high-dollar property we did contracts for. On paper, everything looks like it was a seamless transaction, and the buyer got a good deal. But then once I started digging deeper—going down to the lower level and speaking to actual buyers and sellers—I found the truth."

"He was reporting less than what it was purchased for?"

Chase nods his head slowly and dramatically. "And then pocketing the rest."

I fall back in my chair and give my brother a dumbfounded look. "How?"

"He buried them among other similarly priced properties so it wouldn't stand out in the reports. If it weren't for you having a gut feeling something was off, I don't think even I would've found them. He must have been one sly mother fucker."

I stare down at the damning evidence that my brother had found about the previous CEO. I was not surprised, rather, I was feeling validated by my inexperienced eyes noticing something was amiss right from the start. But still, even with this validation, A sour, sick feeling settles in my gut. If Peterson had been embezzling money *and* getting away with it, who knows what other skeletons we'd uncover if we dug deeper.

I tap my pen on my desk, considering all that my brother has brought to me today. He's watching me expectantly, as if waiting to see what my next move is going to be. I have a lot to consider. Obviously, there's one clear path here, but I know moving forward with it is going to leave a whirlwind of damage in its wake.

Even though I was suspicious from the get-go that there was shady business going on with this office's predecessor, the woman sitting out front did not.

Whitney adored Peterson. He had been the father figure she yearned for in her life, and now I was going to have to be the one to tell her that he wasn't all that he said he was.

I knew this was something I had to do; she deserved to know the truth, but that didn't mean I was going to be happy about it.

And that fact, knowing that I'd purposefully make her unhappy, is like a knife to the gut. But I know I have to do the right thing. I have to tell her.

18

———

WHITNEY

"GOOD MORNING, Theo Hurst's office, this is Whitney speaking," I answer my phone absentmindedly as I pull up a Word document, hoping to get started on an outline for an online presentation Theo is giving at the end of the week.

Silence on the other end of the phone greets me and I glance over at my desk set, to make sure the line didn't disconnect.

"Hello?" I say into the receiver.

Finally, whoever I'm on the call with clears their throat. "Whitney?"

"Yes?" I respond.

"As in, the Whitney I met at my gala last month?"

My eyes grow wide and I twist in my chair looking for something, *anything* that might convince me that I'm not on the phone with Theo's mother right now.

But it's no use.

"Good morning, Mrs. Hurst," I respond, squeezing my eyes shut. Of all the days I had to answer the phone without looking at the caller ID. "What can I do for you this morning?"

"I was hoping to speak with my son," she says. I hear her sniff and I can practically see her staring down her nose at me. "It appears he's not answering any of my calls to his personal phone or answering my texts."

"Theo is in an important meeting right now with regional development," I inform her, keeping my tone professional. "I would be happy to take a message for you and let him know you called as soon as he's free."

"Yes, do that," she says curtly, and I bite my tongue.

"Anything else I can do for you?"

It sounds like she's thinking on the other line. "Yes, answer me this. Why are you answering my son's work phone? I thought you came to the gala as his date. Am I incorrect?"

"No, ma'am," I say, trying to ensure my voice doesn't sound shaky. "I work for Theo. As his assistant."

"I see," she says, her voice dropping an octave. "Well, this is an interesting turn of events. Please do have my son call me at his earliest convenience. It seems I have much to discuss with him."

"Of course," I respond, just in time for her to click off the phone call.

* * *

"ANY MESSAGES?" Theo asks as he shuffles through a few of the note cards I wrote up for him for his meeting this afternoon.

"Yes, actually." I shift uncomfortably in my seat. "Your mother called, and she seemed most perturbed that I was the one answering your office phone."

Theo's eyes snap to mine and his eyebrows pull in at the middle. "What did she say?"

"Not much, but she gave off the impression that she was about to have words with you for bringing your *assistant* to her charity gala last month." I grimace as I say it, then bury my face in my hands. "I'm sorry, I wasn't sure what I was supposed to do."

Theo's large hand rests on my shoulder drawing my attention back to him. When I look at him, I see a soft expression on his face. He crouches down so he's at eye level, his knees cracking as he goes, making me want to make a joke about his old age. But I don't, my mind too distraught at the thought of his mother despising me for being beneath her son's station.

"I'll talk to her," he says, holding my gaze steady. "Don't let this bother you too much. For someone so focused on class, she can be very..." he hesitates, "uncouth, sometimes."

"I don't want her to hate me."

"She couldn't. Not if she gets the chance to get to know you," he says as he trails his fingers down my arm. "I'm sorry, Whit. I hate that I wasn't available to weather my mother for you."

I give a shrug and force a smile. "It's okay. Hopefully she's not too mad at you."

He laughs. "I can handle my mother, trust me. How about we get dinner tonight? Take your mind off this whole thing?"

"Oh, I can't tonight."

His lips twitch into a smirk. "Back to playing hard to get, huh?"

I laugh now and shake my head. "No, not on purpose. Leila's coming over tonight. We always have a girls' night this first weekend in October. Long-standing plans."

Theo nods grimly. "Well then, I can't intrude. Maybe another night."

"I'll hold you to that promise," I tease.

"Perfect. Enough talk about my mother, please. Let's see if we can find other things to keep that pretty mind of yours busy today."

Theo does find plenty of other ways to keep my mind from straying into the dark thoughts throughout the day. He keeps coming up with excuses to pull me off to the side, out of eyesight, so he can kiss me until I'm melting against me. Or he'll send me funny messages through our messaging application that make me laugh out loud.

I'm grateful for any and all distractions he provides. And they definitely make the day go by quicker. As I'm on my way out, Theo gives me a fond smile and tells me to call him this weekend if I'm missing him.

I wink at him as I wave goodbye, knowing there's a good chance I'll be doing exactly that.

Later that evening, when my doorbell rings, I hurry out of my bedroom and over to the door to unlatch it. Leila stands right at my threshold with a wide, beaming grin on her face. In one hand, she's got a bottle of Rose, and on the other, a to-go bag that is hopefully filled with a wide selection of sushi.

I open the door for her, and she walks into my apartment, going straight to the living space and setting the wine and the food on my small table. Already, I've got *Gilmore Girls* pulled up on my TV, ready to stream.

This is a fall tradition for us—for as long as we both can remember, this first weekend of fall, we always have a dedicated girls' night, complete with our annual discussion of Jess v. Logan and copious amounts of wine.

"I've been waiting all week for this," Leila says as she settles on the couch. She rubs her hands together excitedly before digging into the food bag and pulling out different containers of sushi. "I got a little bit of everything since I wasn't sure what you were feeling this week."

I grab two long-stemmed wine glasses from my glassware cabinet and take a seat next to her. Leila's already got the lids off each container and has made sure we each have our own access to Wasabi, ginger, and soy sauce. As soon as I'm seated, Leila hands me a set of Chopsticks, and we dig in.

We make it through one of our favorite episodes in which the Stars Hollow Gang immerses themselves in a twenty-four-hour dance-a-thon. For these girls' nights, we always run through all of our favorite episodes rather than watch them in order.

We've each seen the show all the way through at *least* five separate times, so we can confidently follow along with the surrounding storyline while still appreciating the shenanigans each favorite episode brings.

When the credits start to roll on the first episode, Leila reaches for the wine bottle to refill. "So—" she says, lingering on the word.

I look over at her questioningly. "What?"

She gives me an expectant shrug. When I don't respond—still fully unaware of what she's talking about—she gives an exasperated sigh. "I haven't seen you in ages. I'm dying to know all the dirty details of you and your guy."

My mouth goes dry, and I have to set down my glass. "What do you mean?"

Leila rolls her eyes. "Come on, Whitney. I've still been hooking up with Chase every other weekend. And he's not shy about sharing just how infatuated his brother is with you."

I feel the heat on my cheeks rise, and I know they're starting to turn pink. "Chase has said that?"

Leila nods, giving me a wicked grin. "Oh, he has. Apparently, you're all Theo can talk about—Chase says it drives him nuts, but I secretly think he's glad to see his brother so happy." I swallow thickly, and Leila tracks the movement. "So don't be shy, tell me everything!"

"I'm not sure what there is to tell," I lie. Leila knows about our weekend getaway for his mother's gala a few weeks ago, but I didn't share all the dirty details with her. As far as she was concerned, it was a trip that was strictly business. I didn't tell her that Theo had invited me specifically as his date rather than his assistant.

"Have you slept with him?"

"Leila!" I gasp, looking at her with wide eyes. I feel the tell-tale heat sliding onto my cheeks, indicating they'll be flushing a rosy pink here any minute.

She snickers and raises her glass to take a sip. "I'll take that as a *yes.*"

"I can neither confirm nor deny these allegations," I say back, doing my best to keep my tone neutral.

Leila's lips pull into a smirk. "So then...how many of your things has Theo checked off?"

Again, I'm dumbfounded by my friend's forwardness. As if she can tell I'm not loving this line of questioning, she pushes even further. "Oh, come on, don't tell me that all of a sudden, you've benched the list. I know you better than that. So, tell me."

I narrow my eyes at her. "You haven't told Chase anything about that, have you?"

She flips her hair over her shoulder and rolls her eyes. "Of course not. I would never. But that doesn't mean I haven't been curious."

I look down at my hands as I knit them together in my lap. Suddenly, I'm embarrassed about the whole thing, which is ridiculous. Leila has known me forever, so she's no stranger to my weird, romantic checklist. And I've never been shy about sharing how my dates have stacked up against my high expectations, but for some reason, when it comes to telling her how Theo ranks, I'm feeling protective.

Leila scrutinizes my face for any subtle hints about what I'm feeling on the inside. She can read me like a book, and I see the moment it dawns on her that Theo is possibly the only man who might score a perfect ten.

I haven't checked lately to get the exact number, but based on the few qualities he has checked off, I know for a fact that if I ever were to find someone who met all of my expectations, Theo would be it.

There's just something about that man that screams at me that he's exactly what I've been looking for all these years. It's terrifying and exhilarating. And I'm not entirely sure what to do with these feelings yet.

All I know is that every minute I spend with Theo, I want to spend a million more. I never knew he was missing in my life, but now that I've gotten to experience what it's like to have him in it, I don't think I can ever go back.

And that is a scary thought.

Especially given our circumstances.

At the end of the day, Theo is still my boss, and I'm still his employee. We're dancing along the line of professionalism—which is sometimes thrilling and exciting, but it's also terrifying.

Though we haven't been together very long, I feel like I've known him much longer. I'm comfortable around him, more so than any other man I've been with. He seems to understand me in a way that I can't describe.

If I don't watch myself, I know I'm going to fall fast and hard for Theo Hurst.

And to make matters worse, I suspect that he feels all of these things about me, too. If not based on the way he treats me, definitely based on the way that he looks at me as if I'm the most beautiful person to him, or how he runs his hands over my body as if he can't get enough of me.

"So, it's like that," Leila whispers, her eyes softening.

My heart thunders in my chest, and panic starts to rise. "What do I do?"

"What do you mean?"

"I can't be falling for Theo," I protest.

She raises an eyebrow at me. "And why not?"

"You know why. It's so—"

"Perfect?" she fills in for me, her lips twisting again. "If it's as perfect as you're hinting to me that it is, then I don't see the problem."

"Maybe he signs my paychecks every two weeks?" I say dismally. "Or that he's way out of my league? He's a CEO, Leila. I'm just an assistant. A fact his mother drilled home for me today in not so many words."

Leila arches an eyebrow. "Okay, well you're going to need to fill me in on that one, but trust me, worse things, far more scandalous things, have happened."

I fall back into the cushions of my couch and cover my face with my hands. "It's not even that. It's just—I feel so insecure about it."

"Maybe that's something you need to talk to him about then," Leila suggests. "He should know how you're feeling."

"He knows," I tell her, uncovering my face and giving her a bland look. "But he's trying to have the best of both worlds. He wants to wait until his ninety-day review before we make anything official with HR."

"Why?" Leila asks the question that's been running through my mind since Theo first suggested it.

"I think it's because he's worried it will affect how the Board sees him before he has a chance to prove himself in their eyes," I explain. "Which I understand. And I agreed to it because it makes sense to me. But still, with every day that passes and he keeps meeting qualities off that stupid list, all I want is for him to say '*Fuck it all*' and claim me as his, for everyone to see."

Leila is quiet for a moment once I finish my big proclamation. She studies me intently, her soft eyes running over every feature of my face as if looking for clues. "Have you told him about your list?"

My eyes close, and I shake my head. When I open my eyes again, Leila's about to say something, but I cut her off. "I thought for a second he might've known about it when we went out of town for his mother's gala, but I think he was just saying things. I haven't told him."

"Do you think you should tell him?"

"I don't know," I admit truthfully. It's something I've done for so long, but still, when faced with someone who might potentially be everything I'm looking for, I've suddenly gotten embarrassed about it.

"If I were a guy and I found out that a woman I cared deeply about routinely measured me up against something so seemingly unattainable, I think I'd be bothered by it, don't you?"

"I don't know..." I say again, trying not to make it obvious that she nailed it right on the head. I don't want to talk about this anymore.

As if she can sense that, Leila raises her hands in surrender.

"Hey, don't get mad at me. I'm just asking the questions that I feel like you need to be asking yourself."

"Just—give me some time," I plead. "I'll tell him. I promise I will. I just have to figure out the best way to do it."

Leila gives me an understanding look. "If Theo is anywhere near how kind his brother is, I don't think you have to worry about that. But again, I get the feeling that you'll want to tell him before he finds out himself. I don't see that going over well when he discovered you've been meticulously checking items off an imaginary list to determine his worth to you."

I want to protest that it has nothing to do with *worth*, but I don't. Leila's probably right. But rather than adding any more to the conversation, I reach for the remote and play the next episode, choosing to stew in the aftermath of everything she said.

While the characters play out their plot lines on screen, I'm still mulling over everything in my head. I know Leila is coming from a place of consideration. She wants to see me happy, and Theo definitely is the man who makes me the happiest. But the thought of divulging my secret list to him makes my stomach twist in ways that have me wanting to do the exact opposite.

The evening rolls by until Leila and I have both had too much wine and way too much fun watching the Gilmore Girls make a mess of everything.

The two of us pad off to bed, not bothering to clean anything up—Leila takes my guest room, and I wander into my own bedroom.

As I lie awake staring at the ceiling, all I can think about is the list sitting in my bag. I decide then and there that I'll come up with a way to tell Theo. I just have to hope that he'll be open to hearing about this quirky side of me rather than getting defensive and shutting down whatever is blooming between us.

I get the feeling that though Theo and I have only known each other a few weeks, this is just the beginning.

19

THEO

THE CAR COMES TO A STOP, and Whitney looks up from her phone. She's been scrolling along her social media the entire drive, occasionally laughing at something that has me watching her in pure amusement.

Today, we are tasked with an on-site visit for a potential new satellite office. One of my employees on the geographical research team scoped out this location and brought it to my attention. I had been feeling awfully cooped up inside the big building downtown, so I figured it wouldn't hurt to take a small field trip for the afternoon with my lovely assistant.

Whitney had been excited about the prospect, hurrying around and grabbing everything she'd need just in case.

It was about a thirty-minute drive outside of the city and into the suburbs. The trip had been mostly quiet, as Whitney was busy attending to her social media, but I didn't mind. For once, I decided not to have my nose buried in my phone, instead choosing to stare out the window and watch the scenery of the city go by.

There is one thing for certain—Chicago drivers are some of the worst ever.

I was immensely grateful that I had a skilled driver to ensure I got places safely, especially with Whitney sitting next to me. I couldn't fathom the idea that something would happen to her while on my watch.

The two of us exit the car in front of our destination. Whitney steps right out onto the sidewalk, and I round the back of the Sedan to stand next to her. She's got her sunglasses on as she peers at the building in front of us, so I can't see her eyes to gauge her reaction.

"What do you think?" I ask her, hopefully. The building is significantly smaller than our building downtown, but it's got charm. At about two stories, I think this building would be a perfect addition to the steadily growing Nexus Group. In the long term, I see our chief executive staff moving out of the city and down here to the more private office, which would free up space in our main location for more jobs.

"It's—" Whitney shakes her head. "I'm not sure what I was expecting, but this wasn't it. What is this for again?"

I chuckle and place my hand on her lower back as I guide her closer to the front door. The building's real estate agent is standing on the stoop, holding the door for us to go look around. I nod at him and let him know we will be fine on our own. He lets us go in, staying down in the main lobby and giving us some privacy.

We take a look around the first floor, noting the few office spaces, a break room, and the main lobby with a reception desk. Whitney is quiet as we glance around the floor plan, but now that I can see her eyes, I know her mind is at work trying to figure out just what I have planned with this space.

"I thought this might be a good satellite office," I finally tell her, putting her out of her mental struggle. My voice echoes throughout the empty building, and Whitney turns to face me, her eyebrows knitted together in the middle.

"For who? Property Management?"

I give her a smile. "I was thinking executive staff."

Whitney doesn't respond right away, but her eyebrows knit together even further. I lead her over to the elevators and press the button to take us to the second floor. When we arrive on the second floor, I hear Whitney suck in a gasp of surprise.

This upper floor has been completely remodeled with the finest architecture. Each office space was walled off with floor-to-ceiling windows to keep the office space open and airy. The exposed ceiling above is sealed with black paint, giving it an industrial but modern feel to it.

Whitney walks around in small circles, taking everything in. I follow after her, sliding my hands into my pockets and trying to fight the smile off of my face. The listing did not do this office justice. It's stunning, and the longer I stand here, the easier it becomes for me to see myself working in a place like this.

At my old job, executive staff had their own separate building from the day-to-day operations. That seemed to work well for them, so I could easily see it working well with Nexus, too. We wouldn't be that far away from the main building anyway, only a quick thirty minutes down the freeway.

"Each executive would get their own office," I tell her as I point out the few large offices. "And there would potentially be room for their assistants to have their own office space as well."

Her eyes go wide. "My own office?"

I grin at her and nod. "Better than just sitting outside my office, huh?"

She nods her head vigorously and clasps her hands in front of her. "It definitely would be." Her face falls rapidly, and her eyes shift off to the side.

"What is it?" I ask, taking a step closer to her. My hand raises to cup her jaw, and I pull her attention back to me.

"Mr. Peterson always wanted to expand to two locations," she says, looking around the top floor once more. Her eyes linger on the big corner office, and she gives a small smile. "I wish he was around to see this. I think he'd be proud of everything you're doing for the company."

Guilt consumes me at the mention of Peterson. I know I have to tell her what I've uncovered soon. It is eating away at my insides. It's the last thing I want to do, but I know I am running out of time. Chase and I have steadily been collecting all that we need to approach the Board of Directors with our findings, and there's no way I'm going to allow her to be blindsided on this matter along with them.

Shoving all of those feelings down, I decide to deal with them later. I reach for Whitney's hand, pulling her into the big corner office she is still eyeing. She chuckles after me, her melancholy thoughts now long forgotten.

"Theo, what are you doing?" She laughs when I close the office door behind us.

I spin her around until her back is to the door. She catches onto what I'm thinking. Her eyes flare, and a seductive smile forms on her lips. Heat trails down my spine, and my cock thickens for her as I lean closer into her space and claim her lips.

Whitney's hands trail up my side and around my shoulders. When we find a pause, she whispers her question again. "What are we doing?"

"I'm claiming this big, beautiful office as the CEO's," I say, kissing her again. "So I figure we better break it in properly. What do you think about that?"

My lips move to her neck, and she tilts her head, giving me

more access. With a soft moan, she says, "Anyone could walk in. What about the agent?"

"He won't if he wants to make the sale," I tease her, tracing my tongue over the sensitive spot below her earlobe.

"I suppose that's a good point," Whitney says. Her hands dip under the collar of my suit jacket, and she slides it over and down my shoulders. It falls to the floor, and then she sets to work on the buttons of my dress shirt. I raise my hand and cup hers, stopping her movements. Her eyes fly to mine but I lean forward and kiss her deeply, distracting her from her task. We don't have the time right now to fully undress each other, though there's nothing I'd love more.

Right now, my mind is set on one goal—to be buried deep inside her and feel her exploding around me.

My hands slide up her thighs, collecting the bottom of her dress and lifting it up around her pelvis. I wrap my arms around her waist, hoisting her up and bracing her against the door as her legs wrap around my hips. "God, I just can't get enough of you," I murmur, capturing her lips again. She wiggles against me, pressing her warm pussy against my steadily hardening length. "Do you want me to fuck you right here?

She whimpers and juts her hips toward me, telling me without words that that's *exactly* what she wants.

I won't prolong this any longer. Nimbly, I undo the belt on my pants with one hand and free my aching cock just long enough to shift her panties to the side and bury myself deep within her. She tosses her head back with a moan as soon as I'm seated fully inside of her.

My hips start moving of their own accord, taking us higher and closer to both of our releases. I try not to get lost in the feel of her nails clawing at my back or how she whispers her broken sighs of pleasure in my ears, but it's no use.

I'm addicted to Whitney, and I don't think that will ever change.

Not long after, we both scream out, hitting that point of climax and falling over the edge together. She clutches herself to me, and our skin sticks together as we're both covered in sweat.

Finally, I let her down, making sure she can stand up straight without falling over. When she's steady, she reaches for her dress, pulling it down over her hips and covering her perfect body, just as I straighten my shirt and redo my buckle.

When we're situated properly again, I reach my hand out to her to lead her out of the office, but she halts me.

"Your jacket," Whitney says, reminding me. I spin around to see my suit jacket crumpled in a heap on the floor.

Chuckling to myself, I bend over and scoop it up, folding it over my forearm and reaching my other hand out to her again. This time, she slides her hand in mine, tangling our fingers together.

Together, we walk out of the empty office and make our way back down to the main floor and the lobby. Whitney glances at me every now and then, her eyes bright and her cheeks flushed, and she gives me a heart-stopping smile each time I catch her. It's something that makes my chest ache with euphoria.

I don't think I'll ever be able to get enough of this woman. Nor do I want to.

We do one last look around before going back downstairs to the car waiting for us. I shake hands with the agent and let him know we'll be in touch before sliding into the car after Whitney. Her cheeks are still rosy colored from the orgasm I gave her in the office, and I find myself itching to take her into my arms again.

So I do.

Extending my arm out across the back seat, Whitney reads my mind and sidles up to me, curling into my side. I wrap my arm around her, holding her to me. I lean my head down, burying my nose in her hair and reveling in her intoxicating scent.

As we drive back into the city, my thoughts are a mess of everything that happened on this little field trip today. I keep getting caught up in her comments about how Peterson would have been proud of me.

I realize I can't keep this secret from her any longer, and I make my mind up. I'll call Chase in tomorrow, and we'll both break the news to her about Peterson and his less-than-ethical money swindling. I just hope that after all is said and done, she won't hate me for shedding light on the not-so-brilliant legacy of her friend and mentor.

It's a risk I'll have to take—even if it means losing her.

20

____

WHITNEY

"WHITNEY." Theo says my name in such a way that has me freezing on the spot. I've never heard him say my name like that —granted, we've only known each other a while, but it's so jarring that it has me halting in my place.

My hand is midway into the bag of chips on my desk. I tilt my head to see him better, and my stomach tightens when I see the steely expression he's giving me. He's standing just a few feet away from my desk, his hands stuck in his pockets. He must've shrugged out of his suit jacket, since all he's wearing now is the charcoal gray vest and his dark violet tie.

Out of my peripheral vision, I see Chase walk up to the threshold of the office and lean against the door frame. The two of them have been holed up in Theo's office for the better part of two hours. I didn't dare interrupt based on the way Chase's face was set into a grim line when he arrived today. He and Theo obviously had something important to discuss—probably whatever he came tearing into the office about last week—which I doubted had anything to do with me.

"Can I get you anything?" I ask Theo, finally finding my words.

He takes a deep breath and exhales it sharply through his nose, the movement making his shoulders rise and fall dramatically. "No, can you step into the office for a few minutes?"

I glance at the clock on my computer, noting there's only a half hour before our workday ends. There is still something so completely off about Theo right now. He isn't the fun, easygoing man I've gotten the pleasure to know over the last few weeks. Something about that fact has me on edge, which is ridiculous in its own right. I've worked with Theo when he's had his CEO hat on, and yet, the deep set of his brows and the way his lips are pulled into a firm line has me thinking this is a different matter altogether.

Carefully, I roll my chair away from my desk, stand up, and brush off my skirt. Theo tilts his head toward his office door, and I fall in line. My heel clicks against the floor as I walk into his office, following after Chase.

Theo closes the door behind us and then strides over to his desk, taking his seat and folding his hands on top of the mess of documents and notes strewn across his workspace.

A sick feeling settles in my gut, making me feel nauseous. Am I about to get reprimanded for something? Did I do something wrong? Has someone found out about our relationship?

Did someone hear about what Theo did to me in the office at the satellite property yesterday?

Surely it can't be that—why would his *brother* be here for that of all reasons?

"What's going on?" I finally get the gall to ask.

Theo studies my face for a moment with a tight expression. "Maybe you should sit."

My heart thunders in my chest but I do as he asks, sitting in one of the chairs in front of his desk and crossing my ankles together. My hands fold in my lap and I clutch my fingers tightly together. I feel frazzled, every nerve ending buzzing with adrenaline.

By the firm set frown on Theo's face, I can tell he'd rather be anywhere else but here. He exhales sharply before he leans back in his chair and motions to his brother. "Chase found something that I believe you need to be aware of."

Chase gives his brother a scathing look, not too pleased to have to be the one to introduce whatever we're discussing. Chase looks at me with his kind, brown eyes—so similar to Theo's—and gives me a sympathetic smile. "Theo brought me on as CFO and requested my help sorting through some of these financial statements from the last few years."

I nod my head. I already knew this.

"There were a few items that left question marks when I was going through it the first time," Theo adds. "A couple of red flags. But I'm not good at the numbers, so I wanted Chase to look them over."

I frown, still not completely understanding what this has to do with me. Theo and Chase share a look, and then Theo continues, though his expression is resigned.

"It appears that the reported numbers versus the listing and selling prices on quite a few properties are not balancing," he explains. I blink a few times, trying to make sense of what this means. "There are a number of commercial properties that sold for significantly higher amounts than what was reported, which means there is a large amount of money that is now missing."

"Someone stole from the company?" I ask, just to clarify. Theo is watching me closely, but he nods his head. "Do you know who it is?"

His jaw ticks, and he takes a moment to answer, but finally, he says, "Yes, we have our suspicions."

I stare at him expectantly. When he doesn't give me

anything else, I feel the need to prompt him again. "Well, who is it?"

Theo closes his eyes and bows his head. I find myself wondering what is wrong with him. He's never acted this strangely before. Usually, Theo is all business and can cut straight to the chase without any additional fanfare.

Long after the air in the room has grown thick, Theo looks up again at me. Fear laces through me at the look of pain in his eyes. My mind starts reeling as I run through worst-case scenarios, preparing for the worst. I'm not about to be accused of stealing, am I?

"Whitney—" his voice cracks, and he clears his throat. "I want to be honest with you, *always*. Even if it's something that I know you don't want to hear."

Number 2: Honesty

My stomach rolls as I gauge his facial expressions. I can see this is paining him a lot, which makes the anticipation of what he's about to say so much worse. Theo braces himself, squares his shoulders, and then delivers the blow. "We suspect that Vance Peterson was listing properties for significantly higher amounts than he was reporting to the company. And then pocketing the difference."

The floor seems to fall out from under me; my ankles go weak, toppling me over in my seat and I put my hand out to brace myself from falling sideways. My head spins, and blood rushes through my ears as Theo's words play on repeat through my mind, jumbled and disorganized.

Vance Peterson—Listing properties—Higher amounts— Pocketing the difference.

My lungs struggle to take in enough oxygen, and I clutch at my chest, trying to force my brain to regain my normal breathing pattern. Vaguely, I recognize that Chase and Theo have moved to crouch on either side of me. A hand runs down my spine until it rests against the small of my back. I suspect it's Theo.

I blink a few times, still unable to focus on my surroundings, reeling in the aftermath of the shots Theo fired at me.

This can't be true.

He wouldn't.

He couldn't.

Flashes of growing up with Mr. Peterson explode behind my eyes, and it makes everything worse. I can see his kind face, the way he would toss his head back and laugh. I can feel his comforting arms wrapping around me and giving me the kind of hug only a protective parent knows how to give.

And to find out that he was not the man I thought he was? Devastating.

"Mr.—Mr. Peterson?" I finally choke out.

Theo's left hand applies pressure to my lower back. I realize he's come to kneel by my side. I didn't even see him move but now that he's near, it provides a hint of comfort. The fingers on his right hand catch under my chin, and he draws my eyes to him. His eyes bring a sense of ease, as though I've found myself in the eye of the storm. Everything stills around me as I stare into his warm, brown eyes.

He searches my face and then releases me before drawing me into his arms and holding me close. I bury my face against his chest and squeeze my eyes shut, willing the memories to stop rolling through my mind.

Theo's hand cups my head. His chest rumbles as he says something to his brother. Distantly, I hear the familiar *click* of his office door closing.

Theo holds me for longer than I can measure, and I clutch

myself to him desperately. My mind buzzes, but I hold onto Theo as if he's the only thing keeping me grounded.

I finally gather the energy to push myself up until I'm standing. I still feel hazy, like my head is full of cotton or I'm running in slow motion. "I think I need to—" I shake my head, trying to alleviate the echo the sound of my own voice creates in my mind. "I need to go home."

"Okay," Theo says, reaching his hand out to me. A part of me knows the day is finished anyway, but it feels like a huge request. "I'll call a car for you."

I shake my head again. "I drove. I'll just drive home."

"Whitney, please let me call a car."

"No, I can drive." I really just wanted to go down to my car, away from Theo, and cry.

"I don't think that's—"

"Theo," I gasp. I want to scream at him to let me be, but I don't have the energy. Something in the way I speak his name has him stopping his protest. His shoulders drop, and he nods, defeated.

"Can I come over later? After you've had some time?"

I massage my fingertips into my temple, where I can feel the telltale throbbing of a headache coming on. "I don't know if that's a good idea."

"Please, Whitney." Theo's voice cracks again, and I close my eyes, feeling my chin waver.

"I just need to be alone for a little bit," I say. When I look at him, he nods once and then takes a step back, letting me stand and move past him.

I don't say another word as I walk out of his office and over to my desk to gather my things. My body feels numb, even as I take the elevator down to the parking garage. Thankfully, no one else steps on, which is a small miracle, given that it's the end of the workday.

When I get in my car, I fall against the seat and try to focus on my breathing.

In, out.

In, out.

I glance at the wall of the parking garage, first seeing the placard assigning my parking spot, and then look at the one next to it. They haven't changed it yet, surprisingly, and I wonder if this small detail has just fallen through the cracks. Especially given that Theo is always driven to work, never driving himself.

Reserved for:
Vance Peterson
CEO, Nexus Realty Group

LIKE THE STRAW that broke the camel's back, this is what finally breaks me. I stare at his name and feel the tears start to roll down my cheeks.

How could he do this?

I want to scream. Theo has to be wrong. He didn't know Mr. Peterson like I did. If he had, he wouldn't have been able to accuse him of something of this magnitude.

But I don't, and somewhere inside, I know Theo would never just tell me this unless he was sure. Unless the evidence was stacked.

But even then, that doesn't make the hurt any less.

I sit in my car, staring at the sign until I know I have to leave. I want to curl up in my bed and wallow in this news. I think that's the only way I'll ever get past it.

My mind is still running through every interaction with

Mr. Peterson that I can remember, looking for clues, hints—any sign that he might not have been as honest as he came off to be.

Does his wife know? Was she a part of this horrible embezzlement scheme? Or would she be just as shocked as I am to find out?

I can't imagine she'd have any part in it. I can barely reconcile the idea that Mr. Peterson himself did. It's like finding out your real knight in shining armor just turned out to be a loser in tinfoil.

Mr. Peterson saved me in more ways than I could have hoped for—taking me in when my mother died, helping me get started in online classes and getting a degree, and giving me a job and a home and a family when I had nothing.

This sense of betrayal hurts more than anything.

I want to melt away into nothingness so I don't have to feel this pain.

When I miraculously make it home without crashing, I drop all of my things on the kitchen counter and go straight to my bedroom. I take a quick shower and scrub at my crawling skin, not finding any type of relief. Gathering my coziest pajamas, I crawl into bed and bury myself under the covers. My head falls into my pillow, and for a second, I hope I can find some comfort.

But I don't.

I don't know if I ever will after this.

THEO

MY FIST POUNDS against her door.

Again, no answer.

I lean forward, resting my forehead against the cool wood of her apartment door. I've been standing out here for the better part of fifteen minutes, knocking, hoping she'll answer. Thankfully, someone left the entry door to her apartment complex slightly ajar, so I didn't have to wait for her to buzz me up. I figured I wouldn't have even made it this far if I had to go through that extra step.

"Whitney, please let me in. Let's talk about this," I shout at the door. I'm sure her neighbors are seconds away from calling the police to file a noise complaint, but I don't give a shit. I'll stay out here all night if that's what it takes to get her to talk to me.

I'll never forget the way she stood straight up when I told her the truth. Nor the way she flew out of the office like a bat out of hell. I barely blinked, and she had thrown my door open and grabbed her stuff. I'm not even sure if she took the elevator, she was gone so fast. Either she chose to run down all eleven flights of stairs, or the elevator happened to be ready on our floor. Whichever it was, she was gone so quickly before I could even react.

She was crazy, but I couldn't blame her. I had dropped a nuclear bomb on her reality. She was allowed to be a little shaken from that. I gave her space, watching the clock as a few hours ticked by before making my way to where I knew she'd be.

But now? Now, it was time to have the hard conversations and figure out how to move forward. And I wasn't letting her escape this time.

Finally, after relentlessly knocking and calling out her name, she graces me with her presence. The lock over the door slides, and then she's cracking it open, peeking her nose through the tiny slit she's created.

"What do you want, Theo?" she asks. Her tone of voice guts me—she sounds so defeated and broken.

"I needed to see you," I tell her, hoping she'll let me in. "The thought of you going through this alone..." I trail off, hoping she can fill in the rest of what I'm trying to say. Thinking about her sitting here all alone tore at my heart the rest of the day. All I wanted was to gather her up in my arms and hold her, and comfort her, and help her through something I know she never wanted to experience.

Her eyes draw up toward the ceiling before falling back to me. Her gaze zeroes onto the potted orchid I'm holding in my free hand, and she sighs.

Slowly, she opens the door the rest of the way and allows me entry. I hesitate for just a moment, watching her walk away from the front door and over to the couch, where she grabs a big, fluffy blanket from the arm, wraps it over her head and shoulders and plops down on the cushions, curling into the fetal position and cocooning herself against the world.

The sight breaks my heart and I want to wrap her up in my arms.

I approach her and she watches me with dubious eyes, as if she doesn't believe that the real reason I'm here is that I truly need to see her. Walking into the kitchen, I set the orchid on the counter and angle it in a way that she can see all the prettiest blooms of the flower. Satisfied, I head over to where she is and fall onto the cushion next to her, still giving her plenty of space but close enough that her foot brushes the side of my leg.

It hurts my heart knowing that she doesn't trust me right now, even though I deserve it. Up until the point where I had to tell her the truth today, I felt that she had slowly started to trust me more and more. I mean, I suppose she had to, giving me access to her body in the way that she had and going along with my plan to wait to speak with HR about our relationship—she had to trust me at least a little bit by principle.

But now?

Now, I'm not so sure.

"Have you eaten?" I ask her after a long beat of silence which danced on the edge of awkwardness.

Whitney had grabbed a pillow just a moment ago and now clutches it tightly to her chest using it like a shield against me. She shakes her head, the only visible part of her from her confines of the blanket and gives me what I can only describe as puppy-dog eyes. Another stab to the heart.

"Are you hungry?" I push further. When she shrugs a single shoulder, I decide that she probably hasn't eaten anything since lunch today, and I pull out my phone, opening up the folder for all my food apps.

"What are you doing?" she asks me eventually. Her head peeks over the edge of the pillow so she can see my phone screen a little better.

"How do you feel about pizza?" The fact that our first official date together was to get pizza isn't lost on me. And based on the wide-eyed expression she gives me, it's not lost on her either.

When she shrugs a single shoulder, I take that as a concession and rapidly order us a pizza to share and a side of garlic breadsticks, because I know Whitney loves her carbs. As soon as the confirmation number pops up on my screen, I push off the couch and saunter into her kitchen, searching. She watches me closely as I search for what I'm looking for.

I locate two wine glasses and go into her fridge, knowing she's got to have at least one bottle of something opened that we can share. I pour us two healthy glasses and then return to where she hasn't moved.

Walking over to her side of the couch, I hand her a glass. Surprisingly, she takes it from me and takes a sip before shooting me a grateful smile that doesn't quite reach her eyes. I settle back on the other side of the couch and raise the glass to my lips.

It's a cheap Pinot Grigio; nothing about it screams high class, but I can't find myself caring. I still drink it as if it's the finest age.

The minutes tick by, and finally, I decide that we need to address the delicate matter at hand.

"We need to talk about what happened today," I say. I study her face as I say this to her, gauging her reaction and watching for any signs that she's going to run and shut herself in her bedroom.

Whitney is watching me just as intently, her lips pulled at the corners at the beginning of a frown. She twists her fingers together nervously, and she does her best to avoid my gaze. "I don't think there's anything to talk about."

"Really?" I prod, leaning closer to her on the couch. Her gaze turns wary, but she doesn't lean back.

"Theo," she says my name as if to ward me off, but it only comes out sounding like a plea. I wish I could have prevented this pain. And what's worse is that I know I could have if I just would have kept the truth from her. But that would have come around in some way and bit us both in the ass.

Secrets have a way of doing that, and I wasn't about to let something so insignificant ruin whatever it was that we were beginning to work toward.

"I think there's plenty to talk about. I'll start." I take a deep breath. "I'm *so* sorry, Whitney." Her eyes go moist, but she doesn't turn away. She doesn't even blink.

"You shouldn't have to be sorry," she whispers.

"But I am. You have no idea." I take a shaky breath as I hold her gaze. "If there was a way for me to protect you from this, I would have. But I knew you deserved to know the truth."

She closes her eyes and turns from me, resting the side of her head against the pillow. I fall back onto the couch, letting the silence surround us once again.

When the pizza arrives, I get up to accept the delivery, handing the delivery guy a crisp fifty from my wallet and telling him to keep the change. I bring our food back to the table and open it up. The smell of greasy, slightly undercooked pizza fills my nose, and I glance at her hopefully. If I can smell it, she can smell it.

Sure enough, she peeks her head over the pillow just so she can get a glimpse at the food. I hand her a slice, and she takes it, muttering a soft *thank you* before digging in and scarfing it down. I want to make a joke about how this is much better pizza than whatever we ate together on our first date, but I refrain. I don't believe this is the time or the place to be cracking jokes, no matter how badly I want to put a smile on her face.

I don't turn the TV on, choosing to let the quiet background noises of the city fill in the gaps. She eats two slices and a piece of garlic bread before she refuses anymore, and I consider that a win. At least I got her to eat something tonight.

The last thing I wanted was for her to go to bed hungry on top of feeling miserable from the news today.

We sit together in silence for what feels like an eternity. I mull over what to say to her and come up short every time. It's the first time in a while that I've found myself at a loss for what to do. I've been in the corporate world for nearly a decade and have had countless encounters with hard conversations.

But still, this is the hardest.

In the past, I've never felt for anyone as I feel for Whitney. And I'm quickly learning that changes everything.

Building up the courage to close the distance to us, I finally take a raspy breath and scoot closer to her on the couch. "Tell me to stop, Whitney."

She blinks at me.

I move closer and whisper, "Tell me to back off. Tell me to leave, and I'll do it."

One slow tear trails down the side of her face. I track its movement, waiting for the moment when she tells me she never wants to see me again.

"Tell me to stop," I say one more time, inching even closer.

Slowly, she shakes her head. "I can't."

That seems to be all the invitation I need. I close the distance between us, reaching forward and pulling her into my arms. "Come here, baby."

She lets out a sob and clutches at me as if I'm her only lifeline. She buries her face in my chest as the emotion and the hurt overwhelms her.

I draw her in, resting my cheek against her hair, noting that it's slightly damp. My body sways back and forth slowly as I rock her, hoping to lull her into a sense of comfort. I press kisses at the crown of her head, trying to put as much of myself into them as possible, in an attempt to portray how I'm here for her. How I'll never leave, and I'll never betray her again.

Each tear that falls feels like a slow, agonizing cut to my heart. But I don't let that deter me. I hold her close to me, unrelenting. I am waiting for the moment when she'll run out of tears and allow me to help her move past this.

It doesn't matter how long it takes.

I resolve right then and there that she'll never have to face anything like this alone ever again.

I'll be by her side for as long as she allows me to be, weathering whatever storm comes our way.

22

WHITNEY

"ARE YOU OKAY?" Theo asks into the darkness when he detects that I'm awake again. I must have dozed off at some point during the night, but now, again, I'm awake and forced to face the aftermath of today.

My eyes burn, and I squeeze them shut, trying to fight off more tears. Theo's arms tighten around me, and he pulls me closer into his chest. I grip onto his shirt for dear life, not caring that I'm getting makeup all over the white fabric.

My whole world was flipped upside down yesterday. Am I okay?

Absolutely not.

But having Theo here with me has been helpful.

He's been holding onto me for the entire night. At some point, he lifted me into his arms and brought me to bed so I didn't spend the entire evening crying on the couch. He tucked me in and curled up against my back, spooning me and whispering soothing words into my ear the entire night.

I barely slept a wink, my mind too perturbed by the news that was delivered yesterday. I was trying to make sense of it all, but it wasn't working. For whatever reason, no matter which way I spun it, I couldn't see why Mr. Peterson would do such a thing. And I couldn't imagine him being in that moment where he made the decision to steal from his company like that.

The version of him that I knew was not the version of him that he actually was.

The worst part of it all is that he's not even here anymore. I wish he was still alive so I could confront him about this. Look him square in the eye and force him to explain to me why he did this. Why would he risk everything he had worked so hard to build?

He leans down and presses a kiss on my forehead. He lingers, breathing me in and exhaling warm breath down against my hair. "I'm so sorry," he whispers.

I've got to give it to Theo—he knew how badly this would hurt me, but he also knew how important it was that I know the truth about this matter. Even though he was the one to rip the rug out from under me, he was simultaneously the one to catch me before I hit the bottom.

Even when it hurts, I always want my partner to tell me the truth. And then I need to be able to trust that they'll be by my side even when things get rough—like they did yesterday.

Number 1: Trustworthy

If I hadn't trusted Theo before this fiasco, I know I can now. He's proven to me that he's not going to turn my life upside down without being there to help me right it again.

With that in mind, I pull back a little until I can see his face. Even in the darkness, I can make out Theo's features and his soft eyes as he studies me. I can see how he is hurting, too. Hurting for me.

"Hi," I whisper to him.

Theo's hand comes up to the side of my face, and he strokes his thumb over my cheek so gently that I almost don't feel it. "Hi."

I swallow, my throat and tongue feeling thick. I could use some water. Crying always seems to dehydrate me more than anything. "What time is it?"

"Almost five-thirty." Theo shifts a little, glancing at his expensive wristwatch. "I should probably get going soon."

I exhale, defeated. "Yeah. I'll need a shower. Do you think we could stop and get coffee—"

"Whitney," Theo cuts me off by saying my name. His voice is so tender that it halts me in my tracks and derails whatever I am about to say. I look up at him with wide eyes. Something flits across Theo's face, regret maybe, before he says, "I think you should take the day off."

"What?" I ask, shocked. "But I can't. We have the meeting coming up, and all those reports have to get finished."

"I can handle it," he says, running his hand down my face again. "I just don't think the office is where you need to be today. Take the day, do something fun—maybe see if Leila is available for a spa day or something."

"She's in school," I say woefully.

"Well then, just take yourself." He looks at me earnestly. "Whatever you want to do, I'll pay for it."

"Theo," I start to protest, but he shuts me up again by leaning down and pressing a kiss to my lips. This is the first time he's ventured into a real kiss since the whole debacle. And I missed him. I sigh happily against him, shifting on the bed until we're closer together. He wraps me up in his arms and holds me like I'm the most precious thing to him.

When we pull apart, my lips feel swollen. Theo's brown eyes are gleaming with desire, but I sense that he's not going to request more of me this morning.

"I'll leave one of my cards on the counter," he tells me. "Do whatever you want to do today, and then I'll come back over tonight, and maybe we can talk some more if you have any other questions. How does that sound?"

I nod, still a little unsure of what to do with this gift. I can't remember the last time I was ever awarded a day off that wasn't a holiday. "Sure."

He kisses me again before rolling out of bed and staggering into my bathroom. I note the shower turning on and contemplate going in to join him. A part of me feels desperate for a shower to help wash away the tears of last night. But I don't. I curl up into my pillows and close my eyes.

I must doze off again because I jolt awake when Theo's lips touch my forehead. I moan and shift a little so I can see him better.

"I'm leaving, baby," he whispers. "Just text me if you need anything today, okay?"

I nod and reach my arms up around his shoulders, drawing him down into a hug. He buries his face in the crook of my neck and breathes me in. After a moment, he untangles himself and then kisses me one more time before sneaking out of my room.

The bed feels lonely now without him. I reach my hand across the mattress, already finding the space where he was lying cold from the time it took him to shower and get ready to leave. I bury my face in my pillows, trying to ward off the familiar burn in my eyes.

When I finally emerge from my bed a few hours later, I feel like I've been run over by a truck. I draw myself a hot bath and let myself soak in the warm water, feeling some of the tension release from my shoulders and neck.

After drying off, I manage to find some of my comfiest clothes and shuck them on before wandering out of my bedroom and into the main living space of my apartment. My eyes immediately find the vibrant purple orchid sitting on my kitchen counter. The sight makes my chest ache, and I wander over to it, my fingers gently stroking over the smooth petals.

Right next to the pot is a black Amex card and a scribbled note from Theo.

WHIT,

TAKE CARE OF YOURSELF TODAY. *Do whatever your heart desires. I can't wait to see you again tonight. I'll be counting the minutes.*

LOVE,
Theo

I TRACE the letters of his sign-off, unable to fight the smile forming on my face. If this were any other man, I'd take the instruction with a grain of salt, but I know Theo means every word, and he wouldn't leave his card for me if he didn't.

With that in mind, I find myself at a salon and spa less than an hour later, checking in for a last-minute massage. After my muscles are certifiably jello and my mind much quieter, I go down the street to Uncommon Grounds and get myself a coffee and breakfast.

While I sit, I try my hardest not to let my mind wander back into the dark place thinking about Mr. Peterson and all of his transgressions, but it's easier said than done. Still, as if my mind is on a constant reel of the past, all I can think about are the good times spent with Mr. Peterson throughout the years. It makes my chest feel tight, and my shoulders slowly start inching their way back up to my ears, undoing all the effects of the relaxing massage I had this morning.

I decide I need to do something else. Sitting here and being alone with my thoughts isn't working. Glancing at my phone, I see it's almost lunchtime already. Finally, my thoughts turn back to Theo, which I'm much more content with.

I wonder how his day is going, if he's being productive or finding himself lost in the stacks of work he still has to complete before his big Board review in the next few weeks. It's so weird not being at the office on a workday. It's weird not being with Theo all day too.

Something deep inside my chest urges me to go see him. I glance at the clock again and then reach for my phone, pulling up the phone number for JT's Pub. Making a quick call, I place an order for both him and myself and then leave the coffee shop to go pick it up.

It's ready by the time I get there, and I thank them before taking it and making my way to the big eleven-story building where I spend most of my days. I get a few surprised hellos from the front desk workers when they see me walk in in regular street clothes. I wave back and go straight to the eleva-tors, clicking the button for the top floor.

It is strange being here off the clock. Like I'm an outsider looking in.

I walk past my desk, not bothering to glance at the to-do list that I had meticulously prepared for today, deciding it will still be there for me to tackle tomorrow.

I knock twice on Theo's door and wait for his invitation to enter. When it comes, I open the door and peek my head in. He's sitting behind his desk, head bowed and curly hair falling forward. Chase stands off to the side of his desk, his finger pointing at something that Theo is reading. Whatever it is, it must be troubling based on the stern expression on Theo's face. But when he looks up, that firm expression morphs into something far more desirable.

The man who is quickly becoming my everything sees me walk in, and his eyes light up with emotion that has my heart stuttering in my chest.

With the pure admiration on his face, I can't help but wonder if I already *am* his everything.

"What are you doing here?" he asks, fighting off a smile. It makes my heart do crazy things, that he's so excited to see me at the office today. Chase is watching the two of us with an amused expression.

I hold up the to-go bag as a way of explanation. "I brought you lunch."

"That's my cue to leave," his brother says before rounding Theo's desk and walking out of his office. He pats my shoulder twice as he passes me, and I shoot him a tight smile.

Once we're alone, Theo stands and walks toward me. I set the food on a small table and melt into Theo's arms as he wraps them tightly around me. He buries his nose in my hair and gives a content sigh once I'm pressed against his chest.

"I decided I couldn't stay away," I mutter into his suit jacket.

His chest rumbles with a chuckle as he releases me and raises his hands to cup my jaw. He tilts my face up until I'm staring directly at him. His expression is soft, pleased.

"I'm so glad. It's been miserable being here today without you. I wasn't sure I was going to last until tonight."

With no further fanfare, Theo leans down and kisses me firmly. When he pulls away, he eyes the bag of food I brought. A mischievous smile plays on his lips, and he reaches for it.

"So what did you bring me?"

"Something incredibly unhealthy," I tease him.

He now grins at me. "I wouldn't expect anything less."

Theo leads me over to his desk and brings a chair off to the side so I can sit next to him. After unpacking our food, we both dig in.

As I sit there next to him, stuffing my face with onion rings and a greasy cheeseburger, I feel content. I'm instantly grateful I decided to listen to the urge that was drawing me to be with him.

We make small talk in between bites, and every once in a while, I'll catch Theo's eyes on me, something indescribable behind that familiar, warm, chocolate brown. My mind flits back to the note he left me on my counter this morning, and a warm ball of *something* blooms into my chest.

I never saw this man coming, but now that he's here, I don't think I can ever picture a life without him.

23

—————

THEO

NEARLY A WEEK LATER, Whitney hurries into my office and closes the door behind her. I catch a glimpse of someone standing at her desk with their arms crossed impatiently over their chest, but I don't have a chance to get a good enough look to identify them.

I had barely seen her today; both of us swamped with tasks that never seemed to end. It feels almost like a relief to see her. I've missed talking to her today. In the back of my mind, I think about maybe suggesting we go to dinner tonight.

But when Whitney spins back around, her face is somewhat pale, setting me on edge. I frown and stand up from my desk. "What's wrong?"

She leans against the door and takes a deep breath. "Elena's here. And she wants to see you."

My frown deepens, and I tilt my head in confusion for why she's having such a reaction to the head of our Board of Directors. "Okay, why don't you let her in?"

"I just wanted to warn you," she whispers, holding my gaze steady. "She's in a *shit* mood, Theo. And that means something in regard to her. She just chewed me out for glancing at my phone while she was walking up. I—"

She stops short when I walk up to her, cupping her cheeks in my hands and tilting her jaw up so I can look into her eyes. "Breathe," I instruct. Her eyelashes flutter closed, and she takes a deep breath through her nose. "Good girl."

Her eyes open again and flare with the familiar primal hunger I love to evoke in her. She reigns it in quickly and whispers. "She wants to see you. I don't know what about."

"Okay." I breathe before leaning down and pressing my lips against hers. Some sick part of me finds joy in the fact that Elena is just a few feet away, behind a mediocre oak door, while I'm kissing Whitney until she's breathless.

And she is.

When I pull away, her chest rises and falls as she breathes in deeply. Her slate blue eyes are sparkling with a newfound desire. While I'd like to clear off my desk and bend her over it, I know this is where I need to draw the line.

At least for now.

With one last peck on those plump lips, I say, "You can send her in."

I let Whitney go with one last longing glance and turn to head back to my desk. I hear her take a deep breath before disappearing to the other side of my office door.

Not even a whole minute later, Elena is sauntering into my office like she owns it—like she owns me.

She stares down her pointed nose at me with a level of disdain that I think is customary for her. I give her a tight smile and motion to the chair in front of my desk. "Elena, please have a seat." To my utter surprise, she does, sitting down and leveling the playing field so we're eye to eye. I fold my hands on my desk and inquire, "What can I do for you?"

Elena reaches into her briefcase at her side and pulls out a manilla folder. "These are the details of your board review and everything we hope to see."

My eyebrows raise up at this. Is this some kind of trap? I open the folder and stare down at the bulleted points on the sheet as well as the date bolded at the top. I'll have to make sure Whitney has this date blocked off on the schedule. I narrow my eyes when I see a few extra points on the list that I haven't yet prepared. "Thank you, that was very considerate of you."

"Oh, it wasn't *my* idea," Elena clarifies, flipping her hair over her shoulder. "If it were up to me, I'd let you walk in there blind and let you crash and burn yourself."

I laugh under my breath. "I bet you would. Tell me, Elena, what is it about me you find so disappointing?"

She tilts her nose up, glaring down at me again. "I do not find you trustworthy, Mr. Hurst. And I do not see you being capable of meeting my personal expectations."

I clench my jaw as I stare her down. *Personal expectations?* "Then why hire me in the first place?"

"I was outvoted," she says matter-of-factly. "As it were, though I do have a lot of sway on the Board of Directors, it seems I don't have total control. Hopefully, that allows you to sleep better at night, knowing that despite my wishes, there's a chance you might prevail."

I fight off the amused smile. She is one hell of an ice queen. Elena glowers at me another moment, likely planning multiple avenues of sabotage. Finally, she stands, smoothes out her dress, and then sniffs. "Consider this your one free chance, Mr. Hurst. We'll see you in a few weeks. I hope you do not disappoint."

Elena walks out of the office, her posture just as rigid as her attitude, leaving me reeling in her wake. She leaves my door wide open, and I see Whitney peer her head around the side of the frame.

She gives me a tight smile and says, "I'm sorry."

I try my best to smile back at her, but something is nagging me at the back of my head. I reach for my phone and dial my brother up.

Chase picks up on the second ring. "Hey, did you know Pinnacle is hiring for an executive position?"

I pause only briefly with the news about Nexus's top competitor. "No, I didn't. I have something I need to talk to you about."

"Okay, shoot." I can hear my brother shuffling around on the other line and can picture him leaning back in his chair.

"I need you to get a hold of a private investigator to look into Elena Dawson."

More shuffling noises and the sound of a pen clicking. "As in, Board of Director Elena Dawson?"

"The one and only," I mutter. "She said something to me today that just kind of had my red flags rising. I think she was involved with Peterson in the embezzling. So I need you to get someone on it. We need to know what happened to that money, where it went, and who it went to."

"On it," my brother says. "I'll get back to you in a week."

I don't know who my brother will hire for this, but I trust him to get the best. If we are going to bring this kind of accusation forward, we need more than just a few stray listing and payment reports. I need to know for sure if any of the Board is involved in this scheme.

As soon as I'm alone again in my office, I rest my elbow on my desk and run my fingers over my brow, trying to ease the ever-growing headache this company is turning out to be. I never saw it coming, and I have to wonder that if I had, would I have taken the position?

But when I catch a glimpse of Whitney outside the office

talking to our receptionist, Charlotte, and seeing the way she tosses her head back in laughter, I have my answer.

Though I never knew the undertaking this company would become, I don't regret a thing, because this position led me to her.

That thought is what seems to drive me for the rest of the day, knowing that I get to go home to her and close out my day lying next to her.

When she knocks on my penthouse door later that evening, I'm filled with anticipation of seeing her again. After we finished work, she said she wanted to head back to her apartment to grab a few things for the weekend. Now, bag in hand, she gives me a wide smile as soon as I swing the door open to face me.

"Miss me?" she teases, and my stomach tightens. I can't help the smile that forms on my face.

"You have no idea. Here, let me grab that." I take her overnight bag and set it on the counter before drawing her into my arms and holding her close.

Aside from the explosive physical attraction I feel for her, I can't get over how wonderful it feels to just hold her in my arms. It's something I don't believe I'll ever tire of.

"I wanted to talk to you about something, but it didn't feel appropriate to discuss it at the office," I explain, holding a hand out to lead her into my home office.

Whitney's brows furrow a bit, but she follows me anyway. Once I'm behind my desk, I pull her into my lap and show her what has been plaguing my mind all day. Up on my computer screen is a small report on Elena. It's not exhaustive, as I'm sure it will eventually become once my private investigator gets deeper into the assignment, but until then, I need to know as much about my new adversary as possible.

"Elena?" Whitney asks, her tone sounding surprised as she turns to me.

I hum deep in my chest as a response. "What do you know about her?"

"Not very much. I mean, she's the head of the Board. She has a lot of financial stake in the company."

"I figured she did," I say, musing.

It must be the way that I say it that has Whitney frowning at me now. "What's going on?"

My hand runs up and down her back, loving the way she leans into my touch as if searching for more. "What do you think the likelihood of Elena being involved in Peterson's scheme is?"

I want her opinion. She has worked at this company far longer than I have and seems to know everyone on a much more personal level than I probably ever will. Even if she had no idea about Peterson's actions before, she does now. So, she may be able to shed light on new information now that she's seeing the world through new lenses.

My eyes study Whitney intently as she rolls over the idea. The corners of her eyes narrow just a little, and then she nods once. "That wouldn't surprise me." Vindicated, I lean back a little in my chair but don't remove my hand from her back. Whitney turns her head to hold my gaze still. "Elena and Mr. Peterson were very close friends. There were many times they'd schedule lunch together or private meetings where I wasn't included. I had no idea what happened in those meetings, just that they were important to Mr. Peterson."

She nods again. "So yes, knowing what I know now about him, I could easily see Elena having a part in it all."

I run my tongue over my bottom lip. "Chase is looking into a private investigator to get us the answers. I want to be totally transparent in the fact that I'm going to bring this all to light. I won't be able to move forward with this company until it's all out in the open."

"I think that's the right thing to do," she says. Her eyes fall to my lower lip where my tongue just ran. "How do you always know what to do?"

Her comment means a lot to me. "I don't. At least not always. I just try to do what feels right in the moment."

She runs her fingers through my hair, her nails scratching lightly against my scalp, which has goosebumps rising up on my arms. Her eyes are emotional as she studies my face. I find myself staring into her eyes, watching her watch me.

Heat blooms throughout my body, and suddenly, I feel a great urge for her. As if nothing will be right in this world until I'm buried deep inside of her.

"But enough about that," I say, leaning toward her until her lips are only a breath from mine. "Ms. Palmer, I believe I have something private of a *more sensitive* nature to discuss with you."

Whitney's eyes flare at the new seductive tone my voice has taken on. She gets on the same page right away, and she wiggles a little in my lap, enhancing my need for her tenfold. Then, her eyes widen, her pupils blowing wide with desire. She licks her lips and says two words that I never knew I needed to hear out of her mouth in such a context.

"Yes, sir."

24

WHITNEY

THEO'S EYES flare as the words roll off my tongue before I can stop them. He looks a little surprised, but not upset. He must like me calling him *sir*. His large hands wrap around my waist, pulling me off of his lap and guiding me to stand before him. He remains in his chair, elegantly crosses one leg, and rests his elbow against his knee. He rubs the edge of his jaw and arches one of his dark brows.

"Close the door."

Need travels down my spine at his deep timbre, and I do what he says. We're the only ones in his home tonight, but the action gives our little scene an extra level of heat with the entendre that we're doing something we shouldn't.

As soon as the door is closed, Theo pushes himself away from his desk and stands. He walks around the frame of his workspace and leans against the front edge, crossing his arms over his chest.

I'm still standing by the door, my hands behind my back now as I wait for what he's going to say next. We seem to be eying each other intently. The room is so quiet I can hear him breathing from all the way across the room. He looks calm and steady—like a man in control. It does things to me that I never thought were possible, and I feel the center of my thighs flare to life.

My body thrums with anticipation. I want him to ask me to come to him. I want him to take me in his arms and tell me that he wants me just as badly as I want him. I want him to bend me over this desk and have his wicked way with me.

It doesn't seem to matter that we're in his office at home rather than at Nexus. I still seem to get off on this dynamic—even if it's wrong—and I don't know if I'll ever get sick of it.

We stay like that, on opposite sides of the room, the only noise the sound of our breathing and my blood rushing through my ears.

Slowly, like an animal stalking its prey, Theo begins to walk toward me. Every step he takes sets me further on edge in the best way. I'm hyper-aware of where he is in relation to me. The hair on my arms raises once he steps into my space, and I tilt my head up, my lips parting with a gasp when I catch sight of his eyes.

His pupils are blown wide, desire written all over his expression.

He's staring at me again in that way that makes me feel seen, coveted, craved.

It's a feeling I don't ever want to end.

I want him to kiss me, to close the distance between us and ravage my mouth, staking his claim. But he doesn't.

"Theo," I gasp his name in surprise when he falls to his knees in front of me.

He looks up at me from under his dark lashes and gives me a wicked grin. His fingers trail up the spanse of my leg, sliding over the smooth skin of my thigh until he reaches the hem of my skirt. "Yeah, baby?"

Those fingers dip under my skirt, and my mind swirls. Leaning my head back, I cover my mouth with my hand so my moan doesn't echo throughout the whole house—which is a ridiculous notion, given that we're the only ones here.

Theo catches onto that fact and reaches one hand up to grab my forearm. When I look down at him in question, he gives me a sinful grin. "Don't hold back; I want to hear every moan from those pretty lips."

Wasting no more time, Theo removes any potential barrier between him and my center. When I'm bare to him, his hand trails up the curve of my calf and lifts the leg, hooking it over his shoulder and spreading me wide for his pleasure.

I can't find it inside of me to be embarrassed by the compromising position he has me in. He doesn't give me a chance before he's diving in and licking me from the bottom of my slit to the top, paying special attention to the small bundle of nerves at the top of my sex.

He continues on this way until my legs are trembling, and my hands are clenched so tightly I suspect I'll see nail marks on my palms. Theo draws me higher and higher up the ladder of pleasure until I'm not sure I can hold on any longer.

With my hands threaded in my hair, his eyes watch my every move, gauging where I'm at and adjusting his speed or his pressure accordingly.

Finally, I'm ready to explode when he removes himself from my pussy. I look down at him in frustration, and my breath hitches. The sight of him on his knees before me makes me feel powerful and cherished.

"Okay, Whitney, I'm going to count you down from three," Theo says before flattening his tongue over my center. "Down from three, and then you're going to come all over my face, do you understand?"

I whimper in response to what he's suggesting. He smiles and then resumes his delicious torture.

"Three."

His tongue enters me and swirls around, sending white-hot sparks of desire down to my toes.

"Two."

With his tongue still performing its dirty task, he raises one hand and circles my clit with his fingers until my knees start to shake. I lean heavily against the wall to hold myself up.

"One."

Simultaneously, he thrusts his tongue inside of me and pinches my clit. I see stars as I plummet over the edge of my climax. Theo doesn't stop, continuing to run his tongue over and through my folds, lapping up every bit of my release.

When, finally, the tremors have stopped rolling through my body at an ungodly pace, Theo stands and cups my face before pressing his lips to mine. I moan, tasting myself over his mouth and loving every second of it.

He pulls away and leans his forehead on mine. His eyes are still crazed with need, and I know he's only just started with me.

"I need to be inside of you. How do you want it, baby?" he asks before he swirls his tongue over me again.

I open my mouth to tell him exactly how I want it, but I snap my jaw shut before I manage to say anything. Theo's eyes narrow, and he nips at my bottom lip in mock punishment. "Don't be shy, tell me."

I close my eyes and whisper exactly what I've been needing. "I want you to bend me over your desk."

Peeking through one eye, I see Theo smirk at me. He's enjoying this way too much. "Yeah? I think that can be arranged."

And it is.

Theo does exactly what I ask of him and clears off a space for me over his desk. Making sure I'm still okay with the scenario at every opportunity, he bends me over the cool, oak furniture and then slides deep inside of me.

He takes me hard, and I love every second of it. Drunk on him and drunk on the sensations he knows how to give my body. He brings us both a pleasure I never thought I'd get to experience with anyone.

Later that night, we're lying in his bed, naked and fully sated. After we finished playing in his office, he scooped me up into his arms, bringing me into his bathroom. He turned on the shower to a nice warm temperature and washed every inch of my body before trailing kisses over every dip and crevice. Then, he carried me over to his big fluffy bed, wrapping me up in his arms and holding me close.

My fingers trace over the left side of his chest. His heart is beating, strong and true, as I lay my palm flat against him, feeling the rhythmic beat. I'm resting my head against his shoulder, and his right arm is wrapped under my neck, his fingers threading in my hair and rubbing my scalp gently.

I'm feeling woozy, satisfied, and blissful. Maybe that's why I ask the question before I have a chance to really think it over.

"Have you ever been in love?"

Theo's hands freeze against my head the second the inquiry passes through my lips. I squeeze my eyes shut, instantly regretting everything. Slowly, his hand regains its motion, and he breathes in deeply through his nose.

"I once thought I was, but I don't think that's what it was," he says. I want to press him for more, but if he wanted to share, I'm sure he would've said more about it. "Have you?"

I shake my head against his shoulder. "I don't think so. I guess I'm the same. I might have thought I was in love, but then—"

I stop my train of thought, not wanting to go too far into the past right now. Not when I'm here with him.

He hums and turns his head to press his lips against his forehead. "What's on your mind?"

I feel immature and childish for this line of thought. Not to mention the inappropriateness, given how short of a time we've known each other. I shouldn't be thinking along these lines just yet. "I just—I wonder how you're supposed to know when it's real."

"I think that's going to be different for every person."

My mind flashes to the little notebook I have at the bottom of my work bag with my perfect man list. I wonder if there are other people out there who do the same thing—or maybe something similar. For a moment, I'm tempted to bring it up to Theo, but I chicken out.

What would he think? Would he be mad, or would he laugh it off before kissing me senselessly until I can no longer remember any type of list?

"I think a lot of it has to do with trust," he continues, unaware of the back-and-forth going on in my mind. "Love takes a lot of trust in another person. Trust that they're going to cherish and protect the vulnerable side of you that is capable of love."

I blink a few times, letting his words sink in and surround me. A part of me is surprised that that's what he said first, yet another part of me is not surprised in the slightest. Sitting up from my position, I stare down into his warm eyes, searching for something. "I trust you," I whisper, thinking back to my revelation in the aftermath of finding out about Mr. Peterson.

His lips curve into a smile, and he leans up to give me a gentle kiss. "I trust you too."

"That means a lot to me," I say to him. I wonder if Theo can tell by the way that I look at him just how much it means. With this admission, a tiny voice in my head reminds me that I'm keeping a secret from him too. The thought of the pink, leather notebook, containing a list with his name on it flashes through my mind. I shove it down, knowing I'll have to tell him but choosing to save it for a later time.

His eyes soften, and my heart aches as he runs his hand over my hair. "Me too." He urges forward and presses a kiss to my forehead before pulling back and giving me a small smile. "You should get some sleep. I don't want you to feel worn out tomorrow."

"Yeah, don't want anyone else knowing you fucked me within an inch of my life tonight," I tease.

He gasps mockingly. "Wow, those are some dirty words coming out of that mouth."

I giggle as he rolls over onto his side, facing me. His arm is still wrapped tightly around my waist, his fingers drawing patterns against my lower back.

"I could get used to this," he says as his heavy eyelids close.

"What?"

"You being the very last thing I see at night and the very first thing in the morning." He peeks one eye open at me to see my reaction.

I'm sure my cheeks heat up and I tease, "Isn't that romantic?"

"Yeah, I thought you'd like that one." Now Theo yawns, and as if picking up on his lead, I yawn, too. "Alright, now we actually need to get some sleep."

He doesn't need to tell me again. Succumbing to the delicious exhaustion of my body and the warm presence of him next to me, I barely make out the sound of his whispered 'goodnight' before I slide into a deep sleep.

25

THEO

"THEO?" Whitney asks from my doorway once I hang up my phone call. I look up to see her frowning at me. "What is this meeting on the schedule before lunch? I don't remember putting it there, and there are no details."

She wouldn't remember, since I was the one who called the last-minute meeting with the Board of Directors. My eyes dart down to the manilla folder Chase delivered to my desk yesterday. She also wouldn't know that the individual I was just speaking with was a liaison from the FBI's corporate fraud division.

What Chase's PI uncovered during his investigation was enough to make sure that Elena and the other two members of the Board who were involved in this white-collar crime are locked away and tried for their transgressions.

Once Chase handed me the smoking gun, it took very little time to get everything rolling into motion. I had scheduled the emergency meeting with the Board of Directors, knowing that the FBI would be hot on my tail, arriving to arrest Elena and the other two.

I stand up out of my chair and button my suit jacket, holding Whitney's gaze. "Yes, I scheduled that."

She blinks but then nods, catching the severity of my tone that I mean business. "With the Board of Directors?"

I nod. "Yes."

"To go over—"

"My ninety-day review, among other things," I tell her, hoping she'll catch on to what I'm saying without saying.

When her face pales, I know she's on the right track. Whitney steps further into my office and then closes the door behind her. "Are you saying what I think you are?"

My lips twist in a smirk. "Perhaps. Are you thinking that I'm going to call Elena out on her shady bullshit in front of the rest of the Board?" Her lips fall open, but I don't give her a chance to say anything yet, but my smirk widens. "Then yes, I am saying precisely that."

She rolls her lips into a thin line, and I can see the wheels of her brain piecing together everything she just heard. "And your review? Have you finished everything?"

I dip my chin. "Everything that matters at this point. With Elena potentially out of my hair and no longer breathing down my neck, I'll be able to have a little more time to complete everything I want to complete. Without the threat of a deadline looming over my head."

"So, this is really it then? You found enough dirt on her that you can confidently say she was involved?"

"Yes. Her, Maxwell, and Kurt. They will all be terminated, effective immediately, after the meeting today. And I'm sure our good friends at the FBI will have a number of important questions to ask them."

"Three of them?" Whitney asks, shock evident on her face now as I list off the members whom the personal investigator found to be involved.

I nod my head grimly. "Indeed."

"That's—" She runs her hand over her neck, shaking her head as if at a loss for words. "That's insane."

"It is," I agree. "Which is why I couldn't sit on this any longer than necessary. After today, we'll begin the search for new members to join our Board of Directors and hopefully move forward and past this indiscretion."

"I think that sounds wonderful," she says.

I clear my throat. "Additionally, I think today would be a good time to announce that we are going to start seeing each other."

Again, her lips fall open, and her chest rises with a deep breath. "You think?"

I move forward then, walking across the length of my office to where she's still standing by the door. When I'm close enough, I reach out and take her hand, threading our fingers together. She watches me with wide, wistful eyes. "I don't think I can go another day without the world knowing you're mine."

"And you don't think they'll see a problem with it?"

"I honestly don't care," I say, dryly. "If they want me to resign simply because I'm in love with you, then so be it."

A breath whooshes past her lips, and I can't help but grin at her. "Theo."

"Yeah?"

"Say it again," she whispers.

I smile wider, taking a step toward her until our fronts are flush against each other. "Say what? That I'm helplessly in love with you? That I think I might've fallen in love with you the very first time I saw you sitting at your desk? And that every day that has passed, I've only fallen more and more in love with everything that is you?"

She looks at me so hopefully it makes my heart hurt. I want

to brand those words on her skin so she might never forget them. "You really mean it?" she asks.

"With every fiber of my being." I hold her gaze steady, unwavering. "I'll love you until I'm old and gray, and even then, that might not be long enough."

"Theo." Her voice is so low I can barely hear her. Her lower eyelids glisten with overwhelming emotion as she looks up at me. "I love you too."

"When you asked me if I'd ever been in love the other night, I should have said yes. Because I loved you then, and I love you now."

She leans up on her toes and kisses me, sealing the promise we just made to each other. Her arms wrap around my neck as she kisses me over and over and over again.

Finally, I have to break away, knowing this isn't the time or the place to get carried away—not with the meeting with the Board of Directors looming over our heads.

"We'll definitely pick this up later," I say, leaning forward and kissing her one last time. "But we need to get back to work."

Whitney pouts at me in a way that makes me want to bend her over my desk, just like I did the other night. But unfortunately, I can't. Though unhappy about it, Whitney agrees and wanders out of my office to gather everything we'll need for our big meeting today.

A few hours later, we find ourselves walking into the conference room. Chase has joined us for backup. He walks in, takes a seat, and whips out his phone, likely to message the FBI agent that we're ready whenever he is. Whitney sets up her items at her usual place. However, I take the position at the head of the table, which is typically occupied by Elena, herself.

When she walks in, she stops mid-stride, seeing me in her place for the first time. Her eyes narrow, and her expression morphs into a scowl. I give her a tight smile and motion to one of the free seats at the table.

"Elena, happy you chose to join us today. Please have a seat."

Out of my periphery, I notice Whitney cover her mouth, and I wonder if it's to stifle a giggle. I won't lie that, although this is not something I ever thought I'd have to face in my professional career, I will be getting some sort of sick pleasure from handing Elena's ass to her on a platter. She's been nothing but rotten to me since the moment I walked into this office.

Justice is always best-served ice cold.

"Thank you all for coming today on such short notice." I begin the meeting once everyone is settled. I feel eight pairs of eyes on me, but really, only a certain pair of blue-ish gray ones seem to matter to me right now. "There are a number of items that we'll need to get to today."

"Let's skip the pleasantries, Mr. Hurst," Elena's frigid voice echoes across the table. All eyes are now on her as she glares me down. "What is the real reason behind this meeting. Was our date not sufficient enough for you?"

I glance at Chase, who is now giving Elena a firm stare of his own. Whitney, next to him, gives me a small nod of her chin, and I feel emboldened to cut right to the chase. "Actually, Elena, it seems that there has been a matter of extreme misconduct that has arisen within this Board."

The room grows eerily silent, and I can hear everyone holding their breaths for me to drop the next bomb.

I stare at Elena straight in her witchy face and square my shoulders. "My brother and I discovered a number of properties that were subjected to improper reporting. We traced that back to Vance Peterson himself. And with the help of a private investigator," I pause for effect, holding Elena's gaze before jumping to Maxwell and Kurt, the other two offenders, "we discovered the others involved in the scheme."

"This is absurd." Elena immediately goes on the defense, her voice rising up an octave into a shrill register. "You're accusing *this* Board of embezzlement?"

"That's exactly what I'm doing," I say calmly. "And I have proof to back it up."

She gives me a stern look while the other two share concerned glances but don't make any effort to defend themselves. I watch her expression morph from that of slight alarm into a cool, frigid collectiveness. She tilts her nose up and sniffs. "I'm not sure if you really want to be going down this path, Mr. Hurst. You're not completely innocent yourself."

Now I frown at her, wondering what she's getting at. "Is that so?"

Elena drums her fingers on a manilla folder and then slides it toward the middle of the table. "I believe your indiscretion is just as damning."

I narrow my eyes and reach for the folder. When I open it, my stomach sinks as I realize it's pictures of Whitney and me. Together.

Chase swears under his breath and Whitney gasps audibly next to me as her pen falls onto the table. She leans forward so she can get a better view of the photos. I flip through the pictures, catching sight of Whitney and myself at my mother's gala, my eyes looking ravenous as I stare at her in her purple dress. In another one we're out to dinner and her head is tossed back as she laughs at something I must've said. And finally, the last one, the two of us standing out on the sidewalk in front of her apartment. I'm cupping her jaw tenderly as I tilt her face up so I can kiss her deeply.

Clearing my throat, I toss the photos back into the center of the table. A few of the other board members lean forward so they can see what Elena has brought forward.

"Did you have us followed?" I ask her, my voice level.

"It was brought to my attention that there may have been some less than professional behavior coming from our CEO, so yes. I had someone look into it," Elena says, tipping her head up so she's looking down at me from across the table.

I fold my hands and lean forward. I can feel Whitney's eyes on me as she waits for how I'll handle this situation. "My love life is not up for speculation at this present moment."

Elena laughs humorlessly. "So, you can accuse me, but you can't take it when I turn the tables on you? I see."

"This is not the same thing." I motion to the pictures. "You have stolen hundreds of thousands of dollars from this company, and the game is over. You're done here."

Elena swiftly snaps her notebook folder shut and stands. "This is ridiculous. I can't believe you'd accuse us of such a horrendous crime. Expect to see termination papers on your desk by the end of the day, Mr. Hurst. We can't possibly have someone in charge of this company who is willing to behave in such a manner."

"Actually," I halt her in her tracks. "I believe those will be directed to you, Elena. There are FBI agents waiting outside for you. I can't say I'd recommend putting up much of a fight; I hear that doesn't always work in your favor."

Elena's face pales, and her chin quivers before she tilts her head up at me, glaring down her long, pointy nose in my direction. "I'll take my chances."

With that, she walks out of the conference room as if completely unaffected by my accusations of her. I look to the other two, Maxwell and Kurt—two stuffy, old men who have no business being on the Board of my company anymore.

"That includes you two," I say, my voice cold. They each

share a glance, knowing they're caught, before gathering their items and walking out of the conference room to meet the same fate.

Another heavy silence falls over the room. The remaining three members stare at me with wide, shocked eyes, but are unable to say anything at this time. I can imagine their heads are spinning at full speed currently.

I unbutton my suit jacket and sit down at the head of the table, folding my hands neatly over the smooth oak. "Well, that was exciting."

Slowly, a few of them release nervous chuckles as if they're unsure what to do with me now. I look to Chase and Whitney, who are watching me with equal amounts of amusement and pride. Pulling my folder with my typed-up agendas, I hand one to each of the remaining participants of the meeting, and I get started.

"I hope that this is the start of a new age where we can work together for the good of this company and its employees. I don't want us to be at odds, but rather, working toward the same goal," I address them.

Together, the four of us go through the process of what enlisting new members for our Board of Directors will look like, and we establish a plan moving forward. They get a chance to look over the reports I have completed as of today, and they seem pleased with all of my hard work.

As things are wrapping up, I bring one last item to the agenda. "Now that we've gotten through that debacle, I believe we need to address the elephant in the room," I say. Whitney's eyes flash to me, knowing exactly where I'm taking this. She drops her eyes down to her notes as her cheeks flush.

My brother leans back in his chair, watching the two of us with amusement, also knowing exactly where I'm taking this.

I clear my throat and address the remaining Board

members, who are watching me with confusion. "I'm in love with Whitney Palmer," I announce, not beating around the bush. "And we would like to move forward with an official relationship, effective immediately."

For the third time that day, the room grows ominously silent. The back of my neck starts to sweat a little bit, but I hold my ground.

They've seen the proof themselves, there's no going back now. Not that I would, anyway.

Whitney is mine, and it's damn well time everyone knows it.

26

WHITNEY

"SEE, THAT WASN'T SO BAD," Theo admonishes me as we walk out of the building at the end of the day.

I roll my eyes at him, sure he wasn't in the same room as I was. "It was exactly as bad as I expected it to be. Those poor people had the rug swept out from beneath them *twice* today."

"Well, they didn't explicitly say no," Theo says, urging me to see the brighter side of things.

"But they didn't say yes either," I point out.

He shrugs as if that's no big deal, which I think is a little ridiculous. Sure, the Board appreciated Theo being so open and honest about the whole thing—little did they know that this relationship had been going on for months prior—but they said this was something we needed to circle back to once the remaining Board positions had been filled.

Theo is to still report our relationship to HR, but whether or not this is still *allowed* is the big question.

There's an obvious power imbalance when one looks at our relationship from the outside. Though Theo has not, and likely will never, exert that power over me, it raises a few warranted red flags. He can't ignore that fact, and neither can I. It's just the nature of a relationship like ours. There have been far too many situations in which the more powerful of the couple would use the relationship as a way to manipulate or control.

But I have no doubt in my gut that Theo would never.

He's too kind, too focused on being equals when it comes to our relationship that he would never exert himself like that.

However, trying to convince everyone else of that might be more difficult.

He agreed that he would report the relationship by the end of the week. That gives him just a few days to figure out how he will present it in a way that doesn't make it seem as though he's taking advantage of me.

I offered to go with him to help smooth the matter over, but he refused, saying that this was something he had to handle on his own. He felt the need to assure them by himself that he had only the best intentions with me.

"Do you want to come over tonight?" Theo asks me once he's standing on the sidewalk in front of his car. "We could swing by your place, and you could get some things. Spend the rest of the week with me."

He stares at me with love in his eyes, and I agree right away, loving the idea of starting and ending each day with Theo. As soon as we're in the car, Theo instructs the driver to swing by my apartment. Theo comes up with me and helps me gather what I need for the next few days.

As I'm packing some of my personal items, I toss a few extra in my bag, deciding that I might as well leave a few things at Theo's place just in case I don't have a chance to run home in between. We seem to be spending most nights together anyway. It only makes sense.

Once I've got what I need, we drive over to Theo's penthouse. He helps me bring up my bags and sets them in his bedroom while I scour his fridge, looking for something to cook up. He's got a package of chicken and everything else that I'll need to make one of my favorite casseroles.

I don't waste any time, listening to my stomach rumble greedily. Pulling out everything I need, I set to work combining everything and heating up the oven to the temperature I'll need to cook. Theo emerges just a few minutes later, now changed into a pair of sweatpants and a white t-shirt.

It's such a stark difference from Work-Theo, as I've fondly started to call the version I get to see during the work day. Relaxed-Theo is just that, relaxed. He looks more human when he's like this, rather than the CEO of a high-level commercial realty company.

"What are you making?"

"Poppyseed chicken casserole," I tell him, pouring everything into a pan and rummaging around in his drawers until I find the aluminum foil.

"I've never had that," he admits.

I raise an eyebrow at him. "Aren't you supposed to have a meal prepper or a private chef?"

He laughs. "No, why do you ask?"

I shrug a shoulder. "All the books I read with big-shot billionaires always have a private chef who prepares their meals for them each week. I figured you'd have one too since you're a—"

"Big shot?" he fills in, amusement laced all over his tone. "I'm capable of cooking myself. In fact, I enjoy it when I'm not eating take-out. So no, I've never felt the need to hire someone to make my meals for me."

He comes to stand behind me as I wrap the casserole pan in foil. His hands find my waist, and he squeezes appreciatively as he leans down until his mouth is right by my ear. "Though I will admit, seeing you cook for me is getting me all hot and bothered."

"You'll be lucky if I don't give you food poisoning," I joke, jabbing him lightly in the stomach as I go back over to his refrigerator. I find a package of frozen broccoli in his fridge and start preparing it in a bowl to serve with the casserole.

By the time the food is finished, I'm absolutely famished. And based on the way Theo is tracking my every move from his position at the breakfast bar, I'd say he's feeling about the same. Wasting no time, I dish up the food onto two plates and pour us each a healthy serving of wine. I set the plates down on the table, and we dig in.

Theo moans out loud as soon as the first bite hits his tongue. He shoots me an accusatory glare as soon as he swallows it. "Are you telling me that you were able to cook like this the entire time?" I laugh to myself and shrug, feeling my cheeks warm under his gaze. "Why the hell have you been holding out on me?"

"Maybe you hadn't deemed yourself worth it yet," I tease him.

Theo smiles at me fondly. "But I have now?"

My eyes fall to my plate, then I look up at him again through my lashes. I think back to how Theo proclaimed to the entire Board (or what was left of them), unashamed, and I know my answer. "Yeah, I think so."

"I can't tell you how happy that makes me to hear that," he says, his tone taking on a tenderness that makes my heart race.

He takes another appreciative bite of his dinner, and I do the same. We polish off our servings, and then Theo helps himself to another. As he's finishing this last bit, something catches my attention out of the corner of my eye.

"It's snowing," I announce, startled, as I see the heavy, white flakes through Theo's large living room windows.

Dishes forgotten, I bolt out of my chair and into the living room to get a better look at the first snowfall of the year. I wasn't expecting snow for a little while longer, but this is a pleasant surprise.

I love snow.

Especially when I'm inside.

I find myself becoming increasingly entranced as I watch the snow fall through the air and down to the earth below.

I feel Theo approach me from behind. His arms wrap around my shoulders, and he pulls my back to his front, holding me tightly. His lips find my neck, and he nibbles at the pulse point, which is now going crazy that he's in my vicinity. My heart seems to turn to mush at his ministrations, and I find myself leaning further and further into him as he continues his explorations with his mouth.

His tongue laps at the sensitive spot behind my ear, and I shiver. A moan escapes my lips, but I don't care. Theo doesn't seem to mind at all either—his arms tighten around me, pulling me impossibly closer to his body.

"God, I love you, Whitney," he whispers as his tongue traces the shell of my ear. My chest aches the sound of those meaningful words. "Move in with me."

I rear back, all sense of desire rolling away with his request —or not request. "What?" I ask, too flabbergasted to say anything else.

He beams at me and strokes his thumb over the ridge of my cheek. "Move in with me, please."

"But—"

"Just hear me out, okay?" Theo protests. I snap my mouth shut and do as he asks, waiting impatiently for him to explain himself. "You're here all the time, or I'm at your place—either way, we seem to spend every night with each other anyway. And I don't think I'll ever be capable of going a night without you by my side. I know it's early still, but I've never been so sure of anything—*anyone*—in my life."

Well, how the hell am I supposed to refuse him when he says things like that? I find my resolve melting away with the warm chocolate gaze of the man I'm ridiculously in love with.

"You want me to move in here?" I ask.

He shrugs his shoulder. "Or I'll move in with you."

I can't help but laugh at the idea of Theo, with his expensive tastes, moving into my small apartment. His lips twitch in amusement as if he can tell exactly what I'm thinking.

"You do have more space here," I admit. "And a great view."

"A *great* view," he agrees, looking out over the large windows on the city below.

"And your bed is much more comfortable than mine."

"It's probably three times the cost of yours," he muses.

"I suppose it's an equal commute either way," I continue, trying to be practical about it. However, it seems Theo has had enough of the games.

"So just say yes then," he says, pushing me into giving a direct answer.

I beam at him, feeling joy explode in my chest at this next step we're taking together. "Yes."

And I think it's one of the easiest yeses I'll ever say in my life.

Theo's face splits into a wide grin, and then he spins me back around so I can see the windows again. Reverently, we watch the snow fall on our city, and secretly, I hope we'll have many more *first snows* together.

27

—————

THEO

THE NEXT FEW weeks pass in a blur of activity. My days are spent mostly finishing off my final reports and meeting new potential board members. My evenings are spent ravaging Whitney all over my apartment—soon to be *our* apartment.

Ever since she agreed to move in with me, the weekends have suddenly filled up with assisting her in packing all of her stuff into boxes and slowly starting to move things from her place over to mine. She's been sleeping in my bed every night and waking up next to me every morning since saying she'd move in, and I can't say I'll ever get tired of seeing her bright eyes first thing in the morning.

It seems that the more time I spend with her, the more I just get greedier and greedier. I want my life to be consumed with everything Whitney Palmer. And for the most part, I think she feels the same way.

Everything seems to be falling into place perfectly.

Honestly, that should be my first clue that something would go haywire. But I was so blissed out in my perfect addiction for her that I never saw it coming.

Until I got blindsided by something so inconsequential, yet still entirely disarming.

"Whitney?" I call out as I walk into our bedroom. I hear her rustling around in the bathroom, and then she emerges with a toothbrush stuck in her mouth.

"Yeah?" she asks, her voice muffled as she brushes her teeth.

The penthouse has been a mess since she officially moved in. All of her items and special memories haven't all found their home amongst my things, either. While she was getting ready for the day, I had been going through a box of some of her desk things, hoping to find a way to turn my office into a shared office space for the two of us. On accident, I swung around too quickly and knocked the box over. It crashed to the floor and I hurried to pick everything up.

But as I was doing that, I came across something entirely too coincidental. I didn't mean to stumble across it or invade her privacy, but when the notebook fell on the floor, it landed halfway open. When I picked it up caught sight of my own name listed on the top, curiosity got the best of me. I stared at it blankly for a few minutes, flipping between the pages with different names at the top then down to the same list over and over, but each having different boxes checked off.

I hold up the small, pink, leather-bound notebook and look at her with a raised eyebrow. Whitney stops mid-brush, her face morphing into an expression of alarm. She spins around and spits out her toothpaste in the sink before stepping back into my bedroom.

"Where did you find that?"

I let a long silence fall between us before admitting, "I was trying to set up your office things and it fell out and landed open on my page, conveniently. Want to explain what this is?"

Panic is evident in her blue eyes as she steps closer and

holds out her hand like she plans to take it from me. I yank it away, keeping a firm grip on it. "It's nothing, Theo. Just something silly."

"Number one," I start, and Whitney looks like she's about to throw up. "*Trustworthy*. Number two—"

"Theo, stop," she protests and takes another step forward.

But I don't, too riled up to stop.

"Honesty and integrity. Oh, or my favorite, *Number Eight: Attentive in the bedroom*. It looks like I've checked off more boxes than just about anyone. Good for me, I guess." I laugh dryly. "Except for this one guy, *Daniel*. He's got just one or two less than me. So what, did he just not meet your expectations and you eventually said enough was enough?" I look up at Whitney standing over me, her face flushed red. Dropping my arm, I stare at her, feeling hopeless, the worst parts of myself raging to the surface and reminding me just how worthless I am. "What is this, Whitney?"

"It's just some dumb thing that I made forever ago," she says.

"Forever ago, huh? Then why do you still have it? Why am I in it? From what it looks like to me, it seems like you're meticulously waiting for me to satisfy your requirements so you can check it off in your little notebook."

She presses her lips together and slowly shakes her head. I push myself up off the mattress and start to pace the room. With a frustrated growl, I turn on her. "I don't want to be measured up to some unattainable expectation. I don't want to go through this relationship with you wondering how I'm ranking against your idea of a 'perfect boyfriend'. How do I know I'm not the next *Daniel*? Are you just going to wake up one day and realize I haven't met enough boxes and then you'll just be done with me like that too?"

"Theo, just listen—"

I hold up a hand and stop her. I'm quickly losing the battle against my irritation and the last thing I want to do is say something to her that I regret. "No. No, we're going to have to do this later." She looks as though I've just slapped her. "You know, I have a board meeting in an hour, and didn't you say something about a dentist appointment this morning? I don't have time to dig into this with you right now."

Her eyes narrow at me. "Then why did you even bring it up?"

I raise an eyebrow at her in response. I did go back and forth, mulling over whether to let it lie or to bring it up. But ultimately, I knew I couldn't just ignore it without knowing what her motive was. "How could I not?"

Now, her expression morphs into one that's pleading. "Theo," she says my name, hesitating as if waiting for me to stop her again. When I don't, she says, "It's just some stupid thing I've always done. It means nothing."

That sparks a small flame of irritation inside of me, and I can't help but frown at her. "Somehow, that makes it worse. So you're saying I've checked off almost every single thing on this *stupid* list, and I'm supposed to believe it means nothing? This makes me feel cheap, Whitney, to see my name stacked up against these guys of your past. As if everything we've done so far is only to meet the requirements of your expectations."

Her eyes widen again, and she shakes her head. "It's not."

I close my eyes and pinch the bridge of my nose. "I'm just not really sure what to do with this right now. So please just—Let's just get through the day, and we can talk about this later, alright?"

When I open my eyes, I note that Whitney looks the complete opposite of alright with my suggestion, but she nods her head anyway, wrapping her arms tightly around her middle in some sort of show of defense. It makes me grit my teeth that she's feeling so vulnerable about this, but I can't find it in me to comfort her just yet.

I will.

I swear I will. I'll spend my whole life doing exactly that.

I just need to stew over this for a minute.

Am I allowed that much?

Closing the distance between us, I lean down and press a kiss on her cheek. When I pull away, she's looking up at me with wide eyes that seem to rip my heart right out of my chest. I have to turn away from her before she brings me to my knees.

"We'll talk later, okay?" I tell her, my voice softening.

I grab my suit jacket off the edge of the bed and swing it over my arm, moving to leave the bedroom. I hear her quiet "Okay" from behind me, and it takes everything in me to keep walking. But I need some space. I need to figure out what the hell she's been doing all this time that we've been together.

The insecurities are raging strong deep inside of me. I mean, how could they not? I'm a thirty-six-year-old millionaire who still hasn't found the right person to settle down with. And it's not for lack of trying. Of course, that makes me feel as though I'm deficient in one way or another.

Then I find Whitney, and everything realigns in my life. Everything feels right.

Only for me to find out that she's been grading me against every other man she's been with to find that potentially perfect match. And this *Daniel* fellow, he only had one box less than me, but obviously that also wasn't enough for her. So what did that mean for me?

The tiny voice in my head that I hate is rampantly whispering that maybe that's the only reason she's put up with me this long. Maybe she's only with me because I check off her damn boxes. That I'm going to be her first 'perfect ten.'

My thoughts fly to my past relationship with Lauren

Farthington, and instantly I remember the unworthiness I felt when she told me over and over again that I wasn't enough for her. That was what ultimately drove her to cheat on me. I didn't give her enough, I wasn't enough.

And now it seems that, yet again, I'm being gauged on my ability to deliver on expectations. Such is my luck.

As soon as I'm downstairs and in my car, I pull out my phone, dialing my brother.

He answers right away, but he doesn't sound happy about it. "What do you need? I'm kind of busy right now."

In the distance, I can hear a female voice asking him who's on the phone. I jump to the conclusion that he spent the night with Leila. *Again.*

At some point, I'll need to grill my brother about what the heck he's doing with Leila. She seems to be able to match him in his wild child ways, and I suspect that anything between them could be perfect or catastrophic. But he doesn't seem to be worried about any of that.

But at this moment, I'm too frazzled by the road bump in my own relationship to care about whatever he's doing.

"Whitney's apparently been keeping track of all of my good qualities," I spit out. It sounds so comical when I say it out loud. And again, a part of me wonders why I'm so bothered by this, and another part reassures me that I should be bothered.

Chase laughs on the other end of the line. "That's weird."

I want to roll my eyes. Weird doesn't even begin to describe how I feel about this newfound information. "That's one way to put it."

He laughs again, and it grates at my nerves. "You sound pissed."

"I am a little," I admit, gritting my teeth so tightly my jaw starts to hurt. I force myself to release it and then take a breath. "I guess I'm more just confused about everything now."

"I think you're probably thinking too much on it. It just sounds like some weird, girly thing to me," Chase says.

I glower out the window. "I just hate feeling like I'm being compared to every other guy she's been with. There were pages of them with different names on the top of each one."

"And?"

I shrug even though he can't see me. "And I guess I meet more of her little requirements than all the others. I checked." My mind keeps flashing back to *fucking Daniel* and my irritation mounts again. I didn't even know the guy, but somehow I figured I didn't like him. In the back of my mind, I wondered if he had been the source of one of her disastrous date stories she had told me. Yet at the same time, I knew he had to have been more significant to her if she had enough time to check off seven of her ten little boxes.

"See, that sounds like a good thing to me."

"Except the fact that she's been tracking all these things throughout our entire relationship," I grumble. "Like she's been grading me on my performance as a potential suitor."

"Maybe you're looking at it wrong," Chase says. I let out a frustrated sigh, knowing my brother—ever the voice of reason—is probably right. "Just calm down and try to think rationally about it. Will she be at the Board meeting today?"

"No, she has a dentist appointment. She probably won't be in until after lunch."

"Great, well, there you go. That will give you some time to mull it over and chill out about it."

"As if I don't have a million other things I need to be using brain power on," I say.

"Well, I could argue that this is probably more important. At least to you. In the long run."

"Yeah, I suppose you're right."

"I'm always right," my brother says smugly. "That's why you called me."

We hang up the call just as my driver pulls up in front of our building. I thank him and step out onto the sidewalk, buttoning up my suit jacket and looking up at the large skyscraper in front of me. The air is still frigid, and winter is now in full swing here in Chicago. I'm quickly learning that in the Windy City, the colder months come with a vengeance.

Not wasting any more time standing out on the cold sidewalk, I hurry into the warm building. I say hello to the reception desk down in the lobby as I step into the elevator. When I make it to my office, I drop my suit jacket down over the back of my chair and pull up my email and agenda, scanning over what the day's schedule looks like.

Already, I'm due into the Board meeting in a little under an hour and a half. I busy myself by collecting everything I'll need for that meeting. It will be different not having Whitney there to help keep me organized or give gentle reminders when we're getting off task.

When I'm less than half an hour out, I'm confident I'm as well prepared as I'm going to be, so I pack up my things and wander down to the conference room. As expected, I'm the first one there. As I'm setting up—getting my presentation pulled up, and the note packets handed out to each position at the table—my mind continuously wanders back to the events of this morning and my conversation with my brother.

I replay everything he said to me as he attempted to talk me down out of the panic I was feeling. Though I'm not sure I'll be able to take a step back and view it how he wants me to, I'm grateful that he was readily available to lend an ear.

However, as I think about it more, I think he might be right that I need to look at it from a different perspective. So that's exactly what I try to do.

Eventually, though, the three remaining Board members walk into the conference room together. I stand up and shake each of their hands. They take their seats, and then we dive right into work. Our main agenda for today is to look at some of the possibilities to fill the open positions on our Board.

We run through each of the candidates, and then I catch them up on where I am in my transition period as well. The meeting goes smoothly for the first time since I've been here. I think that largely has to do with Elena no longer having a looming presence.

As the meeting is wrapping up, I'm busy sliding my papers into my folder and powering down my laptop when the last matter of business is brought to the table unexpectedly.

"Mr. Hurst," Johnson, now the oldest member on the Board of directors, addresses me as he folds his hands on the table. His expression is grim, and I brace myself for whatever he's about to say. "We have been discussing your—predicament with your assistant, and unfortunately, we cannot condone a relationship of that matter in your position."

I nod my head slowly, trying my best to take this curveball in stride. "Okay, so what does that mean moving forward?"

The Board members share a quick, uneasy look, and then Johnson continues, "You'll have to end the relationship if you'd like Ms. Palmer to continue to work under you, or resign."

I lean back in my chair. Those are not great options.

I stare at them silently, running over the potential outcomes of either of those decisions. The first one, I'd have to publicly stop dating Whitney. We'd go back to keeping our relationship a secret, and it would be vital that no one was aware of otherwise. No one would know how much she means to me.

Or, I resign from my position as CEO.

As I mull it over, I really only see one option here.

But now, it's a matter of making it happen.

28

WHITNEY

MY NERVES ARE SHOT for the rest of the morning. As I drive from my dentist appointment to the office, my stomach churns, and my mind swirls with vertigo. Every molecule of my body feels like it's stuck in fight or flight mode. I want to run. I want to hide, but I know the best thing is to face this issue head-on.

Theo said we'd talk about it later, so while I sit at a traffic light, I rehearse what I'm going to say to him over and over, perfecting my words and working through the best way to say how I'm feeling.

Even as I sit in the elevator, waiting to get to our floor, I mouth my speech to myself over and over so I don't forget it.

But it's a useless endeavor.

Outside Theo's office, there is a flurry of activity. People in matching 'Mike's Moving Co.' shirts are stacking boxes onto a dolly and wheeling them down the hallway to the elevator.

"What's going on?" I ask as soon as I'm standing in front of our office space. I glance down at my desk to see everything completely untouched. But there's still a stack of boxes outside

Theo's office. A few of the movers each have a box in their arms as they walk down the hallway to the elevator to go down.

I step closer and frown. "This is Theo Hurst's office, you know that, right? He's the CEO of this company?" I ask them, wondering if they've gotten lost from where they were supposed to be moving things out of.

"Not anymore," a familiar, sinfully sexy, deep voice says from his doorway.

I turn to see Theo leaning against the frame with his hands in his pockets. He's not wearing his suit jacket and has the cuffs of his baby blue dress shirt rolled up, making the veins in his forearms stand out.

"Theo..." I trail off, hoping my tone states that I'm not interested in playing games.

"Whitney," he says back, almost like he's bored of this conversation already.

"What's happening? Why are you moving out of your office?" I ask him, trying to sound polite, though secretly wanting to scream at him and shove this girl away from my chair.

"It's not my office anymore," Theo says, his tone flat. "I've resigned."

"Theo," I protest, and I'm embarrassed when my voice breaks. It seems to work out in my favor, though, because his cold eyes soften ever so slightly.

"Come in, let's talk." He nods his head back toward his office. I follow after him, my posture stiff as I brace for the worst. As soon as I've stepped into his office, he closes the door behind me and then sticks his hands in his pockets, watching me apprehensively. Something about his expression has my already frayed nerves imploding into panic.

"Are we going to break up?" I ask him, my voice timid.

Theo stares at me blankly. His silence is making everything

worse, and helplessness sets in. Finally, he says, "Why would we do that?"

I knot my fingers together in front of me, feeling an overwhelming sense of shame. "Because you're mad."

He still gives me that blank stare, but he takes a step toward him while I simultaneously step back from him. He catches my hand before I can get too far and pulls me back into his chest, wrapping me tightly in his arms. His familiar scent overwhelms me, and I circle my arms around his waist, gripping him for dear life.

I squeeze my eyes shut and try to hold onto everything that we've become together. I don't know what my life will look like if he decides to end things right here and now. Though it's been such a short time, Theo has ingrained himself into the very essence of my being.

"No, Whitney," he finally says after we've been holding onto each other for a few minutes. "We're not breaking up."

He releases me but holds me at arm's length so he can look me dead in the eyes. "And I don't want you ever thinking that just because I'm *mad* or any other emotion, the first thing I'm going to jump to is a breakup. Do you hear me?"

I nod my head slowly, letting his words wash over me.

He cracks a side smile, then. "Sorry, baby, but you're stuck with me. For forever, if you'll have me. I have no plans on going anywhere."

My heart soars.

And just like that, Theo has checked off the ninth item on my list.

Number 9: Committed.

But still, my mind is spinning, trying to catch up with

everything I seemed to miss by taking the morning off. "You said you resigned?" I ask.

He gives me a tight smile. "I did."

"But—why?"

Theo runs his hands up and down my arms and takes a deep breath. "I was given an ultimatum: either I resign, or we could no longer have a relationship given our positions here at the company." I open my mouth to protest, but he doesn't give me the chance. "There was only one correct choice. And it was you."

As I study his face and recognize the sincerity behind his words, my heart starts to race, and my eyes begin to sting. "Theo—"

"That's why I've resigned and recommended Chase for the job. He'll get it, of course, but it's a courtesy anyway."

"Chase?" I ask, dumbfounded. My head is still spinning with all the changes that have happened in such a short time.

"Yes, you'll be working under Chase now. Granted, the Board chooses him to fill my place."

"What about you?"

Theo takes a breath and walks around to me. "I'll be applying to fill the CEO position at Pinnacle. I made a few calls and pulled a few strings. I'll likely be given the position there."

My mouth opens and then closes. "Theo, that's—"

"I know, it's not ideal," he says. "Things will be different for us. But I do think it's for the best."

"It's going to be so weird walking in here and not seeing you behind this desk," I say, glancing at the big oak desk at the end of the room.

"And I swear no one will ever be as good to me as you are." He smiles before leaning in and pressing his lips to my cheek.

"But now we'll have the opportunity to focus on what makes us *us* outside of these walls."

Uncertainty sets in again, and I give him a wary look. "We still need to talk about what happened this morning."

"We will," he says as he tucks a strand of hair behind my ear. "Tonight. Preferably with a bottle of wine."

"You're not mad?" I ask hesitantly.

He studies me for a second but then shakes his head. "No. I'm not sure I could be mad at you. And even aside from that, I don't have the whole story. We'll talk about it. Tonight, okay?"

I nod and step forward, pressing myself into his chest again. Theo wraps his arms tightly around me, holding me close enough that I can hear his heart beating against my ear. He tucks his cheek against the crown of my head. We stay that way for a few minutes, holding tightly onto each other when he finally breaks away again.

I raise an eyebrow when a mischievous smirk appears on his face. "Just promise me you won't tell Chase we had sex in his office whenever you move to the new building," he says with a wink, and I can't help the laugh that bubbles out of me.

A KNOCK on my door has me flying off the couch and crossing my apartment in record time. When I swing open the door, Theo is leaning against the frame in a way that has my heart skipping a beat. He's watching me with his warm, brown eyes, and his lips twitch up. He raises his hand, showing me the bottle of white wine—likely an expensive one—that he brought, just like he said he would.

I open the door further, inviting him inside. I grab two wine glasses and then join him on the couch. Theo pours us each a healthy glass and then hands me mine. Right away, I take a big gulp, feeling the alcohol warm me all the way down. Then I settle into the cushions of my couch and turn to him expectantly.

As if this was the silent encouragement he needed, he jumps right in. "So, tell me about this list."

Even though I know I can trust Theo in every possible meaning of the word, I'm still entirely too self-conscious about this. My eyes fall to my glass as I steel myself to tell him the truth.

"I don't know how it started. I think it was when I was a freshman or sophomore in high school." My eyes find him again, and I give him a wry smile. "In other words, a teenage girl with fantastic ideas about what love should be."

"And so that's what that is?" he asks as he turns toward me. He hooks his arm over the back of the couch and folds one of his legs elegantly underneath him. The picture of ease. "A checklist for true love?"

I give him a shrug. "Maybe? I don't know. I think it started off because the boys I dated in high school were utter jerks. And so, I made this list of all the things I wanted my 'Perfect Man' to have. And then, for whatever reason, I just continued it."

Theo watches me thoughtfully. "You had other guys' names in there, but they didn't have as many checkmarks as me."

My cheeks heat with embarrassment. "No, they didn't."

"So what does that mean? Am I 'your perfect guy?'" he asks, twitching his fingers as he makes air quotations.

"It would seem that way," I say softly.

Theo's still holding my gaze as he takes a deep breath in, which makes his shoulders rise. He lets it go with a *whoosh* and then looks down at his hands. "I don't like to be compared to other people. It makes me feel like I'm under a microscope or that every little thing I do is being evaluated."

"No, Theo, that's not—"

"I mean, how would you feel if you found out I had been outwardly comparing you to Lauren?" he asks. I frown at the mention of his ex-girlfriend.

"I'd feel pretty terrible."

"Right," he says, his lips curving into a small empathetic smile. "I want whatever we've found between us to be genuine."

"It is," I argue.

He laughs under his breath and shakes his head. "But when I see my name stacked up against all those other boyfriends, I feel insignificant. And I'd like to think that what we have is significant. *Very* significant. At least, it is to me."

"It is to me, too," I say, my voice soft.

He takes another breath. "I may have overreacted about this whole thing this morning, and I apologize for letting my feelings get the better of me."

Now I shake my head. "You didn't. You had every right to be upset. I should have told you about it instead of hiding it from you."

His lips twitch into a smile. "Maybe. But what's done is done. So now we have to decide how to move forward."

"Cause we're not breaking up," I say, reassured by what he told me in his office earlier today. It's weird to think that those private moments we had together today would be our last together in that building. After today, Theo will no longer be the CEO of Nexus Realty Group. Or my boss.

He'll just be Theo.

My Theo.

"No," his voice grows firm. "We're definitely not breaking up."

A warm, fuzzy feeling explodes in my chest and radiates down to my toes. I can't help the smile that's forming on my face. It's something about the way he says it so surely that has any sense of doubt dissipating into nothingness.

I lean forward and set the glass of wine down on the coffee table. Then, once my hands are free, I crawl across the length of the sofa until I'm curled up to his side. Theo shuffles his glass to his other hand and then wraps his arm around me. His hand settles on my hip, his thumb dipping under the hem of my worn-out t-shirt until he's rubbing soothing circles on my skin.

I nestle myself against his chest and close my eyes, basking in the lovely feeling of being this close to him. His clean scent overwhelms me in the best way possible, and I find myself wanting to be consumed by everything *Theo*.

We sit like that for a few minutes together, basking in this newfound security of our relationship. Finally, Theo breaks the silence by asking, "So how many things did I actually check off of your damn list?" Then he pauses, and his chest rumbles. "Actually, I'm not sure I want to know."

I fight off the smile. "Are you sure? It's a new world record."

He exhales. "Fine, tell me."

"Nine," I tell him.

"You're telling me I'm not a perfect ten?"

I lean back so I can see him, "Not according to the list. But in real life, you absolutely are."

He smiles and bends toward me, pressing his lips to mine. When he pulls away, he's still smiling. "I guess I can live with that. My competitive nature will just have to get over it."

I kiss him again, content with how this evening—this *day*— has turned out. "I'm sorry if I hurt you. That was never my intention."

He runs his free hand over my hair. "It's okay. I'm glad we talked about it. Just promise me this will be the end of that. I don't want to feel like every little thing I do is being measured or weighed up against something else."

"I promise," I say, wondering if I've ever meant something as much as I do now. "I'll never even think about that list again. All I want is you. Even if you're not a perfect ten."

Now Theo laughs and shakes his head. "You sure know how to make a guy feel good about himself."

I quirk a smile. "I do my best."

He gives me another fond look before setting his glass down and drawing me into him. He kisses me until I no longer can even think about numbers, let alone any kind of list.

And later that night, when we're lying in bed and Theo gathers me into his arms, I can't help but smile.

Because this handsome, trustworthy, honest, successful, attentive, committed man is mine.

All mine.

29

THEO

"I PROPOSE A TOAST," Leila announces the minute the server walks away after leaving our drinks on the table. She reaches for her glass of white wine and raises it toward Whitney and me sitting across from her. Chase looks at Leila in amusement but follows her lead, picking up his glass and raising it, too.

"What are we toasting to?" Whitney asks, though she plays along as well.

"The end of the school year," Leila raises her glass to her lips and then takes a large gulp.

The table erupts in laughter from Leila's sense of humor. Among other things, the last day of school for Leila is one of the many reasons we decided to come out tonight to celebrate.

Additionally, Whitney just got a promotion to more of an executive role. She'll now be overseeing a number of tasks and functions throughout the company. Though I don't know the exact details of the ins and outs of the inner workings of Nexus anymore after being fully engulfed with my position at their lead competitor, I know she's excited about it.

And I know she'll excel.

Just like she does at everything else.

I follow suit, and we raise our glasses, clinking them together and toasting for this new chapter that is steadily approaching.

There is another thing that Whitney doesn't realize we're toasting to. But I found a home outside of the city, which I think will be a perfect place for us to start this next chapter. She and I will be traveling out there tomorrow to take a look at it and determine if it's the right fit for us. Hopefully, she agrees that it's everything we need, and we can put an offer in right then and there.

I smile to myself as I sip my wine, excited for the moment I get to share this surprise and—hopefully—watch as her face lights up with an equal measure of excitement.

We've been together nearly eight months now, but that feels like nothing. When I close my eyes and picture what my life looks like, all I can see is her and the life we're going to build together. I'm eager to see everything come together and watch all the pieces fall into place—but I'm also content to enjoy every individual day that I get to spend with her.

It's hard for me to imagine that there was a time in my life that I didn't know her. I didn't know what it was like to count down every second of the day until I got to see her again. I suppose it's a good thing because if I had, I'm not sure anything could have stopped me from scouring the Earth until I found her. Until we were together and everything was how it should be.

Something so simple as running into each other at the workplace turned out to be exactly what we both needed.

Our group makes small talk once the waiter comes by and takes our orders. Mostly talk of work, or in Leila's case, what her plans are while she's off school for the summer.

"I don't know, man. I think Melinda has the hots for you," Chase says before reaching for a piece of the complimentary bread provided by the restaurant. I make a face at the mention of one of the older members of the Board of Directors at Nexus.

"She definitely doesn't," I argue back.

He laughs. "Oh, she does. Every time I run across her, she makes a point of asking how you are."

"She does, I've seen it happen," Whitney adds. I shoot a glance at my girlfriend and grin wickedly.

"And how does that make you feel?"

She waves me off. "If you want to leave me for her, I'd probably let you. She's got to be a millionaire or something."

I quirk a brow at her. "I'm already a millionaire."

"Well, then you two would be perfect for each other," she says, sticking her tongue out at me.

"You two are sickening," Leila says, shaking her head. "I don't know why we even hang out with you."

"Because you love us," Whitney admonishes her friend.

Leila rolls her eyes but fights off a smile. "I suppose you're right. I'm so bummed you can't come with me to the Bahamas, Whitney."

Whitney laughs and then gives Chase a pointed stare. "You better talk to this one about that. He's got a strict, no Caribbean vacations policy."

"Unless I'm invited," Chase teases with a wink.

Leila looks like she's pondering it, inviting Chase and Whitney on her vacation, but then she shakes her head and changes the topic before anyone else can say anything else on the matter. Our food arrives not long after, and we all dig into our meals, laughing and joking away the remainder of the night.

As we walk out of the restaurant and start making our way back toward home, the girls take off ahead of us, looping their arms through each other and then leaning close to speak softly. Chase and I stay a few feet behind them, walking side by side. I have my hands tucked into my pants pockets as we stroll across the sidewalk. Surprisingly, the city isn't too busy tonight, giving us plenty of room to meander and enjoy the spring evening.

"You're happy, right?" my brother asks me out of the blue, in a rare show of vulnerability for him.

I don't look away from Whitney, watching the way her long hair swings against her back with every step. I nod my head. "Yeah, I am."

"Do you miss being at Nexus?"

I ponder his question, wondering if I do. I sometimes look up from my desk when someone walks into my office, still expecting to see Whitney standing there expectantly. I'm always a little disappointed when it's not her, but then I remember that I get to spend every night and every morning with her, and that eases any type of longing for our past surreptitious relationship.

"Not especially," I finally respond. And it's true. Aside from getting to see Whitney every day, the work at Nexus compared to my new company, Pinnacle, is essentially the same. The only difference is that Pinnacle has been around much longer than Nexus and has a far wider reach as far as property demographics. Other than that, the workload is identical.

"Must be nice to have someone you can be so confident in," Chase says, his voice whimsical.

Now, I do look over at him and catch his gaze lingering on Leila as she walks right next to my girlfriend. Chase and Leila have been on and off for the last eight months that I've been seeing Whitney. When they're on, they're *on*. But when they're off, I try my hardest not to get in the crossfire because it can get messy real quick.

Though, by the way, my brother is looking at her now, I wonder if he's yearning for something a little more sturdy. Something more stable.

"You should talk to her," I suggest, reading between the lines. Though Chase and Leila were on good terms for this evening's festivities, I know they're not actively seeing each other right now. No matter how much either of them wants it.

Chase exhales. "I don't know what good that'd do. She's a free spirit. All I can do is hope that she'll come around to the idea of something eventually."

I tighten my lips into a thin line. I definitely am not familiar with Leila the way Chase, or even Whitney, is. I can only attempt to be a support when he needs it, but even then, I feel like I'm always shooting in the dark.

Finally, we arrive in front of my building, where Chase and Leila both parked their cars so we could walk to the restaurant. Whitney gives Leila a big goodbye hug while I pat my brother on the shoulder in farewell.

Chase and Leila walk away into the parking garage together. As soon as they're out of sight, Whitney and I make our way into the elevator and press the button for our level. Once the doors close, Whitney tucks herself into my side. I kiss the top of her hair, breathing in the sweet scent of her shampoo. I don't think I'll ever grow tired of this.

When we make it to our level, Whitney shoots me a smile before unlocking the door with her key. She glances back at me as she steps inside, shrugging her coat off from her shoulders. I follow after her, transfixed, wondering if I'll chase after her like this forever.

When she makes it into the bedroom, she reaches behind her back, fiddling with the clasp of the zipper. I step up and help her, pulling the zipper down until her back is exposed. I lean down and press a kiss to her shoulder, breathing in the sensual scent of her skin.

"I think I'm going to take a shower," she says, her voice breathy. "Do you want to join me?"

"Is that even a question?"

Whitney giggles as I follow hot on her heels into our large master bathroom. While she's shucking off the rest of her clothes, I reach into the walk-in shower stall and turn it on. Since living together, I've learned that Whitney likes the shower as hot as humanly possible.

Unfortunately for her, I can hardly stand the water as hot as she prefers it, so we have to find some middle ground whenever we share.

Once steam is billowing out from the top of the shower and I rid myself of my clothes, we both step in. Whitney grabs my hand and pulls me closer so we're both standing close enough to the stream from the shower head. She closes the distance between us and presses her steadily soaking body close to mine.

I rest my chin on top of her head and tighten my arms around her, loving the way our bodies feel pressed together like this.

"I had a good time tonight," she says against my chest.

"I did, too. Leila and Chase always make things interesting."

Whitney makes an exasperated sound in the back of her throat. "She's so frustrating. I know she's crazy about Chase, she just won't admit it."

"I think he's crazy about her, too," I muse. "Maybe even as crazy as I am about you."

Pulling away from our embrace, I can't help my eyes from wandering down the length of her body. Her skin is soaked, and her chest is slowly starting to flush from the heat. My hands move on their own accord from their position on her hips up to cup her full breasts. Whitney's eyes flutter shut as I tweak her nipples until they're hardened peaks.

"You're breathtaking," I say to her, my voice loud enough that the sound of the shower doesn't drown it out. "I love you, Whitney. I want to spend forever with you like this." Her eyes open again, and she gazes at me with such adoration that it makes my chest hurt. I bend over and kiss her nose.

"That sounds perfect to me," she says back, bracing her hands on my shoulders as she stands on her toes to kiss me. I let myself get lost in the kiss, holding her to me and letting her take over my every waking thought.

Or *almost* every thought. Though I can easily see this shower progressing into more sensual territory, I suddenly can't hold back the surprise I've been sitting on all night long. The need to share with her is overwhelming.

I pull away from her. She gives me an adorable pout that makes me laugh as I say, "I have a surprise for you."

Whitney's eyes glitter with anticipation. "What is it?"

I smooth my hand down her wet hair until I'm cupping the edge of her jaw. "You remember how you mentioned you were thinking about getting out of the city?" I ask her, referring to a conversation she and I had about a month ago. Whitney nods, now remembering what I'm talking about. "Well, I found us a place—potentially—if you were really serious about that. It would make your commute a bit longer, but you said you might be able to work from home for a few days. And it's closer to my office, too."

That last bit didn't really matter to me. I'd commute however far I needed to. But it was an added bonus.

Her eyebrows raise on her forehead. "You found us a house?"

I nod. "Yes. And I think it's perfect, but I need your

opinion before I do anything further. So what do you say about taking a little road trip down there tomorrow to see it?"

"Are you serious?" she asks after a beat. I can't make out the tone of her voice if she's excited or put off that I did this without asking her. It wasn't as if I *bought* the house, but maybe even taking the steps without her input was enough of a transgression for her.

"More than I think I ever have been. What do you say?"

"I can't wait," she says, her voice raising a bit with her increasing excitement. "I can't believe this is really happening!"

"Well, let's see what you think about the house first before we get too excited. Who knows if you'll even like it."

"I bet I will," she says confidently. "You always seem to know exactly what I like without me needing to tell you."

I smile at her. She doesn't need to know the lengths I go to ensure that I am the expert on all things *Whitney*. Above everything else, she is my priority, first and always. I could spend the rest of my days striving to make her the happiest version of her that I can, and never grow weary of it.

Strong desire pulls at me and again, urgency takes over, encouraging me to close the distance and make her happy in a completely other way now.

I don't say anything else as I capture her lips again. Whitney responds immediately, wrapping her arms around me and pressing her naked body languidly against mine. I maneuver us so her back is pressed up against the tile wall. She makes a small sound—probably at the shocking coolness of the tile—but I swallow it down until it morphs into a moan.

My hands continue their roaming and exploring. I don't stop until she's shattering around me for the first time, her pussy clenching at my fingers buried deep inside of her.

"Fuck, you're so pretty when you come around my fingers,"

I whisper huskily into her ear. Whitney gasps and rolls her hips against my hand, still looking for that last bit of friction to draw out the remainder of her orgasm.

When her body has finally ceased trembling, I slowly remove my hand and look down at her. Need is still coursing through me, and I see it reflected right back at me in her eyes.

"How about we get dried off and continue this elsewhere," I suggest.

Her cheeks are flushed, and this time, I don't think it's from the heat of the shower. Her eyes are still dilated, and she nods her head in a daze. "I think that sounds like a great idea."

I don't waste any time. The shower is off within a minute, and shortly thereafter, I have Whitney wrapped up in one of the fluffy, purple towels she recently bought for our bathroom. She gives me a seductive smile as she dries off before scampering out of the bathroom, hopefully to our bed.

As I'm following her into our room, my eyes catch on the orchid plant sitting proudly on a table by the large window. I got this one for her a few weeks ago, regretfully, after the last one lost its last petal. Both Whitney and I have gotten attached to having the vibrant purple flower around—I even have one sitting on my desk at my office, just like I know she still has one on her desk, too.

Somehow, it has become the symbol of our relationship. It started off as a friendly welcome gift to my new assistant, and without us even realizing it at the time, it was the precursor to so much more.

As my eyes move from the flower to Whitney, sprawled so gloriously on our mattress, I can't help but be thankful for every little moment that led up to this one.

I never saw Whitney Palmer coming, but now, I can't imagine my life without her.

30

WHITNEY

"THIS IS INSANE," I say with a laugh as I look out over the balcony of our hotel. Right in front of me is the Eiffel Tower, standing tall and proud, lit up so beautifully that I can't seem to take my eyes off of it. "I still can't believe we're here."

Theo comes up to stand behind me, his arm wrapping around his waist. Another laugh bubbles out of me at the crazy realization that this is my life. Theo and I have been together slightly over a year, but still, sometimes his privilege surprises me. I know the depth of the Hurst wealth, but it always feels a little surreal when I'm on the receiving end of the benefits of that wealth.

Just last week, Theo announced that he had booked us a flight to France, where we'd be spending time in Paris, hitting all the must-sees like the Louvre and the Cathedral of Notre Dame. All things I always wanted to do but never imagined I'd get the opportunity.

I was more than shocked, given that with this trip, we'd be missing his mother's annual gala. I had been so relieved at the event last year when his mother finally welcomed me with open arms. I'm not sure what changed for her to finally realize that Theo was never going to go back to his ex-girlfriend, and that I was around to stay, but regardless, I was grateful that she had a much warmer welcome for me than in the past few years.

When I asked Theo why he picked Paris so suddenly, his blunt response was, "Well I love you, and Paris is the city of Love so why not?"

I hadn't pushed him, finding that answer to be perfectly satisfactory.

It still hadn't felt real, until we checked into our hotel room today and I saw the Eiffel Tower right outside my window for the first time. We spent the day exploring, trying out some cafes and visiting some of the shops. We ended the night at a gourmet restaurant, toasting champagne flutes over a delightful dessert.

I was so stuffed as we made it back to our hotel, but I couldn't resist another look out at the Tower before we call it a night. As I stare out at the landmark, I decide that I don't think I could ever get tired of that view.

I sigh whimsically and lean back against Theo's chest. The hand wrapped around me holds me tighter, his thumb rubbing small circles over my hip bone.

We stand together in a comfortable silence, only the sound of the city beneath us breaking through the quiet. In this moment, I feel more content than I think I ever have before. There's no thought of work or responsibilities lingering in the back of my mind, only Theo's presence, and the realization that I'm in a beautiful city.

"I met almost every single one of your requirements," Theo says into the night. I blink a few times, still looking out over the balcony.

Somehow, though, the urge to look at Theo is greater than the twinkling lights. Slowly, I drag my eyes away from the

Tower and over to him. He's watching me with such a gentle expression that it makes my chest ache. I'd always dreamed of having a man look at me like that, never would I have imagined that it would have been my former boss.

"You know I'm not doing that anymore," I whisper.

A smile threatens on Theo's lips and he leans forward to press a kiss to my cheek. Instantly, my skin heats under his touch and my breath hitches. "I know. I just think it's somewhat disappointing that I didn't meet all ten."

"Which one didn't you meet?" I ask him, still breathless from his proximity. It continued to blow my mind that even a few years later, Theo could bring this type of reaction out of me. Every time he touched me was like the very first time. He still made my stomach clench and my skin prickle with even the simplest brush of his fingers.

"Hmm," he murmured, in a low rumble which made goosebumps erupt on my forearms. "I think it was something about being spontaneous."

Number 3: Spontaneous

I look up to meet his eyes, now confused. "You don't think a random trip to Paris is spontaneous enough?"

"I think I could do better."

Before I know what is happening, Theo is stepping away from me. He reaches into his back pocket and gets down on one knee, in such a smooth motion that I have to blink a few times to make sure I am seeing things correctly.

"Theo," I whisper as my fingers flutter up to my lips.

When he's solidly down on his knee, he holds out a black, velvet box. My eyes widen and I suck in a breath. He opens the lid of the box for me and the world spins a little as I stare down at the ring he's chosen for me.

Sitting on a beautiful, white gold ring is an Asscher cut amethyst stone, surrounded by two small, round, and marquis shaped diamonds on either side of the band.

My jaw goes slack as I continue to stare at it, getting lost in the dimension and the complexity of the purple stone.

"Whitney, I know I don't need to keep telling you how much I love you, but that doesn't mean I'm ever going to stop," Theo says. I notice his voice is shaky and I tear my eyes away from the glittering ring to gaze at him. His eyes are teary as he stares up at me, nothing but pure love emanating from his eyes. "Somehow, I find more and more reasons to love you as each day goes by, and I want to spend my whole life doing exactly that—loving you endlessly."

I take a shaky breath and feel my eyes start to burn with the intensity of this moment. "Is this really happening?"

Theo chuckles and nods his head. "Well, I thought you'd might like some new jewelry to sport around while we're exploring Paris," he says, his voice now teasing. "What do you say, Whitney? Will you be my wife?"

I don't hesitate even a bit in my answer.

"Yes of course," I gush. Theo stands up and wraps me up in a hug, picking me up and spinning me in a circle right there on the balcony. I laugh out loud, pure joy circulating through my body.

When he puts me down, he holds out the box again, plucking the ring from its little nest and holding it out for me. I extend my left hand, watching in awe as he slides the ring onto my finger, where it belongs.

I hold it out, testing the way the statement looks on my finger and my heart swells with love for this man. "I love it."

"I love you," he says, firmly, making sure there is absolutely no questioning that fact.

I squeal as Theo scoops me up in his arms, carrying me

bridal style from the balcony into our room. He drops me on the mattress and crawls over me, looking positively starved for me. I squirm under his heated gaze, loving the way that his eyes caress every square inch of my body.

Slowly, Theo helps me out of my clothes, and I do the same, unbuckling his belt and pushing the waistband of his pants over his hips. When I'm bare to him, Theo trails his lips over every divot and swell of my body, paying special attention to the places he knows drive me absolutely mad.

I shiver when he nibbles at the small spot under my ear and arch up into him with an aggravated moan. "Don't tease," I whine.

He laughs huskily, which sends another shiver across my body. "If you don't like my teasing, then why are you moaning?"

He doesn't give me a chance to respond before he's sliding down my body again, pressing kisses everywhere.

"Well, I guess you've done it," I say, squeezing my eyes shut and enjoying the pleasure Theo is delivering to me. "You've officially hit that perfect ten."

I can practically picture the satisfied smirk on his face, but that quickly goes away when he presses a firm kiss to the center of my thighs. My back arches off the mattress and I moan again. When he pulls away, letting me catch my breath, I notice his eyes are still gleaming with amusement. "Was that ever even a question?"

"No," I say, surely, as my heart rate starts to settle slightly. "Even without that stupid list, you're perfect. Far more perfect than I ever could have dreamed up."

"I'd say the same about you, but I feel like it's not enough," he murmurs, thumb stroking over my hip bone reverently. "Perfect doesn't begin to describe you."

My cheeks warm. "I can't wait to be your wife."

"I love the way that sounds on your lips." He leans down and kisses my belly, making me squirm all over again. "I can't wait to worship you every day of our lives."

"I could probably get used to that."

His lips twitch and his eyes darken just a smidge. "Yeah, I bet you could. So, *Future* Mrs. Hurst. How do you feel about consummating this newfound engagement on every surface of this room?"

A full body tingle travels down my spine and into my toes and I nod my head. "I think that's a perfect idea."

EPILOGUE

Whitney — *Three Years Later*

MY FINGERS DRUM against the countertop as I impatiently stare at the wall. I tried mindlessly scrolling through social media to keep my mind busy, but it was useless. I couldn't focus on what I saw, so I gave up.

My eyes dart to my phone screen, where I watch the clock for the signal that enough time has passed.

It's almost noon, which means Theo will be home for lunch any minute. Thankfully, Chase let me leave work after throwing up three times this morning. That was enough to finally spur me into action.

On the way home, I stopped at the drugstore and bought three packs of pregnancy tests. When I got home, I hurried into the bathroom and set to work.

This is only the first one, and the box said I had to wait a maximum of five minutes for results, but this has been the longest five minutes of my life.

Getting pregnant hasn't been easy for me. Theo and I have

been married for two years, and we've been trying for a baby just as long. After so many late periods with negative pregnancy tests, I started getting discouraged. This was going to be our last attempt to go about it naturally before we started looking into different options.

Having a family has been my dream for so long. I want it so badly that I don't know how I will react if this test is negative, too. Theo has been more than supportive, but I know it's weighing on him, too, not being able to help us achieve this dream.

I squeeze my eyes shut and pray that this time, I'll finally be pregnant.

Finally, the timer on my phone goes off, and I jump up, grabbing the stick and looking down at it hopefully.

"Oh my god," I whisper as I take in the results, staring right back at me from the pregnancy test. Excitement blooms through my chest right at the same time as another wave of nausea.

I quickly curl over the toilet and throw up for the fourth time today. When it's finally passed, I sit back and lean against the cool ceramic of the bathtub. I reach for some toilet paper and wipe my mouth before dropping it in the toilet and flushing it away.

My hands feel clammy as I press them to my cheeks, taking deep breaths and trying to calm my racing heart.

Theo's timing can't have been better. I hear the familiar *click* of the front door closing and the sound of Theo setting down his keys on the stand by the door.

"What?" He calls through the house. I can hear the concern lacing his tone. I was supposed to be in the city today to work with Chase at the main building, so I wouldn't have been able to come home for lunch like I would've if we were at the satellite office.

"I'm in the bathroom," I call back.

His footsteps echo through the hallway into our bedroom, and then he opens the bathroom door. His movements are careful, and he slowly peeks his head in first, his eyes widening when he sees me hugging my knees to my chest.

Theo steps into the bathroom and crouches in front of me. His hand reaches out and cups my shoulder, then slides up to the side of my neck and my jaw. I look into his warm brown eyes and try not to immediately burst into tears.

His eyebrows are threaded together with that same concern I heard in his voice before I saw him. "Whitney, what's wrong? Are you okay?"

I lose my battle against my emotions, and tears start to steadily stream down my cheeks. I wipe my face and shake my head. "I'm sorry."

"Whitney," Theo urges. He moves until he's sitting next to me, pulling me into his lap and wrapping his arms around me tightly. "You're worrying me. Please tell me what's wrong."

The soothing back and forth of Theo's hand on my back just spurs me to cry harder. This is ridiculous. I know we should be celebrating right now, but the overwhelming emotions of how much we've been wanting this is too much for me to deal with.

Thankfully, Theo stops prodding, choosing to just hold me until my tears subside, and my breathing returns to normal. When I finally have a grasp on myself again, I pull myself out of his arms and stand up. I can feel his eyes on me as I walk over to the sink where the test is lying. I can't believe he didn't see it when he first walked in.

With the stick in hand, I sit down next to Theo again and hold it out for him, putting the results side down so he can't see it.

Theo's eyes widen when he sees the pregnancy test in my

outstretched hand. His gaze flashes to me warily before he takes it from me and flips it over.

There, he sees the second pink line, clear as day, right in front of him. He sucks in a sharp gasp and then drops the test on the floor before scooping me into his arms once again.

The gesture spurs more tears to fall, though this time, I know they're out of joy rather than the overpowering emotion.

I wrap my arms around Theo's back and hold onto him tightly. His shoulders shake, and it takes me a moment, but I realize that he's crying now, too. We grasp onto each other, silently basking in the joyous moment.

When he pulls away from me, his warm brown eyes are tinged pink, and he wipes his nose while smiling widely.

"You're pregnant?" he whispers.

I nod, the gesture feeling too good to be true. "I am."

Theo hugs me again, and I squeeze my eyes shut, immensely grateful that we made it to this point together. It's all I've ever wanted, and I'm so glad he's the one I get to experience life with.

In the coming days, months, and years, I somehow fall more and more in love with him.

Every day in the years following, Theo gives me more and more reasons to recognize that he's the perfect match for me. And with every single one that he shows me, I find myself looking back and wondering why I ever thought ten little things would be enough.

Theo — *Six Years Later*

"Shh, be very quiet." I recognize my wife's voice outside my door, but I don't look up from my work, familiar with this routine. My lips twitch as I try my hardest to fight off a smile.

"If you be very quiet, he won't hear you, and you can sneak up and surprise him!"

The sweet giggles of my children ring through my office, and my chest tightens with the realization of how lucky I am.

Eliza and Elliot, my five-year-old twins, and Riley, my three-year-old, have no concept of the word *quiet*. Their little feet thump against my carpeted floor as they make a bee-line toward where I'm sitting at my desk, pretending that I don't hear them rushing toward me like tiny, unconfined animals. The three of them roar, and I laugh as they jump around me excitedly. Laughing, I scoot my chair back a little. The older two of the three hurry to my sides. Each grabs an arm while Riley ambles toward me and falls onto my lap.

My wife is just a little behind them. I look up at her, my heart doing the familiar stutter, which it still seems to do every time I see her. She gives me a blinding smile and scoops up Riley before setting her on top of my lap. Then, she leans against the edge of my desk and crosses her arms, watching the four of us with amusement.

I give each of my children an equal amount of attention, listening to Eliza and Elliot tell me about their day at kindergarten. While her older siblings babble on, Riley busies herself with my tie, wrapping it around her hand and tugging on it occasionally.

"They were dying to surprise you at work," Whitney adds after the older two recount their school adventures. "I hope we didn't interrupt anything important."

"Nothing is more important than seeing you four," I say, leaning down to kiss Riley's soft brown curls.

I'm not sure I've ever said truer words. Every day, though my job is demanding as CEO of Pinnacle Realty, my primary focus is being a good husband and an even better father. Whitney and I have built this beautiful life together, and it's everything to me. More so than anything else I've ever accomplished in my life. Our little family has become my entire world, and I can't remember a time when I didn't get to experience the joy and love that they bring to my life each and every day.

I look up at my wife and stare at her in wonder, struck by the realization of how perfect it was that we crossed paths at the moment we did. When I accepted the position at Nexus all those years ago, I never thought I'd be gaining so much more than a job title. But now, there isn't a version of my life that I'd ever want without her. She and our children remind me just how happy they are to have me in their lives. And even though they don't do it on purpose, they find ways to reassure me that I'm more than enough for all of them.

The End.

CHASING INFINITY BY ARIA HARDING

Read Ahead for a Sneak Peak into another Standalone Romance by Aria Harding

---

Chapter 1 — Noah — Now

Thunder rattles outside, making the frame of my car shake. The rain bombards the windows and I groan, pulling the edges of my flimsy pillow across my ears to drown it out. Shifting around in the backseat of the pathetic run-down car, I try to get comfortable. It takes great effort not to let my situation weigh me down too far.

My life is a shit show. Nothing about where I am right now would have been on my plan for my life. I never imagined the catalyst to bring me back to this godforsaken town would be my mother's funeral. But here we are. Life has a funny way of turning the tables around on you.

Almost ten years have passed since the last time I set foot in this town. While the threat of knowing I'd have to return at some point lingered in my mind like a foul odor, I generally did a fair job of keeping myself distracted. I was living in a happy little fantasy outside this picturesque place. Unfortunately, now that I'm back, the bubble has burst.

Willow Heights is where I was born, where I grew up, and where I crashed and burned. The residents of this town probably still walk around whispering my name like a legend. This place elicits too many memories for me to be comfortable hanging around for too long. But it's home. This is why I begrudgingly parked in front of Monty's Market & Pharmacy when I rolled up to the city limits last night. As I slowed to a stop, I attempted to deter myself from recalling when old Monty caught me buying a pack of condoms at fourteen. I was mortified.

Throughout the rest of the night, the memories of growing up in this town flood my brain as I attempt to get some sleep. I keep tossing and turning, trying to get comfortable, but it's pointless. There is nothing left for me in this town, and reliving all those years here is a stark reminder.

I sit up in the car with a groan and lean my head against the window. Rain is pelting down on the frame of my vehicle. The clatter of the raindrops on the metal soothes me. Usually, it would lull me to sleep, but I've concluded that it likely won't be happening at this point. I peer out the window at the giant clock tower looming like a beacon on the Main Street square. I squint my eyes, trying to read the hands. Six-thirty. The heavy clouds hanging over the town give the morning an ominous air.

I weigh my options: I could stay in my car and hope that sleep comes to me for another few hours, or I could leave my car and brave the rain. I'm camped out a few storefronts down from a cozy-looking café. The lights are on, and I see people walking in and out holding coffees and bagels. They're all much too cheery for it being six-thirty on a Thursday. I can't blame them; their world hasn't tilted on its axis like mine.

I sigh and reach for my wallet, throwing the worn leather open and peering inside. I have fifty bucks sitting in there. A coffee and a muffin would be what, seven? I estimate no more than ten dollars. It's not all I have to my name, but contributing to Willow Heights's economy makes me want to barf. But my stomach growls in a pathetic pleading noise, and I concede. I need to get something to eat.

With a wince at my aching back, I open the door of my car and clamber out into the rain. I pull the hood of my sweatshirt up to cover my head. My feet slosh in the puddles on the street, and I grimace. The puddle water will seep through the holes in my boots and ruin my entire day.

I schlep down the sidewalk to the diner, keeping my head low and hoping no one will recognize me. The last time I was here, I was a teenager, now I'm a man. I hope the maturity is considerable enough that identification won't be too quick.

In such a small town as Willow Heights, it's impossible not to know everything and everyone. Not to mention, my father's been the mayor since I was fifteen. Makes me kind of a small-town name, despite my utter reluctance. It wasn't much later that I realized that having a name associated with the mayor of Willow Heights wasn't all it cracked up to be.

I pull open the door to the diner and step in. Immediately, the warmth from the little restaurant seeps inside of me. My muscles relax as the atmosphere warms me to the bones. The scent of fresh omelets and greasy bacon hits my nose. My stomach rumbles again, begging me for something to eat. I peruse the layout, looking for the best place to sit, but the diner is packed. I finally settle on the last seat at the bar. It's off to the side, so hopefully, I'll stay out of everyone's way.

As I head towards my targeted seat, a flash of red and

brown flies into my line of drive. Her toe catches on the tip of my boot, and she stumbles. My arms reach out instinctively to steady her.

"Oh my gosh, I'm so sorry!" she exclaims, looking down and trying to straighten the food she has on her tray. It doesn't take much to put together that she works here and was mid-stride to delivering someone's breakfast when she tripped.

I let her go, frowning at the now-occupied seat I was aiming for. Someone else snagged it right from under me during the fiasco. I exhale, frustrated as I say, "All good, sorry for getting in your way. I was trying to find a seat."

"I think there's one over in that corner if you want," the woman says, finally satisfied with the tray. "I'll be over to take your order in just a moment—" her sentence cuts off with a gasp. I drag my glare from the douche who took my seat. My own breath catches in my throat when I glance down at her.

"Noah," she gasps, now gazing directly at me, her plump lips falling open on my name. Her eyes flutter across my face as she appraises me standing in front of her. She studies me as if she's re-committing me to memory. Or upgrading her old memory of me to the newer version, filling in the pieces that have changed.

"Parks," I say back with an edge of surprise. Her name on my tongue recalls the memories of her I've held at bay for so long. They come rushing into my brain like a tsunami, triggered by the familiarity of her hazel eyes on me once more. Those hazel eyes have haunted my dreams all these years. Always hazel, with flecks of gold flaring from the pupil and a dark freckle on the left iris. So familiar after all this time, but yet unfamiliar.

"Long time no see." I recompose myself as best as possible. I slide my hands into my pocket and grip my fingers into tight fists, my eyes never leaving her.

Parks stares at me, shell-shocked. Her silence draws out the moment before she shakes herself out of it and shifts the tray around to settle on her hip. "You're back."

"So it would seem," I mutter, my eyes still roving her. Out of all the people, I figured I would run into here, she was not one of them. She is supposed to be far, far away from here. She should have left and never looked back. "As are you."

Parks has the decency to blush a little bit at my blunt statement. "Yeah, I am. Um," she looks back at the table in the corner, taking her bottom lip between her teeth and worrying at it. "If you want to grab that seat, I'll bring you a coffee or something in just a minute."

The corners of my lips pull up into a smirk, and I dip my chin at her. "Sure thing, Parks."

Parks inhales, her chest rising with a deep breath, and she nods. Her eyes peek at me for a second longer before she hurries off to deliver the food so it doesn't get cold.

My eyes follow after her for a second too long, then I saunter over to the lonely table in the corner. I pull out the chair and make myself comfortable, flipping through the menu sitting in front of me. I only manage to peruse the menu's first page before she comes over. She's holding a pot of coffee and an empty white ceramic mug.

"Cream and sugar are on the table. Have you had a chance to look at the menu?" she asks, giving me a tight smile as she pours a cup of coffee for me. Parks' expression develops into a more professional demeanor. She can pretend it's not just her and me, but I don't know how long that will work.

"Yeah, I'll have the French toast with a side of sausage," I tell her, folding up the plastic menu and sliding it away from me.

A smile plays on her lips as she sets the now full mug of coffee in front of me. The steam swirling from it hits my chin, and the aroma of the coffee is enough to make up for my missing hours of sleep. My brain is already re-energizing from the scent of it.

"I'll get that right in for you," she says briskly. She spins on her heel and heads to the back. With her exit, she leaves me to my own devices. As she walks away, I watch her go, a familiar constriction forming around my heart. My hand unconsciously rubs on my sternum to ease some of the ache.

Addison Parks was the greatest thing to happen and not happen to me. We could have had it all together, but it wasn't the right time. I ended up leaving Willow Heights, and she was supposed to pursue her dreams elsewhere. Yet here she is, standing in front of me.

My eyes roam around the quaint little diner, and as I look around, my memory jogs. I remember that this was the exact storefront that used to be Parks' parents' café once upon a time. My deductive skills fill in the blanks, and I determine she must have bought out the space and made it her own.

It's small, but there are enough tables to keep the staff busy. It has that classy hometown atmosphere. The employees look energetic and happy to be there. They greet every customer by name as they walk through the door.

One of the other workers delivers my breakfast a few minutes later. I thank them before digging in, not remembering when I last had a serving of French Toast this delicious. Addison comes over again as I finish up, bracing a black square bucket on her hip that's half full of dirty dishes. I raise an eyebrow at her as she stares at me.

"I was sorry to hear about your mom," Addison says carefully after an awkward moment of ogling at me as if she can't believe I'm truly right in front of her. I can tell she's uncomfortable at how distant we are, not sure how to approach the conversation. Well, that makes two of us, sweetheart. "I didn't even realize that she was...."

"Suicidal?" I fill in for her, chuckling humorlessly under my breath. "Me neither, but I can't say it's out of character, given who she was married to."

Addison's dark eyebrows pull in at the middle as she frowns, unsure how to respond. "But even so, I know your mom means a lot to you."

"She does."

"Charlie told me," she informs me. "He was the one who got called onto the scene first. He said he tried everything to resuscitate her but—"

"Yeah," I reply and shift in my seat, the wooden chair putting uncomfortable pressure on my low back.

Jesus H. Christ, get me out of this conversation.

I glance around the diner, searching for something to comment on to move off this topic. I clear my throat when I find nothing worth talking about. "Well, this has been... I'm not sure. But I need to go. Maybe we can catch up another time."

I don't mean to brush her off, but I know it is likely how my brusque tone translates for her. God, that's the last thing I'd ever want to do, but distance is my friend now. I have to keep my mind on my reason for being here. I can't let myself fall back into old habits. If I did, I'd never leave this diner again—or her.

"Oh," Addison says, the brightness in her eyes dimming slightly.

"I have a meeting with Sullivan to talk about—you know," I inform her, surveying her.

The brightness slowly returns when she realizes that I'm not trying to jump ship on her again. "Are you going to be staying long?"

"I'm not sure. I haven't decided yet." I sigh and rub the back of my neck, meeting her eyes and shrugging a shoulder.

"Okay," she responds, clearly unsure what else to say, her eyes tracking my every movement as I ball up my napkin and drop it on the empty plate. "Can I get you anything else before you go?"

"I'm good, Parks. Thank you, though." I stand up and brush off my jeans, reaching into my back pocket for my wallet. "How much do I owe you?"

Parks is still staring at me with her wide hazel eyes as she waves her hand in a blow-off manner. "It's fine. It's on me today."

"You don't have to do that," I argue.

"We're friends, Noah. And this is my diner. I can do what I want."

"Thank you," I shoot her a grin as I head toward the door. I raise my hand in her direction before I leave. "I'll see you around, yeah?"

Addison presses her lips together, narrowing her eyes and tilting her head at me. "Yeah, I'll see you around. Bye, Noah."

***

"Sully!" I shout as I throw open the front door to the Sheriff's department. "Get your ass out here."

I hear a scuffle in the other room. Charlie fucking Sullivan walks out holding—and I'm not even making this shit up—a glazed chocolate doughnut and a to-go cup of what I'm assuming was coffee. The coffee has the *Sunny Side Up Diner* logo pasted on the side, and I realize he got it from Addison's diner. I try to school my features as best as possible, remaining impassive. Still, despite my best efforts, I'm sure my upper lip curls into the signature sneer I reserve just for Charlie Sullivan.

Sullivan raises his eyebrows in surprise and struggles to gulp down his massive bite of doughnut. "Lockwood, you're here."

I hold up the folded business card in my hand. "You rang?"

Sully sets his coffee down on a neighboring desk and gently places his doughnut on top. "Yeah, but I didn't think you'd be here that quickly."

I roll my eyes and take a few steps towards him, noticing the shiny new badge under his nameplate: Sheriff. "Whoa, man, congrats on the promotion. Dear old Dad, finally hand over the reins?"

Charlie grimaces and shakes his head. "Ah, no. He passed away last year heart attack."

I press my lips together and freeze for a brief second before regaining my mojo. "Well, shit, man. I'm sorry to hear that."

"It was pretty sudden, like someone just pointed their finger at him and muttered a curse or something. One second he was here, and then he was gone. Kind of like what happened with your mom, I guess," he says sheepishly, looking up at me like he's afraid I'm going to punch him in the throat. "I'm sorry, by the way."

I cross my arms over my chest and hold his gaze. "Thanks, it was a bit of a shock."

"Understandable. I was the one who arrived on the scene first, you know?"

I know, I say to myself, my mind darting back to Addison this morning. "Well, I'm glad you were there."

"Me too," he says, his eyes locked on mine.

"I'm not really sure how to do this." As I stare at my old schoolmate, I stay quiet for another moment. I clear my throat and he glances back at me with an eyebrow raised.

Charlie laughs humorlessly. "It's okay. I'm not looking for a hug or anything."

"Okay, good," I say with a sigh of relief. "Now, can we get to business?"

"By all means, my office is this way."

He leads us back past all the desks belonging to his deputies into an office. His workspace is spotless, of course. I follow him in, and he shuts the door behind me, reaching over to pull the blinds closed.

"First things first, thanks for the note; you know I love a cryptic message," I shoot at him. He opens his mouth to retort, but I hold up a hand, not finished. "Second, would you care to explain to me why I ran into Parks? Here in Willow Heights, of all places?"

Charlie grimaces again and moves around to sit in his chair, taking a moment to answer me. "I was hoping to talk to you before you ran into her."

"So this is a thing then," I speculate. "She's actually still here. After you told me you'd convince her to leave?"

"Noah, listen, it's not that—"

"You gave me your word, Charlie," I growl back at him. "How the fuck are we supposed to do this when she's still here, still at risk? My dad knows about her and isn't afraid to risk her life again to prove a point. Especially with me being back here."

"She wouldn't leave."

"Well, then, you did a shitty job of convincing her."

"It's more complicated than that. Look, I'll be the first to admit I could have done more, but she wouldn't leave. Not after she saw you in New York a few years back. She was set to go, but I dunno, man, that gave her hope or something."

"Is that it? That's the story you're sticking to?"

He hesitates a moment too long. "Yep."

"I can tell you're hiding something, Sullivan. You're a shit liar, and you always have been. What, has she found someone else?"

By his expression, I already know the answer. That's fine. I told her not to wait for me. Honestly, I'd be surprised if she didn't have another man. Parks is a catch. "Who is it?"

"Don't ask me that."

"Okay, you've just narrowed it down to about five people. Go ahead and just rip the bandaid off."

He holds up a single finger. "I want to make it known for the record that I didn't want to tell you this, but you basically forced it out of me." I roll my eyes, and he continues, "It's Eli."

Mother fucker.

I bark out a laugh and grip the back of my neck. "You've got to be fucking kidding me. This guy again?"

"Things are a little more complicated than that."

"This is a small town, Charlie. Of course, things are complicated. Spill it, then we can get to the real reason I'm here," I order. I choose to ignore that we resemble a pair of two old ladies gossiping about the town's juicy business right now.

He sighs loudly, as if this is the last thing he wants to do, but concedes, "They're not dating per se, but just seeing each other. They both have different ideas of how they want their relationship to progress. You know Eli, he's been in love with her since he first saw her."

"I'm aware," I say through gritted teeth.

"But Addie is more just looking for a friends-with-benefits deal, I think. Something to take the edge off when she has a bad day." I grit my teeth at his phrasing, not liking the mental image that gives me. "I can't imagine she sees herself settling down with him. She's always had eyes for someone else, you know? And as history has shown, Eli doesn't live up to that for her."

I scrub my hand over my face, trying not to dwell too hard

on the fact that I want to throw up at this recent development. "Okay."

"That's it? Okay?"

I scowl at my not-so-much friend. "I don't know what else you want me to do. Your bestie and his incessant puppy-love isn't my problem."

"What about Addie?"

"Parks is a grown woman." And a fucking beautiful woman at that. The image of her plump lips falling open when she ran into me this morning pops into my brain, and I shake my head, trying to clear it, focusing on where I am. "She can handle herself."

I've spent way too long daydreaming about Addison Parks, and I know that despite it all, I'll spend much more time continuing to do just that. Later tonight, when I'm alone, I'll break apart every second of our interaction today, analyzing all aspects of what we said to each other. But, for now, I shove it to the back of my mind so I can focus on the task at hand.

"So, about this nice card you sent me," I begin. About a week and a half ago, I received a plain white envelope with my name and address written on it. I found a Willow Heights City Hall business card when I opened it. Nothing was written on the card. It was enough to send a message and confirm that my coming back for my mother's funeral was not the only reason I was supposed to be back here.

Sullivan steeples his fingers and looks at me, his green eyes turning severe. I realize I'm now talking to the Sheriff of Willow Heights, the Charlie I grew up with, now pushed to the sidelines. "I think I have him."

"You think? What does that mean?" I ask him, praying to whatever God is up there that I didn't come back to this godforsaken town for a hunch.

"I had someone undercover at the right place at the right time, and I think we have a lead."

"Again, with the 'you think' bit. Charlie, drop the façade and just tell me what the hell you got."

"My guy heard Mayor McCoy talking about delivery to someone named Orville Marks. I haven't heard of anyone in that town, but I'm looking into it. We'll check databases for neighboring towns and go larger if we have to. I think this might be our way in."

I frown. I guess there might be something here. It's not much to go on, but something, at least. "Did he allude to anything illegal? Or literally, anything else that could get us a warrant?"

Charlie looks contrite as he shakes his head. "Unfortunately, no, but I'm hoping that now you're back in town, we'll be able to smoke him out a little. Hopefully, he'll think we're onto him—which we are—and he'll trip himself up."

I fall into the chair in front of his desk. My hand rubs at the back of my neck to soothe the tension. "He'll definitely know we're onto something."

"Why's that?"

"Because I basically said as much," I mutter, looking out the window at a squirrel climbing a tree. I try to dampen the white-hot fiery anger that boils in my chest whenever my father crosses my mind, but it's no use. "He might believe that my mother's death gives him a free pass, which, sure. I'll give him that one. But I told him he'd be in cuffs the next time he'd see me."

"Well, that might be a little extreme. We still have a long way to go before we get there. We don't have any solid proof yet."

"So, what's the plan then, Chief?" I say, turning back to him.

"Just lie low for now. I have my guys out there with their ears peeled, just in case he slips up again. I want you to re-acclimatize yourself here in town, maybe rattle him up a bit, but don't pursue anything. Then he'll let his guard down, and we'll get him."

"Do you want me to—" I shrug my shoulders, unsure, "Make him think I'm not after him or what? That I've given up?"

Charlie's eyebrows pull in. "No, I don't think that would be the best course of action. You two have always been at each other's throats. If you pulled a full one-eighty on him, he would know something was up. I think you should just go back to how it was before."

"Before?" I scoff. "Sorry, man, with all due respect, but that's a bullshit plan. Not only am I a completely different man than I was then, but now my mother's gone. Before is nonexistent."

"That's all I got right now, Noah. Don't make it obvious that we're trying to nab him, and we'll be fine."

"And not to mention if I go back to 'before' as you say," I twitch my fingers into quotations, still on a roll, "I'm knowingly putting Addison back in danger. Or have you forgotten what happened to her parents when my father thought I was onto him the last time?"

He narrows his eyes at me. "I haven't forgotten."

I lean back into the chair. "My point. I don't want anything to happen to her. She's suffered enough because of me."

"We'll just have to play it a certain way. Like I told you, Addie is in some sort of weird arrangement with Eli. Let's just let that come to a head, so you don't have to worry about that. Just stay away from her. If your father doesn't think she means anything to you anymore, there won't be a problem."

My chest squeezes tightly. Visuals of wide hazel eyes come to mind, and I frown. "I'm not sure if I can promise that."

"You can't just stay away from her for a little longer? I

thought that wouldn't be much to ask of you." I glare at him at his unspoken words, and his eyebrows heighten.

"It's asking a lot for me to pretend that she's not everything to me, Charlie," I growl.

"You're hung up on her still, then?" I remain silent, which is answer enough. "Okay, whatever. Just try," he pleads with me. "I don't want to see Addie hurt any more than you do. She's my best friend."

"Why do I feel like I'm just a pawn in your game here?"

"Because that's what I need you to be right now," Charlie says bluntly, holding my eyes with a heavy stare. "We'll get him, Noah. We will. I promise you that."

Read the Rest of Noah and Addison's Story in Chasing Infinity on Amazon and Kindle Unlimited

ACKNOWLEDGMENTS

Thank you so much to everyone who has been involved with creating and perfecting *Wonderstruck*!

Wonderstruck, once upon a time ago, was my very first go-around in the NaNoWriMo competition. This story will always hold a special place in my heart, and though the story has changed significantly since that first draft, a lot of the elements haven't changed one bit.

Writing Theo and Whitney was such a great experience, and I loved getting to watch their story unfold. I hope you enjoyed reading it as much as I enjoyed writing it.

I have many people to thank for assisting me in this process:

Thank you to my dear friend Kris Wood who provided a sounding board and editing for this book throughout this entire writing process. Thank you to my lovely beta-readers who gave me such great feedback on how to fully tell Theo and Whitney's story.

And thank you to my editors Cassandra and Emi who helped me in various stages of the editing process.

Another big thank you to Graziana with Chris Covers for designing this beautiful cover and the alternative paperback cover.

And as always thank you to my husband for always being a support for me with my passion for writing. I can't imagine life without you.

I can't wait to see what's next!

ABOUT THE AUTHOR

Aria Harding is an up-and-coming romance novelist from the Midwest, USA. Aria has been a long-time lover of romance novels and is excited to join the ranks as a romance writer. Her first book, "Chasing Infinity" was published in May of 2023 and there are many more exciting projects to come. Her goal is to write stories that make readers feel as though they are immersed in the world and experiencing the same highs and lows as the characters on the pages. Her favorite tropes to write include slow burn, enemies-to-lovers and second-chance romances. Aria always looks forward to hearing from readers, so feel free to reach out and have a chat!

Instagram: @ariaharding_author